THE CODE OF MANAVAS

Arpit Bakshi has studied electrical engineering and has an MBA in finance from the University of RPI, Troy, New York. He now works for a prominent Indian bank. Arpit had initially wanted to pursue a career in theoretical physics, but ended up opting for engineering (as most students of science in India tend to do).

Since his childhood, two things have never failed to amaze him—the vast expanse of the cosmos; and the unfathomable depth of Indian mythology and spirituality. He believes that one should never stop learning, and it is his love for science that has gravitated him towards writing this mythology-inspired science fiction.

MAHA VISHNU TRILOGY: PART I

THE CODE OF MANAVAS

ARPIT BAKSHI

RUPA

Published by
Rupa Publications India Pvt. Ltd 2018
7/16, Ansari Road, Daryaganj
New Delhi 110002

Sales centres:
Allahabad Bengaluru Chennai
Hyderabad Jaipur Kathmandu
Kolkata Mumbai

Copyright © Arpit Bakshi 2018

This is a work of fiction. Names, characters,
places and incidents are either the product of the author's
imagination or are used fictitiously and any resemblance to any actual person,
living or dead, events or locales is entirely coincidental

All rights reserved.
No part of this publication may be reproduced, transmitted, or stored in a retrieval
system, in any form or by any means, electronic, mechanical, photocopying, recording
or otherwise, without the prior permission of the publisher.

ISBN: 978-93-5304-120-5

First impression 2018

10 9 8 7 6 5 4 3 2 1

The moral right of the author has been asserted.

Printed by Parksons Graphics Pvt.Ltd., Mumbai.

This book is sold subject to the condition that it shall not,
by way of trade or otherwise, be lent, resold, hired out, or otherwise circulated,
without the publisher's prior consent, in any form of binding or cover
other than that in which it is published.

To my parents,
Anil Kumar Bakshi and Vinita Bakshi,
All this has been possible only because of
your love and support.

Contents

Prologue ix

1. The Half Moon 1
2. The City of Hopes 9
3. The Chant of Forefathers 17
4. The Yocto Magic 24
5. New York to Albany 34
6. Love by the Lakeshore 47
7. The Elusive Vandal 59
8. The Berry Affair 71
9. The Dance of the Cosmos 83
10. A Foe among Friends 94
11. The Jurassic Summer 105
12. The Interactive Map 122
13. The Nefarious Plans 137
14. The Eternal Song 149
15. The Erstwhile Earth 162
16. Taming the Tides 176
17. The Belligerent Love 186
18. The New-Found Love 197

19. Hope Besieged	205
20. The Deluded Wisdom	217
21. Betrayal: Best Served Cold	225
22. No Holds Barred	240
23. The Kakudmi Manoeuvre	251
24. The Much-Awaited Reunion	260
25. Beyond the Realm	269

Glossary 281

Prologue

Throughout history, the modern man was not the only human species to have thrived on earth. His many cousins roamed the vastness of this planet aeons before him. The Neanderthals, the Denisovan, and the Flores Man to name a few. They all were very special in their own ways. They were mean survival beings adapting to the harshness of their environment.

Then came along the modern man who, rather than adapting to the prevalent environment, began carving it to suit his own needs. He had thought he would live forever and dominate the world, unquestioned. But his reign, his unchallenged dominance was to run out of steam soon. Around the middle of the twenty-first century he finally began to run out of time. The food was scarce, freshwater was hard to find; even his genome grew weaker. All this happened because he took liberty with the Nature beyond any limits. And Nature, no matter how passive it may seem, always retaliates when pushed to an extreme corner.

Around AD 2050, Man had to voluntarily give way to a new human species. Man's population had been dwindling at alarming levels and his last attempts at saving his own kind were failing to produce any results. It was then that he participated in an experiment. Consequently, the modern man then transformed into a much wiser immortal being.

All that we know about the ancient predecessors of humans is from archaeological findings. And what we know about the modern man, comes from his own writings. But, what we don't know is the story of his successor—the wiser immortal being.

This story is set in 2050.2.0000001 FV,[1] about two million solar years past the base year of AD 2050 (the last of the AD years). The Kali-Yuga has transformed into Swarnim-Yuga. And, Bhoomi (the erstwhile Earth) has been inherited by the new successors—the Manavas. Although Manavas are immortal and have evolved beyond primordial emotions such as—anger, rage, and jealousy; they do have their own issues to deal with. Despite being the epitome of human evolution, they continue to deal with the modern man's legacy left behind from over two million years ago.

The Manavas are few in number and geographically restricted to the last of the continents on Bhoomi. While some of them are quite liberal and rational, few others are highly spiritual. But, what they have in common is their unwavering faith in Lord Vishnu (or his various avatars). Come what may, they believe Lord Vishnu will always be there for them.

This is the story that has never been told before, and for which there were no records up until now. The story of what happened after the modern man's dominance ended and his world crashed—the story of the Manavas.

---

[1] For Vishnu

1

The Half Moon

A cool, balmy gust of air unsettled its antennas and wings. It raised its forelegs and then brushed its antennas in a hurried manner. It then flapped its beautiful big wings twice to regain its balance.

The wings had wave-like patches of yellow amid cerulean blue, which faded into lavender grey towards the middle of the wings. There were beautiful tangerine-coloured eyespots all over the outer edge of the wings. The eyespots added colour and splendour to the wings and kept the predators away, which were mostly medium-sized birds that would confuse the colourful creature for the nectar-loaded flowers.

Sitting atop a big banyan tree, it was trying to find flowers to feed onto their nectar. Little did it know that the flowers were well concealed in the figs growing in abundance on the tree.

The cool wind gusts were growing stronger with the coming of dusk. The leaves of the tree were dancing to the tune of the wind blowing down the mountain slope. The winged creature was now perturbed and finally decided to give up its search and fly away.

It started descending down the dense tree, manoeuvring through the aerial shoots and branches. The wind was now swinging the creature in both the directions as it floated in the air. It flew down the length of the tree and finally found a sleek piece of bamboo in the shadow of the giant trunk.

Krishna stopped playing his flute, turned his head to his right and noticed something sitting atop his flute. A butterfly was resting on it, between the last two air vents, gently flapping its wings. He was amused at the sight, a beautiful blue-greyish butterfly sitting right atop his 'Venu'.

Up until now, he was long lost playing his flute, with the cool spring-evening winds ruffling his hair. But now, he was looking at the beautiful patterns on the wings of the butterfly, like a spellbound child. He was careful enough not to unsettle the little one, and held the flute steadfast and still. He patiently held his breathe too, already heavy from incessant playing.

The butterfly was touching the flute with its proboscis and legs looking around for nectar. With the air vents now calm, the butterfly started probing them. Its forelegs got stuck in the penultimate vent, and it started flapping its wing vigorously to free itself. Seeing this made an already smiling Krishna laugh. The puff from his laughter startled the fly; it then untangled its legs, with all its might, from the vent and took off.

Krishna now looked at the setting sun. The clouds marked the horizon, with their peripheries displaying yellowish hues from the refracting sunlight. The birds were on retreating march and the shadows of the nearby kadam trees were now growing longer and fainter.

Krishna got up dusting his yellow silk robe and tucked his Venu under his saffron waistband. He raised his head and saw the peak of the Govardhan hill, which was now glowing in the slant sunlight. He wanted to view the sunset from the peak. The banyan tree was on the foot of the hill, and it was nearly 500 feet of steep ascent to the hilltop. He smiled and raced forward like an unfurled spring. A minute or so of sprinting and he was on the hilltop.

The view was magnificent, and the winds were more enthusiastic at the top. The sweet fragrant smell of banyan fruits, from the other side of the hill, filled his nostrils. A strange feeling of connect encompassed his consciousness and a nostalgia of belongingness overpowered him. The feeling, the cool breeze, and the sweet figs' fragrance gave him goosebumps.

He pulled out the flute from under his waistband and started playing again a soft composition of his own. The music filled the air, and a mélange of birds chirping along, created a melody of its own. He stood there, on top of Govardhan, with his eyes closed, playing his Venu relentlessly.

On hearing the music, an old man with flowing white beard came out of his hut. The music brought a smile to his face. He could hardly see (as to) who was standing at the top of Govardhan, from his hut situated on the summit of Mount Meru (a few hundred feet from the Govardhan). Krishna sensed someone looking at him; and opened his eyes while still playing the flute.

It was probably the first time Krishna saw the old man of the fables. People in the city called him the 'Archaic hermit'. He was a recluse who had no interactions with the city dwellers of Jambhu-Dweep. The hermit usually had least interest in the outside world and rarely ventured among people, but today was unusual. He stood there as if enchanted by Krishna's flute, smiling as if a mirage-seeking deer finally found his oasis. Krishna found this quite bizarre and lowered the Venu.

He was still wondering what had brought the hermit out of his hut, when his left wrist began to shake. A watch-like device on his wrist was vibrating. The device was a wrist-phone, and everyone in the city owned one. But Krishna's was a special issue and was named 'Mani-Bandh'. When it came to appearance, Mani-Bandh was like all other standard issue devices—made of solid steel bracelet with a big oval-shaped yellow sapphire-like crystal adorning it. The crystal was smooth and translucent, and looked like a shimmering piece of jewellery. The wrist-phone would vibrate when receiving an incoming call. And on user's acceptance the crystal surface would clear up and a beam of light would start projecting images from the caller's end. The one Krishna wore was the first of such device to be manufactured and differed vastly in its features and capabilities, compared to the standard issues.

He looked at his Mani-Bandh and nodded. It was now projecting a holographic video at a foot's distance from his face. It was Mohan, his childhood friend and colleague.

'Krishna, the set-up is ready. I was wondering where you have been the whole evening,' said Mohan.

'I came out for a walk,' Krishna replied.

'When do we initiate the sequence?' he replied.

'I will be there in an hour or so, if it's ready we need to initiate it tonight,' Krishna said and disconnected the call. He then looked back towards Mount Meru, but the hermit was gone.

Some other day then.

He tucked his flute again in his wristband and began the descent from the eastern side of Govardhan. He could see the city lights and faint silhouettes of people walking on the streets. It was almost dark now, and the city was at least four kilometres from the hill.

The moon was now rising from the east. Krishna could already see the upper crest of the big and bright summer moon from the heights of the mountain. Its rim was glistening with a blue halo and its surface appeared carrot orange in colour. The moonrise now occupied the majority of the eastern horizon.

It was a magnificent view. But the visuals only reminded Krishna that it wasn't the original one. Not the moon he used to watch and wonder about in his childhood.

Some 1.5 million years ago, after the end of Kali-Yuga, a giant inter-planetary rock came hurling toward the Bhoomi. The city dwellers had been preparing to shoot the asteroid down to avoid the impact. But something happened midway and the asteroid soon disappeared.

No tracking device on Bhoomi was then able to trace the asteroid for the next twenty-four hours. And then it struck.

It had impacted the dark side of the moon. Bhoomi had been saved but the collision had split the moon into two. The smaller half had moved away from Bhoomi tangentially, and the bigger half had started orbiting at a faster pace.

The fragmented moon had then begun spiraling in. City dwellers now had a bigger dilemma at hand, either to wait for moon's orbit to stabilize or to shoot it down too. Shooting down the moon would have sent innumerable debris and rock towards Bhoomi. After a month of anxious waiting, things had stabilized. The moon's orbit had lowered to half its original. Rounded by the resetting of its molten surface, the moon (with its lowered orbit) had grown bigger and brighter (in appearance).

•◆

Krishna's Lab, Café Evolution, was on the eastern end of the city of Madhavpur. While the hill range adorned the western fronts of the city. He took the shortest walking route to the lab avoiding the MagVahn (the magnetically levitated circular public transportation, crisscrossing the city).

He could have gotten to his lab faster on a MagVahn, but he chose to walk. He wanted the evening to sink into him; he wanted to be part of the present. By the time Krishna reached his lab, evening had metamorphosed into night. The sky was ablaze with stars of the Milky Way.

He entered the lab and placed his flute on the desk beside the main door. Mohan was still busy configuring the bell jars placed into the compartments that were made into one of the walls.

The main hall of the lab was huge with a high ceiling. On the left of the main door was a big screen on the wall, displaying outputs from the computers placed below it. Between the computers and the screen was a touch panel with various controls on it. The lab was commissioned on a special decree of the Council, for the namesake project 'Café Evolution'.

Mohan was busy calibrating the compartments, and did not notice when Krishna entered the lab. He walked up to Mohan and patted on his shoulder.

'Oh! Hello there, Krishna,' said a startled Mohan.

Krishna walked up to the control panel and started punching some commands. The compartments got covered behind glass in a near vacuum. The screen began showing progress for the parameter test for all the twenty-eight compartments.

'Krishna, I have done the set-up as instructed by you, still these payloads do not seem like they could go for an inter-galactic mission. As a matter of fact, of all projects we have done together, I have never seen any projectile or payload like this before. How do these work?' Mohan asked.

Krishna was busy writing some sort of code on the touch panel. The codes were getting displayed on the screen in encrypted form, leaving Mohan further perplexed.

'Do you wish to initiate the sequence?' displayed the screen.

Krishna pressed 'Yes' on the panel.

'Copying Evolutionary Sequences to the Payloads'—read the screen.

As the status bar on the screen was progressing, a green light started glowing over each compartment. The count was growing at a fair speed, within a few seconds all the lights got illuminated.

The screen now read—'System Ready'.

'What are these evolutionary sequences all about?' asked Mohan.

Krishna turned, walked towards Mohan and asked him, 'Do you trust me?'

'But I thought we were sending inter-galactic probes,' said Mohan.

'Can you keep secrets?' asked Krishna, to which Mohan nodded in affirmation. 'Then just hold back all your questions for a while,' he said further.

Mohan drew a heavy breath and nodded again. He stepped back and stood silently.

Krishna moved back to the panel, and started keying in some more encrypted code sequences. The screen now read—'Launch'. He hesitated for a moment, looking back at the empty chambers. He then initiated the sequence.

Ten, nine, eight, seven, six, five, four, three, two, one.

'Phooffph' was the sound as the scant air molecules in the depressurized chamber moved in to occupy the space left behind by the payload. The payloads were gone.

Mohan was staring at the empty chamber with his eyes wide open, in extreme amazement and disbelief. Krishna resumed his work on the computer panel. The screen was now showing a map resembling a solar system, with a glowing red-hot ball in centre and many more revolving around it.

'Is this the new kind of launch mechanism that you were working on?'

Krishna nodded, while still busy working.

'Is that a solar system on the screen?'

'Those are universes orbiting around the core,' said Krishna.

Suddenly, the graphical representation of the universes started blinking on the map. The payloads were now placed into the alternate universes. The mission was not what Mohan had been anticipating; it was not meant to probe galaxies.

The payloads now started sending back home massive loads of data stream. Krishna felt a sense of pride, his immense toil was now set on a remarkable journey. The payloads were travelling in altogether different universes. Mohan was slowly beginning to grasp the situation; the rest of the operation was now to follow the standard procedures.

'Do you want me to throttle the sampling rate up?' asked Mohan.

'You can, but it would take some time before any meaningful data makes its way back.'

Mohan increased the sampling rate, allowing data and parameters to get stored and logged. Of the numerous signals being displayed below the simulated map, one particular equation sequence caught Krishna's interest—1408. It was a small blinking sphere revolving around the core.

Realizing that the operation had gained some momentum and the rest of it will still take some time, Krishna turned and said, 'Let's go to the terrace and get some fresh air, Mohan.'

2

The City of Hopes

Krishna stood near the edge of the terrace with his arms folded and elbows resting on the parapet. He could see the whole city from the terrace of his lab. The city was abuzz with flickering lights and crowd. It was a typical evening for Bhoomi inhabitants, most of them out in the local markets.

The city of Madhavpur was octagonal in shape, with each border facing one of the eight directions. Then there were avenues, each parallel to one another and running east to west. The avenues were then, intersected by lanes running north to south. Madhavpur was thus designed like a lattice. All residential houses were located in lanes while institutes, commercial ventures, and offices were located in the perpendicular avenues.

The basement of the city was divided into three parts. The uppermost housed manufacturing plants, the middle one had power production and storage units, and the lower basement had all kind of waste disposal and renewal units. The multi-layered city design facilitated the best possible use of limited inhabitable space that Manavas had on Bhoomi.

'What's the matter Krishna, why did you keep this mission a secret?' said Mohan.

'Do you see all these people hustling and bustling all around the city, what do you feel about them?'

Mohan smiled and said, 'They are happy after a long day of work and are enjoying their evening.'

'The truth is things aren't as smooth. Had I not kept all this a secret, there would have been panic around.'

'Bhoomidium?' asked Mohan.

'Yes! Bhoomidium indeed.'

'Are the levels already low?'

'Too low! Infact I fear that low levels of Bhoomidium in the crust could trigger deficiencies in Manavas too,' said a worried Krishna.

'I thought our plan was good to go. We were to inject stable isotopes of Bhoomidium to the crust, and buy ourselves some more time to find new planets to colonize.'

'Ah! The Bhoomidium-1008. The stable isotope! You do remember what happened last time we injected Bhoomidium to the crust, right?'

'But that was Bhoomidium-1007 and it had mild radioactivity, which went unnoticed back then. This one is stable,' argued Mohan.

'My studies showed that it was not about radioactivity after all that lead to such violent reactions the last time around. It had more to do with intrinsic properties of Bhoomidium. It is the only known element to have Conscious Control. It can sense things around, and has a sort of life in it and surprisingly Bhoomi was resisting it.'

'And now you fear doing the same might destroy our last bastions too?' asked Mohan.

'It could have, if not for a fix that I devised. Instead of delivering Bhoomidium-1008 into Bhoomi's crust directly, I have encapsulated it into smart carriers which let Bhoomidium dissolve into the crust in a quantity- and time-controlled manner in batches smaller than critical mass, thus not upsetting Bhoomi,' said Krishna.

'Problem solved then?' asked Mohan.

'But not before paving way for another to arise.'

'What does that mean?' asked Mohan.

'Funnily enough, the ideal rate of release is too slow to catch up with decomposing Bhoomidium. It won't get replenished, before bringing about substantial damages.'

'Of what kind, what ensues?' said Mohan.

'Come on, Mohan! Look at yourself! But for Bhoomidium, we wouldn't even exist today. We wouldn't have remained young and healthy since the past two million years. We live in a just and rational society with no suffering, we owe all this to it.'

'You mean all this could vanish?'

'Just like a thin film of water on a hot sunny day! The Bhoomidium isotope we used was unstable; as a result all that was planted in the crust and our bodies including our Epi-Cortex has been disintegrating all this while. I am still trying to figure out how to fix all this before it spins out of control.'

•◆

The night was growing darker, and only few people could now be seen on the streets. Mohan looked up to see the clear night sky studded with stars. The Milky Way was now a more prominent visual.

Krishna was lost deep in these very thoughts. The very idea of Manavas losing their characteristic Epi-Cortex was disturbing to him. The aeon's worth of cortical development would be lost, if he did not do anything about it. The whole society would crumble into realms and chaos. His years of labour and endeavour would go to waste. What use would be his cortical development level of CD1++, if he could not save his own kind?

'Are you sure about this plan of yours?' Mohan then said.

Krishna took a fraction of a second to withdraw himself from his thoughts and focus on Mohan's question. 'I won't say I am too sure, but yes my calculations show that we might have a way out. All those deep probe ships we sent into different galaxies, point towards one thing. That we are not alone and there are other universes out there. No two universes are exactly the same; they differ in their age and maturity. But fate of each universe is not random, they are tied together.'

'Implying?' asked Mohan.

'The occurrences in our universe could very well shape the fate of other newer universes.'

'Let us assume there are multiple universes. And you say that fate of each universe is governed by the fate of others, right?' Mohan said.

Krishna nodded in affirmation.

'Is that the reason we could not find life or habitable conditions on any other planet in any of those galaxies?' asked Mohan.

'Exactly! It turns out that life can exist just once in a universe. Apart from Bhoomi our universe is as barren as it can get.'

'So, basically we are stuck,' Mohan sighed.

'Partly yes and partly no. All the universes known and unknown alike are but a solution to a very complex equation—a sort of mathematical representation. They are just a condensation of different possibilities, so to speak. Life can exist in universes younger than ours. I am just reaching out to those with life potential.'

'We have seen days more difficult than these. Had it not been for you, none of us would have made it through. We already owe you a lot and if you choose to reveal the present situation to the Council, I am sure you will have their full support,' Mohan suggested.

'The time is not right to do so, any kind of panic won't help.'

'Trust me on this one,' said Mohan with a gleam of elation in his eyes.

'Do you remember the seven continents? What remained? Just Jambhu-Dweep? I cannot risk losing that too.'

Mohan nodded in agreement. The painful memory of those particular incidents was still evident in Krishna's eyes. Mohan understood how he felt, and thus choose not to carry the convincing part any further.

Krishna was now blankly staring at the city lights, only to be interrupted by a MagVahn passing by, some hundred feet from the lab. The sound of the passing MagVahn was alternated by the sound of hustling leaves and branches, rubbing against each other. The newly grown tender leaves, the bright coral coloured ones were the most enthusiastic among them all, swinging away to the tune of sweetly fragranced spring winds that were sweeping across Madhavpur.

The sidewalks of each lane and avenue of the city were paved with kadam and aragvadha trees. They provided much-needed break from the monotony of the conch-shaped houses and cone-shaped offices, made of glass and steel, throughout the city. The splendid greens and yellows of the kadam and aragvadha interlaced the streets, a pleasing contrast to the steel-greyish look of the structure-clad city.

A light started blinking on Krishna's Mani-Bandh. 'Touchdown'—read the device screen. That got him smiling.

'Mohan, give me your wrist-phone. I am pairing it with my phone and the Samganak.[1] Krishna took Mohan's wrist-phone and waved its screen over his own, and punched in an authorization

---

[1] Samganak is the Mother Computer, controlling all the systems in Café Evolution.

code into it before returning it to him.

'It will remain connected to the system as long as it is on your wrist. This is crucial—the payloads have started attaching themselves to the targets. We now need to monitor the whole project with an unprecedented attention to the details,' Krishna couldn't stress enough.

Both returned to the lab and hurried towards the main hall. 'It's beautiful!' exclaimed Mohan looking at the screen as Krishna stood next to him and smiled.

'Why would the projectile go and attach itself to such a restless and ever-erupting planet…?' Mohan wondered aloud. The screen was displaying some stunning images of a young planet, with a big landmass shifting places on an all-encompassing blue ocean. The landmass was huge and looked like a clay sculpture gone wrong, with magma overflowing and spurting out of big open vents.

'The components, Mohan! The essential components.'

Mohan smiled gleefully, highlighting the fact that he was not questioning Krishna, but that he was rather amazed. The restlessness of that young planet was spellbinding.

'Why are the pictures moving at such a fast pace?' said Mohan.

'In the Universe-1408, time runs faster. It is a younger universe and thus closer to the core, and revolving around it at a speed much faster than ours. Events worth millions and millions of years are taking place in our Bhoomi's one day and night.'

'You mean the picture stream we are seeing is already slowed down?' he then asked.

'They are! We will be able to see climates becoming conducive and life taking Conscious Control of Prithvi, if all goes right, within a few weeks.'

'Prithvi? Is that what you call this planet?' said Mohan.

'Yes! Samganak has chosen that name for this planet.'

Mohan leaned forward, and touched the bottom right corner of the screen where it said 'Prithvi Universe-1408'.

'Where did it get that name from? I have a vague feeling that it was our planet Bhoomi's ancient name,' said Mohan.

'Samganak randomly picked it out of many other old names of our own planet.'

The conversation exchange was followed by an uncanny silence, as both witnessed another spectacular view. The angry ever-erupting planet started cooling, and started getting covered beneath stratums of fragmented grey specks. Even before Mohan could add any interjections, those tiny grey specks started spreading on the face of the blue planet. In a matter of minutes, they had conquered the oceans and landmasses alike. They were now expanding and growing thicker and darker.

'This is indeed our Prithvi, Mohan!' announced Krishna as he watched his dreams come to life.

'What follows?' asked Mohan.

'It has already started; the payload has initiated the sequences. The marvel of our mathematical precision is at work. The cloud formation has started, soon amicable conditions will prevail both on land and oceans for Conscious Control.'

It was now the turn of those fluffy grey clouds to act grumpy. Intermittent blazes of lightning emerged from the heart of those floating cotton-like clouds. As if Prithvi has encased all its anger and rage into those flying masses of vapour, and now in turn those newborn clouds were spewing lightning bolts all over Prithvi.

'What a colour riot is going on down there, Krishna!'

'A total eye candy, Mohan!'

The thunderbolt strikes were now incessant, scorching the face of Prithvi left, right, and centre; churning the primordial soup in the process and working as the catalyst in the formation of complex molecules from the simpler ones. The brilliant blue oceans covering almost the entire surface of Prithvi seemed so free and untameable. Yet they were now being prepared as a hot bed for series of reactions, the result of which (in the distant future) would tame not only those oceans but also the entire Prithvi at large.

The mission was using a complex set of mathematical manoeuvres to gather information from Universe-1408. The information thus gathered was being documented at the lab, to be reconstructed as 'Time Shift-able' live stream. The very interaction of the payload with Universe-1408 was sensing, creating and sending massive load of data back home. The systems were smart enough to pick only the relevant realms, where inceptions from Bhoomi were interacting with and affecting Prithvi.

3

The Chant of Forefathers

Dressed in his signature yellow flowing silk robe, Krishna entered the hall. A momentary silence prevailed as he moved to the centre and bowed to the Council at large. As he took his seat, the chatter continued from where it had taken a pause. Few councillors were even whispering into each other's ear. The atmosphere was clearly tense.

It wasn't very often that the Council witnessed such a level of enthusiasm and apprehension. Only matters on which referendums were to be called generated such anxiety—which had councillors consulting Manavas of their domain, and then debating with each other on merits. But that was not the case today, because the matter that had come to the Council for discussion was a State secret and had been kept from the general public.

The cymbals and windpipes started playing, enforcing an instant silence across the hall. Everybody stood up for the 'Chant of Forefathers':

> *Samano mantrah samitih samani!*
> *Samanam manah sahacittamesam!*
> *Samanam mantramabhimantraye vah!*
> *Samanena vo havisa juhomi!*
> *Samani va akutih samana hrdayani vah!*
> *Samanamastu vo mano yatha vah susahasati!*

> *May our place be common, common be our assemblies,*
> *common be the mind and united be our thoughts.*
> *A common purpose should we propose, and may our worships*
> *and aspirations be common too.*
> *May one and the same be our resolve (for the betterment of*
> *all), and may our minds always be in agreement.*
> *May united be our thoughts so that we all may agree on*
> *everything important and coexist happily.*

Long after the choir was done with the chant, those words and their melody reverberated through the air.

Everybody on Bhoomi knew the chant by heart. Yet if you ever asked people about the origin of the 'Chants of Forefathers', chances were rare you would get an answer that didn't sound like folklore.

Every Manava agreed upon two things about the chant—first, that it was sacred and demanded veneration; and second, its origins were unknown. Their forefathers had kept it close to their hearts for millions of years and the chant had bonded the Manavas from the dawn of the civilization.

The purpose of the sacred chant was to bind every consciousness across the universe in a single string. It echoed in every throbbing heart. The people with intellect deep enough could grasp the message being relayed and others who couldn't, lead ephemeral lives. The echoes of the chant were immortal and pervaded through every corner of space and time, like an invisible binding force, like a string holding every pearl in place.

Shyam stood and took the centre stage of the hall. He was the head of the Council since its inception. He was the one who had conceptualized the Manava society. He was also instrumental in drafting the Code and had brought everyone on the same page;

without which there would have been no peace between factions of differing ideologies.

'My dear councillors…' began Shyam in his baritone, 'We have all gathered here today for updates on the Project Café Evolution. I would request your patience and would like to declare that the Q&A would be held at the end of this session. Now, I invite Krishna, our Chief Scientific Advisor, to come onstage and brief us about the progress of the project.'

Krishna walked towards the stage with a sense of calm on his face and in his gait. Councillors were eager to hear him out, and were secretly wishing that the progress report would not be anything like the rumours that had been doing the rounds.

'Good morning, everyone! As we all know, the Bhoomidium levels have dropped to the point where they cannot be increased without disrupting life on our planet.' Whispers and chatter followed among councillors, as Krishna reaffirmed their fear. 'But,' continued Krishna, 'my honourable councillors, this is not the end of the story. As a matter of fact, we were able to infuse some Bhoomidium-1008 isotope to the core of the Bhoomi. I can narrate all the probable outcomes of the manoeuvres carried out, but let time and Nature play their own course. The core of our planet is stable for now and has accommodated the injection of the new isotope quite well.'

The Council now seemed less anxious, though a level of scepticism still prevailed. 'This was the status report I had for our own planet to address the current crisis. On the extra-planetary front, I have got some exciting news to share with you,' said Krishna.

But before Krishna could speak any further, an elderly councillor rose from his seat and said, 'We face a very perilous situation here, Krishna. Would you let us know what direct and explicit actions are we thinking about? What are our chances and what alternatives are we exploring?'

'Please everyone! Let us maintain the sanctity of the house. We would all get a chance to ask all our questions and I am sure our Chief Scientific Advisor would address all our concerns,' said Shyam.

He then turned toward the centre stage where Krishna was standing calmly and said, 'My apologies on behalf of the Council. Please do continue with the brief.'

'As I mentioned, we are exploring all options and alternatives. We have sent probes to all known possible targets, and to my delight we have got what we were looking for. As a matter of fact, the probe has attached itself to a planet. The probe has already started the evolutionary sequences as per our precise calculations. The planet in concern is quite younger to ours, and it would take some while for the sequences to mature and take control of its environment. We are keeping a close watch on the developments and would not refrain from interventions and carrying out manoeuvres if and when required. I would like to reassure the Council, that all possible measures are being taken. And, please be rest assured that we have planned the whole course of action. Thank you,' Krishna concluded.

As he stepped down from the centre stage and proceeded towards his seat, Shyam rose to say, 'That was all Krishna had for us this evening. Gentlemen, you may now ask your questions.' Krishna was standing by his designated seat, calmly waiting for those questions.

'We are content with the briefing and again reiterate that we have completely entrusted our faith in our Chief (Scientific) Advisor,' said the elderly Councillor who at the beginning of the brief was the most sceptical of all. A loud roar of applause filled the hall. Everybody was cheering not only the work being carried out by Krishna, but also the show of unity and harmony in these trying times.

The Council members then gathered in the dining hall of the building. It was a big hall with brightly coloured walls. Its ceiling had beautiful paintings depicting decorated elephants, blossoming lotuses, and peacocks in vibrant colours. The wall paintings were widely spaced and the space was filled with motifs of a mother figure sitting on a giant lotus. The hall as well as the Council building was as old as one could remember. The building was monumental and historical. It was one of its kind, solely powered by solar energy. Bhoomi was abundant with many sources of energy, but this building was more of an ode to the sun.

The building's dome was fitted with a huge glass. The gems encrusted in the motifs on the slope of the dome would capture sunrays and sparkle in sun's glory. At daybreak, the whole building would light up in colour.

As everybody in the hall was eating and chatting, Krishna found himself a quiet corner with his coffee. He wasn't eating, and was probably still thinking about Universe-1408. The planet, amazingly, was a clone of Bhoomi's. The probe would not have selected Prithvi of all planets in all the universes, had it not been one. What he saw was probably an action replay of what Bhoomi went through in its formative years. He knew that he had a long list of manoeuvres and tasks ahead of him in the coming weeks. He also knew that he would not be able to meet all his challenges within the walls of Café Evolution. After all what happened today at the Council assembly was not a normal incident, but it was in Krishna's best interest to play it down.

His left-brain was already calculating what lay ahead of him. The conscious realization of what part of your brain was doing what was a unique capability of Bhoomi inhabitants. The Manavas were equally intuitive and logical. They were no longer slaves to their Palaeolithic basic instincts. The highly developed Epi-Cortex of their brain could subjugate any irrational or emotionally charged thought. Unlike Kali-Yuga humans who perceived only danger around them and worked only out of self-interest, for Manavas it was not a constant fight or flight world.

Bhoomidium had not only nourished their brains, fought illnesses, reversed damages done by the environmental toxins, but had also given Manavas immortality. It had acted on cellular level to alleviate fear of harshness from the cellular memory. Instead of self-destruction after a certain number of cell divisions, the cells now kept themselves young. It was altogether a new chapter in the saga of life's evolution.

'Krishna!' shouted a fast-approaching voice. The tone of that voice was more like an announcement of self-arrival. As Krishna turned, he saw Vasudevan (the same old councillor who had interrupted him during his brief) walking towards him.

Krishna greeted him in return by nodding his head.

'So Krishna, we are finally working on the options which I have been championing for a while now,' said Vasudevan with a smile.

'Yes, we finally are!' replied Krishna with a reciprocating smile.

'I have always made it known to the Council that finding a new planet has to be on top of our priorities. Everybody should have a right to get a new beginning. It would be partial justice to place all our bets on isotopic implants while waiting for people to face perilous situations.' Vasudevan had a hint of seriousness on his face and, he was right in his concern—waiting for new isotope to kick in would have aged him (and many people like him) and left him vulnerable.

'I agree with your sense of justice and impartiality, and appreciate your vision,' Krishna said.

'Agreeing' was all he thought would be best for now. It was not as simple as Vasudevan wanted it to sound, but arguments and discussions were not what Krishna thought to be a solution.

The year Krishna was made the Chief Scientific Advisor to the Council, was the year when the whole race of Manavas reached the landmark Criticality—after which they stopped ageing any further. But for him, something else too had changed. His interactions with his acquaintances became limited too. Any overlap and political will of the City Council could have overshadowed his office.

'The Council would be requiring regular updates, Krishna. We hope things go on smoothly, and as soon as the new-found planet becomes inhabitable, we will work on further plans of action,' Vasudevan said.

'I think there is still some time and effort left before we reach that stage. It is a one of its kind project.' As he finished the sentence, there was a gentle tap on Krishna's shoulder. It was Mohan.

'We must make a move back to the lab,' Mohan said, while simultaneously greeting Vasudevan with a gentle nod.

Krishna nodded at Vasudevan with a smile, then turned and walked out of the building. It was well past noon and the sun was on its descent. There was still some chill in the breeze and the sky was clear. It was a typical early spring's late afternoon.

'The De-Accelerator chambers are ready, Krishna.'

He nodded.

'I think it's time we took a closer look,' said Mohan.

4

The Yocto Magic

The data stream was continuously playing on Samganak's large screens. Krishna, meanwhile, noticed that his stuff on the desk had been shuffled and asked, 'Were there any guests here?'

'I might have left the window open. It could have been a strong gust of wind that had tossed the stuff around. Is it a concern?'

Krishna glanced back at him and asked in a perplexed manner, 'Wind?'

But before Mohan could offer further explanations, Krishna was already busy looking at the screen. The live stream was displaying images of huge gas bubbles bursting on the surface of an ocean on Prithvi.

'I noticed them too and that's what made me run to the Council meeting to get you,' Mohan said as he rearranged the desk. Krishna was still glued on to the screen, but the bubbles were only intermittent. Given the fact that data stream was being played at a very fast pace, even successive bubble bursts meant a gap of thousands of years. This could be an early sign of life on Prithvi.

'Can I get access to the cached data stream?' Krishna asked.

'Are you thinking, what I am thinking?' said a puzzled Mohan.

Krishna laughed; it was a rather hearty laugh. Krishna grabbed the arm of the chair and sank into it, while still laughing. Meanwhile, lines of puzzlement grew more ostensible on Mohan's forehead.

'What is it?' asked Mohan, albeit, with hesitation.

Krishna was now recollecting the rhythm of his breath, as his laughter slowly faded like a damping tuning fork. He chuckled and said, 'How would I know what you are or were thinking about?' Mohan smiled, too.

'We are childhood friends, you need to relax more and be less formal,' Krishna said and meant it, because he had begun to sense that designation and cortical categorization was gradually drifting them apart.

Perfection almost always brings along isolation was what Krishna had learned early in his youth, from days when his newly discovered genius brought him some rapid recognition. That recognition, more than anything else, gave him a sense of where his focus will have to be. Since then Krishna had neither the time nor much audience beyond his close friends and mentors to share stories of his monotonous life with.

How could Krishna now allow time to dent whatever camaraderie he was left with? After Criticality was reached, there was baggage to be left behind. But whatever he could carry along, meant a lot to him. But for Mohan and Shyam, his life would have been a treadmill run.

'All right then! You want me to run servers for Bionic Data Analysis?' asked Mohan.

'Infact we both should go to the server room. Even I am curious to see what those gas bubbles were about.'

'You mean "are",' said Mohan pointing toward the screen where a series of bubble were still bursting. Krishna and Mohan both froze, as if awestruck. The bubbles were of orange-yellowish hues illuminated by bright sunlight, with a contrasting background of dark-greyish clouds, lining the horizon.

Those impromptu bubbles covering the face of the ocean

were like small mandarin oranges, suddenly appearing on a pool of molten emerald. They were not intermittent now, but were in rapid succession. The size of bubble burst had also decreased. They seemed as if somebody was launching colourful pearls from the ocean bed. And they appeared on the ocean surface, only to burst and display yet more colours and hues. That somebody was to be enquired.

Krishna and Mohan began walking to the server room, which was located across the hall, on the right wing of the Café Evolution. It was required to be kept at a specific level of temperature, humidity, and radio-interference. It was sealed with twin vault systems and air curtains. The access to the room was absolutely limited to the two of them.

As both of them stood at the door of the room, Mohan took the step forward and placed his finger on the DNA analyser. The security system took a while in sequencing his DNA matching the same with the database. After a moment or so, the light above the sensor turned bright green from a pale red and the first sealed door opened.

As they both entered the alley between first and second door, the Envo-Monitor systems started operations to bring back the temperature, humidity, and radio-interference level to normal. A little chime beeped thrice (ensuring parameter check completion) and the second door to the room opened.

Both entered the server room, it was cold and dry. Krishna raised his left arm and touched the dial of his Mani-Bandh, and a thick layer of fabric started growing over his yellow robe. The fabric was made up of Yocto-particles. The particles used to rest hidden in voids between the fabric of his robe and when commanded would form the Yocto-Suit over the robe. A complex array of magnetic field bonded particles together to form a thermo-insulator cover.

Mohan followed and activated his own Yocto-Suit. The suit was one of the lab's best-kept secrets.

Krishna took a look around the room. That cold dry air brought a familiar tinge of nostalgia along with it. A peculiar feeling of visiting a place, after a while, which you feel you belong to.

Mohan, meanwhile, reached out to a cupboard beside the wall of the room, and pulled out two helmet-like hats made of a translucent material.

'Here! The Interface,' Mohan said.

Krishna grabbed the hat, which Mohan had swung in his direction. Both proceeded to the end of the room. An array of boxes were placed atop each other. In the centre, there was a screen with two cords on both sides of it. Both sat in the chair in front of the screen and attached the cord to the back of the Interface hat. The screen now started displaying two distinct brain scans.

A quick check started appearing on the screen.

'Prefrontal Cortex—ENGAGED'.

'Occipital Lobe—ENGAGED'.

'Olfactory Lobe—ENGAGED'.

'Somatosensory Cortex—ENGAGED'.

'Auditory Lobe—ENGAGED'.

'Amygdala—ENGAGED'.

'Temporal Lobe—ENGAGED'.

'BIONIC DATA ANALYSIS—STARTED'.

The computer was now playing old data stream again and was directly relaying data to their brains. It was parallel threading its own CPU with their brain. They could think and choose what recorded data interested them.

Krishna re-ran the data stream from the ocean surface. The gas being emitted constituted of high levels of sulfur and methane. The source of the gas emission could have been either primordial life or any gas mixture venting out of the earth's crust below the sea surface.

He then changed his focus from sea surface to the seabed, and the computer started displaying the data. The bed was clear, no sign of any movement, except for rock shifting along with the current and time. It was an unending stretch of a barren land under the saline water. He drew his voluntary thoughts toward the source of the gas vent on the seabed. The vent was glowing with molten lava all around it. Huge gas bubbles were oozing out of the vent at random intervals. He gave a thought command, to run the spectrum analyser for detecting the presence of organic substances like nucleotides. But systems could not detect any organic chemical bearing signs of life.

Krishna raised his arm and disconnected the cord from his Interface hat, and then turned to his right to pat Mohan's shoulder. Mohan unplugged his interface too and rose from his seat.

'That was magma and gases leaking into the ocean from a vent. Nothing more, nothing less!' Krishna declared pre-emptively.

'Perilous?' asked Mohan.

'In and around molten lava, life wouldn't exist anyway. Nothing to worry about; let Prithvi cool first. It might take some time before the Conscious Control.'

Both exited the server room, and were back into the more amiable room temperature. The Yocto-Suits, now no longer required, receded back to the intra-fabric void.

Krishna could still see bubbles rising on the ocean surface. But, these were definitely different than what he saw in the server room.

He raised his hand to point his finger towards the screen, and said, 'This is tricking us, Mohan. This is not what we saw inside the server room. I need access to the De-Acceleration Chamber now.'

'Let the fun begin, for you are not plugging in alone.' Mohan was almost looking forward to it. Krishna gave him a momentary skewed glance and then smiled.

The De-Acceleration Chamber was right next to the server room, protected with the same amount of security. The chamber was not cooled, as no data servers were housed in there.

Both entered the room. Inside the usual security doors, there was a glass globe, big enough to house equipment and two sitting chairs. The chairs had big red buttons on the right armrest, by pressing which the experiment would have stopped and chairs would have auto-evicted the glass globe on a rail underneath. Glass sections just behind the two seats parted and came down to let them both in.

Mohan looked around and said, 'So, this is why you made me leave my office space?'

'I wanted the De-Acceleration Chamber just next to the server room. I wanted as low latency as possible.'

'I will require my office back.'

'You will get a new one. Now the coordinates of time and space—that I won't be able to assure,' said a gleeful Krishna. Mohan was now brimming with frustration.

'Come on, Mohan! Sit on the chair, wear the Interface hat and relax. You can press the red button on your right to shut off data stream to your interface in case of emergency or if you feel claustrophobic. The chair will release for you, and will evict you gently out of the glass structure.'

'What emergency? You are making me anxious!' Mohan said worriedly.

'Focus, Mohan! You are a CD2++, you control your nerves and not the other way around.'

'But why does it require an emergency eject button?' persisted Mohan.

'That is a very rare possibility, just procedural safety standards.'

'What does it do?' said Mohan.

'It will connect to your thalamus, and will synchronize with your brain pulse. It will then raise your brain pulse rate from 40 per second to 4,000,000,000 per second gradually.'

'Which means?'

'That your brain will become superfast, and would process all information billions of times faster.'

Mohan sighed with a thick air of concern.

'I am making you hypersmart, now you stay calm.'

'Stay calm? It won't cook my brain, right?' Mohan asked.

'The Interface has cooling devices in it. I have used and tested the device extensively. Now we have to find out what those gas bubbles are, Mohan. I need you to be perfectly calm to begin the experiment.'

They both then took their seats with their Interface hats on.

'On my count of five! One, two, three, four, and five.' Krishna then activated the De-Accelerator using his thought command.

Fast moving images of the ocean bed started relaying to their brains. The images were beautiful, with an indistinguishable humming sound in the background. The visual treat began relaxing Mohan, and his breathing rate became steadier. The De-Accelerator started synchronizing with the thalamus and was progressively increasing the brainwave rate originating from it.

The images began to grow slower in pace. The De-Accelerator was enabling Krishna and Mohan to view images from Prithvi at their near-actual pace. The white noise of the background also started becoming intelligible. They were sounds of ocean's waves and of gas bubbling on its surface.

Krishna redirected the data stream to the source of the bubbles. The source was now a group of rocks on a shallow bed of the ocean. Krishna zoomed in further and reached in between the rocks. There was nothing.

Zoom 1000x, he thought.

Yet he found nothing out of the ordinary. Krishna kept on zooming till he reached 10^6 X of zooming. He could now make out a few blobby specks—inconsistent in shape, lightly pigmented, and in huge numbers (forming a sort of colony). The colony ran for miles under the rock. They were the source of the recent bubbling.

Run nucleotide check, Krishna thought again.

The systems started analysing the incoming data stream. Arrays of them were detected. What Krishna saw then was self-evident and needed no complex analysis. Few of the blobby specks were dividing asynchronously. The colony, which now had various hues, was growing on some frontiers and receding on others.

End the run, Krishna issued a thought command and opened his eyes. He turned to the left but Mohan was not there. He removed his Interface hat, placed it aside, and quickly looked around.

Mohan was standing outside the glass globe, arms folded and next to his experiment chair. Krishna came out of the De-Accelerator. 'The experiment has begun showing results,' said Mohan.

Krishna nodded. He could notice the unease in Mohan's eyes. But he still could not figure out what was bothering him. Mohan too should have been happy, with the results of their finding. But apparently he was not.

'Have you factored this in?' asked Mohan.

'Factored in what?'

'Your brainwaves are actually bending the rules!' Mohan then said.

'What made you say that?'

'Your thought commands, I was able to hear them,' Mohan explained.

'I must have been vocalizing them too!'

'No! Not like that, I mean they actually made their way back to Prithvi. They were like echoes. I could hear them along with the ocean waves,' he explained.

'No, I didn't factor that in.'

'Strange, isn't it?' Mohan said.

'If you could hear them, then yes it is.'

'I mean when Bhoomidium levels are going down, how come your brainwaves are growing stronger?' Mohan asked.

Krishna kept his calm while admitting, 'To this I have no explanation.'

'Did you consider telling these latest developments to Shyam?' Mohan enquired.

'He is a busy man; administration takes most of his time. The next time we meet, I will seek his assistance.'

'I am worried for you, I am now not sure what this Bhoomidium deficiency will do,' Mohan said.

'Heightened brain activity is not what you look for, when you do look for the deficiency. And you can check the logged data stream, to make sure how my brainwaves made its way to Universe-1408, if they actually did.'

Mohan went to the auxiliary chamber just outside the server room, and fetched the data on to a hand-held device. 'Here are the results.'

He was right, Krishna's brainwaves were making their way back to Prithvi. Krishna was able to see the dots connecting, but kept silent.

'How about this? We call it a day, you go home and I will go get some rest.'

'I will place the data by your desk, and see you tomorrow morning,' Mohan said.

'Tomorrow morning it is!'

Mohan left the lab and boarded the last MagVahn to his way back home.

5

New York to Albany

Krishna leaped up, and sat on his bed. Drenched in his own sweat, he looked at his Mani-Bandh. It was three in the morning.

He was still trying to pull himself out of what he had seen and heard in his dreams. He could remember all of it quite vividly. It has been going on for a while now. Those voices in his dreams had been guiding him throughout Project Café Evolution. He didn't know the source of those voices, whether it was his brain running amok or if these were some kind of messages he was receiving. All that he knew was that they were guiding him, and were making him see things in new light. The voices were even able to convince him to alter the course of his research; these dreams had a strange but strong undercurrent of conviction in them, and always gave him the urge to follow them to the tee.

Krishna was now wide awake now. His brain was racing like a wild horse let loose. He sat in his bed and wondered about the course of his life, and how one event had led to another.

Almost two million years ago, Bhoomi had not been as nice a place to live on. A race of humans, known as the Modern Man ruled the Earth (the then name of Bhoomi). And Bhoomi was divided into seven major continents, out of which Man inhabited six permanently. These continents were conjoined to begin with and with gradual sliding over Earth's liquid core, drifted and got separated from each other. And, what species of animals or plants inhabited which continents, depended solely on when that species had originated and its adaptability. The rule never applied to Man, who being a creature of curiosity travelled and occupied each of the inhabitable continents. He travelled through land, water, and at the later stages of his evolution, even in air.

Man lived in near harmony with Nature for thousands of years. A meek creature he was, who used his new mental ways to get along the day. But as he slowly and gradually made his place on Earth and devised means for his safety, he branched outward and started occupying land for planned cultivation. He crafted magnificent civilizations, which were masterpieces of art. There used to be skirmishes amongst different races and cults of man, but nothing to upset the ecosystem around.

But somewhere down the line, things went awry. Technology coupled with hunger for personal gains made Man insensitive. The natural ways of evolution started crumbling, with man-made materials interfering with the delicate balance of life on the planet. The rivers turned bad, the air suffocating, and even the farthest corners of the planet bore marks of man-generated toxins.

By the turn of the twenty-first century, the progress (or quite the opposite of it) made by man was too fast and too ferocious to be dealt by natural course of selective evolution. Now, evolution works on trials and errors; while Man's frantic growth left no space for trials, only errors prevailed. A better quality of personal life drove him reckless. But he was preparing a toxic soup in whose venomous broth he was about to get boiled.

·•·

The year was 2050. It was an early October noon. Cool winds swept the ocean-trapped island city of New York. Krishna was posing in front of the Times Square and Mohan was the one behind the lens. Krishna had then walked towards Mohan in a hasty manner, took the camera and checked his pictures.

'Aren't these cool?'

'Except for that flashy red billboard in the background,' said Krishna, as he zoomed into it—'Xididium' appeared in bold.

They both turned. 'Xididium®—Friendly Chemical Company,' read Mohan aloud. 'What's this Xididium thing, Krishna?'

'A new product, they are organizing some inaugural events for and calling up science grads to come for the event. I read somewhere, it is some kind of food's shelf life enhancing product—they call it groundbreaking.'

'You would go?' said Mohan.

'Nah! Let's go to Central Park. I want to capture some autumn colours.'

They then took a cab to the Park, which was abuzz with people all around. The walkways were carpeted with foliage, rendering it yellow and red. As Krishna walked on them, the hustling of the leaves amused him. The haughty colour exhibition of the maple trees, standing tall on both sides of the walkway, was something he could gaze at the whole day.

This was not his first autumn in the United States, but he was happier than ever before. It was the final year of his Master's, and he had been newly inducted into the elite research programme code named 'Amrit'.

Uncle Shyam, the director of 'Human Longevity Research Department' at New York College of Advanced Research (NYCAR), had referred him to the most glorious and challenging project of his department. The referral was a mere formality; the fact was NYCAR needed him. He was one of the most brilliant minds of the time.

Mohan, meanwhile, was referred to Project 'Bhoomi' of Geo-

Sciences lab, headed by Vasudevan. 'Bhoomi' was Earth's tectonic plate movement-tracking programme.

Mohan pointed at a bench by the walkway, 'Let's sit there.'

Behind them were skyscrapers and in front of them were rows of maple and oak trees. Krishna's glance was fixed on the vacant bench on his left. The freshly done black varnish was gleaming in contrast to the yellow background of the autumn colours. The sunrays filtering through the dense trees made those colours look more vibrant and pleasing to the eye.

That brilliant play of colours and contrasts, made Krishna remember someone, utmost dear to him. He longed for her, and all he wished for in that moment was to be with her. Krishna was deep in his reverie, not paying attention to anything else around him.

Mohan snapped his fingers, just a few inches from Krishna's face, 'Did you even hear what I said?'

'What?'

'That girl is hot!'

'Which girl?'

'That one there in the red t-shirt and beige shorts, whom you have been ogling so audaciously,' chuckled Mohan.

'I have been doing what?' Krishna readjusted his focus, from foreground to the background. A cute-looking girl holding the leash of an adorable pug puppy was whom Mohan was referring to. He laughed, 'I was thinking about something else.'

'Let's go talk to her. I am pretty sure, if we begin with anything to do with that funny-looking pug she will talk to us for at least twenty minutes,' Mohan was beginning to get excited.

'Don't call him funny, he is cute.'

'What thoughts were you lost in?' said Mohan.

Krishna didn't say anything, and was about to get up and leave when Mohan said, 'Oh! Come on, tell me.'

Krishna gave him a crooked glare with one eyebrow raised, 'Radhika. I miss her.'

'Now, that's cute,' Mohan said.

'I wish she was here with me.'

'That's a problem in this case. Boy's a geek. Girl's a daddy's girl. Girl's dad won't hand over her hand, unless Boy gets his hands on a desk job paying him a handful of money,' Mohan said with a broad smile on his face.

'Whoa! That's some handy way to put it.'

'Why do you worry, next year you will be done with your degree. And Uncle Shyam will make sure you get a full-time job in the lab. I too am counting on the same,' Mohan stated matter-of-factly.

'Got a girl?'

'Not yet, but they are going to go crazy over me once I become a full-time geo-scientist,' Mohan said cheerfully.

'Yes! The geo-scientists are always such a catch,' Krishna said sarcastically. 'I know studying tectonic plates is not cool, especially with lava oozing out of those fault lines.'

Krishna chuckled and got up from the bench, dusting his trousers, 'For now I video chat with her, and that is sufficient for me. I need to concentrate on my project and academics. Priorities!'

'Priorities!' echoed Mohan.

'Let's get going. Let me call Uncle, he must be done with his seminar by now.' Krishna pulled out his phone. 'Uncle will meet us at Penn,' he said after he hung up the phone and the two friends started walking towards the Park's exit.

The hot girl in the red t-shirt was just ahead of them. She was finding it hard to convince the pug to walk beside her. It was racing ahead, lugging her along in the process. And here Krishna was having hard time grabbing Mohan by his arm to make sure he didn't ram into the girl, and Mohan too was racing ahead towing him along. Nonetheless, Mohan managed (walking fast enough) to walk past her, 'Hey! He is cute.'

'Nah! He is funny,' replied the girl cheekily.

'I am Mohan. Got any plans for lunch?'

'If it's Italian that you have in mind, then yes,' she promptly said.

'Garden of Olives?'

She smiled and nodded.

'We need to reach Penn Station in another 150 minutes, to be precise, Mr Pick-up-expert,' Krishna muttered under his breath.

'I know that, Mr I-am-jealous,' Mohan replied. The trio went to Times Square for lunch. Mohan spoke to her (at length), fully compensating the lack of interest that Krishna was projecting with each string of spaghetti that he was gobbling down.

'She is a fashion journalist,' Mohan said, as they left for the station.

'We will discuss that once aboard,' Krishna replied and increased his walking pace.

Shyam was waiting for them in the central lobby area near platform. There were still about ten minutes for the train to be announced. Krishna saw Shyam first and waved.

'Train will be announced any minute now. I need to reach Albany on this one. I have an update and certain instructions for you,' Shyam said.

'What is it all about, Uncle?' Krishna asked.

'We will discuss that once aboard,' Shyam replied.

Mohan smiled in nirvana. Uncle Shyam had scored it even for him.

Mohan occupied the window seat facing the Hudson River (running parallel to the tracks). It was around four in the evening and the sun had just started its descent. The slanted sunrays made those tiny wave fronts shine with golden hues. Mohan was still lost in that girl's charming ways—her golden hair, her blush, and to top it all her sweet smile.

'I have been promoted to head all projects being run at NYCAR.'

'That's great news, Uncle,' Krishna said.

'That calls for a celebration, Uncle Shyam,' Mohan added.

'Sure, it does. But before any of that, I want to know how his behaviour was with you.'

'Even the word "super" doesn't begin to describe her. The way she talks, the way she looks, and the way she smiles. Super smooth,' replied Mohan, half-smiling as he recalled his lunch date.

'What is he talking about?' asked a bewildered Shyam.

'"His" is the word, Mohan! Uncle is not talking about the girl with the great legs,' Krishna said to Mohan.

'Oops! It's my bad. Whose behaviour do you want to know about, Uncle?'

'Vasudevan's. And who is this girl with the great legs, Krishna?'

'We just had lunch with Mohan's new-found friend. And it seems his tectonic plates have gone faulty since then.'

Shyam kept on looking at them both. He was even more perplexed then before.

'Never mind all of that, Uncle! What's with Vasudevan?' said Krishna.

'He was vying for the same post; I am not sure how he will react to me being promoted. He had a close eye on all the developments, he must have known about this beforehand,' said Shyam.

'Don't worry, he is an old colleague of yours. He is a nice fellow.'

'I agree, he has always been cordial with me. Not an iota of fishiness,' Mohan remarked and Shyam nodded in agreement.

The three got down at the Albany Train station, and took a cab to NYCAR.

'There will be a brief in S&T Hall in another two hours. I want you two and your fellows to join in,' Shyam said to them. Both nodded and left for their dorm.

'What is it going to be about?' Mohan wondered.

'Will have to wait and see,' Krishna replied.

Both reached the S&T hall fifteen minutes before the schedule. Shyam entered the hall wearing a cream-coloured suit with a striped shirt and a red tie, the colours of NYCAR.

'Good evening, ladies and gentlemen! This is my first address as Director of NYCAR. First, let me just assure you all that nothing would change, except for two things—our focus and dedication. We will have to challenge our own limits. As you all know, this institute is one of the finest in the world, but it was not established to churn out only graduates. This institute is an answer to an SOS call. It was established by the mandate of the seven leaders. The last thirty years have been a grim warning for humanity and our planet. The chemicals, the additives, the food colours and the meal replacements, which were passed by authorities as GCAS (Generally Considered as Safe), boomeranged. The cumulative toxicity of every error of ours has come back to haunt us. The world's human population has drastically declined to less than one billion, and has been restricted to the seven nations. Half of the animal and plant species have disappeared; rivers in major parts of the world are now polluted beyond reclamation. All the industrial effluents and artificial chemical exposures have weakened our immune system.

'But, my friends we do have some hope. Hope for the coming decades and, that is, science and technology—the application of our acumen for betterment of mankind and life of our co-inhabitants, flora, and fauna.'

Shyam took a brief pause, and started a presentation projection on the main wall of the hall.

'Longevity, Environmental Enrichment and Geo-Sciences, funding for all the three departments have been doubled this year. We need to work with double the focus and commitment. My colleague Vasudevan will now handle Environmental Enrichment and Geo-Sciences. With fine staff, well-versed researchers, and the best of graduates we all wish to see NYCAR achieving its goals within the stipulated time frame. This slideshow contains few more formal details about our vision for the coming years, and would be circulated to you in a mailer. I would like to thank you all for taking out time for this brief.' Shyam concluded as he flipped through the slides.

Post his presentation; Shyam was collecting his belongings when Vasudevan approached him.

'My heartiest congratulations, Shyam!' Vasudevan said as he shook Shyam's hand.

'Vasu, my being appointed as the new director is not as important as us working in a team to achieve our common goal. The directorship is rather a throne of thorns for me, as majority of my time would now be consumed in liaising outside the labs with people who understand neither technology nor how research works. I need your complete support.'

'You don't have to ask for it,' Vasudevan assured him. Shyam smiled, patted him on the shoulder and left. As he exited the hall, he pulled out his phone and texted—'106, in ten minutes.'

Shyam was standing at the end of the aisle near the window overlooking the lawn. It was now dark outside. Few cars passing by were gleaming under the street lamp's light, every now and then. It was not too breezy and definitely not too cold either. The otherwise quiet foliage of the autumn would hustle and crackle under the tire of the passing cars.

Shyam was almost startled as Krishna approached.

'Uncle, you seem tense. What's the matter?'

'Not here kid, come on, show me your lab. It has been a while since I last saw your set-up.' They both walked towards room 106, Krishna's lab was situated at the beginning of the corridor.

'Impressive! It hasn't changed a bit. How is the work coming along?'

'We have prepared the side chains of the compound, we are now working on carrier's backbone chain.' Krishna's theory predicted a compound centred on a heavy metal, which could repair the human cell. 'There is a small glitch, though,' he confessed.

'What's that?' Shyam asked.

'Further probe and simulations indicate that any element that could work as backbone chain does not exist.'

'So, we have hit an impasse. Have we?'

'I will need more time. I am working on it.'

Shyam stepped forward and rested both his hands on Krishna's shoulders. 'I have news for you. The equipment you requested has been ordered. Now you will have enough space to house your new set-up. The whole floor is now yours, including the adjacent 107 and 108.'

108 was the biggest hall in the building, and Krishna had always wanted it. 'Thanks, Uncle,' Krishna said earnestly.

Shyam waved it off saying, 'I am talking to you as Director of NYCAR, and not your uncle, and I need results. I am putting my faith and resources into you, not because I know you. But because I see merit in your work.'

'Yes, sir.'

Shyam nodded and started walking towards the door. Just when he was about to leave the lab, he halted and turned his head back. 'I wish times were more favourable, but they are not. I wish situations were better, but they are grimmer than ever before. Our race is shrinking, our gene pool diversity is dwindling, and with each passing day more species of plants and animals are vanishing into oblivion.'

'I understand the gravity of the situation, sir.'

'I know you want to visit Madhavpur. Let me assure you, kid, that you and Mohan are going to get a fully-paid holiday, once we make some substantial headway in our projects,' Shyam said and left the room, heading back to his house.

•◆

Krishna resumed his work. He was eager to draw the layout for the new lab set-up. He pulled out some drawing sheets and started scribbling notes and sketches, completely forgetting in the process that he had to meet Mohan for dinner. He was neck-deep in drawing the layouts, when he heard people talking and some metal moving against the hard concrete floor. He quickly came out of his lab and saw two security personnel and two other people, who appeared to be from the tech support team, moving a big shipment on carts.

'Is this meant for labs 107 and 108?'

'Yes, it is,' replied one of the security personnel.

'Maybe I can help you out with arranging those then.'

He was amazed at the speed with which the equipment had been arranged for him. It was almost eleven in the night by the time they put everything in place, just as he wanted them to be. It was midnight when he reached his room. He was in no mood to eat, and just wanted to drop on his bed and sleep. He changed and slipped into his bed, trying his best not to disturb Mohan on the other side of the room. But Mohan moved and asked, 'How is the new set-up?'

'It's good, sparkling new toys to play with. Uncle told you about it?'

'I had to pick a mail from the front desk. I saw the cargo for you there. Besides, I always knew that once Uncle had the power he would make sure that you faced no hindrance in your work.'

'Looks like, you know him better than me,' Krishna said and smiled.

'Did you tell him about the backbone chain problem?' Mohan asked.

'I did.'

'Okay. Get some sleep for now then.'

'I am sorry, I could not make it to the dinner,' said Krishna.

Mohan just smiled. Within a minute, both were fast asleep. Glistening under the light of a proximate night lamp, a maple tree was all that could be seen from the window. The young maple (which was now almost reaching the first floor window of the room) was rustling every now and then, as a mildly cold wind carrying the scent of cedar was circumventing its way around the dorm building.

A few hours later Krishna woke up gasping for air, drenched in his own sweat. His hands were trembling and his heart was racing. After a minute or so of being in a state of trance, he started processing what it actually was. Was it a dream, or someone actually was whispering into his ears, or was he transposed to some other transcendental plane? It was probably just a dream, a lucid dream after a long and tiring day. Krishna raised his arm to fetch his wristwatch, lying on the table next to his bed just under the window. It was three in the morning.

Suddenly something else caught his attention under the brilliant moonlight—his hands had turned blue. Maybe he had slept with his body weight over his arms, and had thus interrupted the blood flow. That could also explain his lucid dreaming. *I am too stressed. I need to take it a bit easy.*

He then tried going back to bed, but sleep evaded him. He got up from his bed. *Those voices have to mean something… Why don't I think of such ideas when I'm awake?* Krishna grabbed his jacket and lab keys, and headed straight to the lab.

He now knew exactly how to get the backbone chain for his longevity compound and couldn't wait to get it.

6

Love by the Lakeshore

The sound of flute playing and birds chirping caught Krishna's attention, and brought him out of his nostalgia for his college days. It was his six o'clock alarm tune.

The MagVahn had already started plying again on the tracks. The branches of the aragvadha tree outside Krishna's window were abuzz with birds. The brown-coloured birds with strong beaks were pecking the very branches and shoots they were perching upon. The yet smaller fork-tailed birds with hues of brilliant blue and green were busy singing. As they chirped, their small head would dip forward and their tails would tweak up. The slant sunrays made the tree shine in golden hues. The early buds of the yellow flowers, hanging like a woven garland, were shining as if they were made out of real gold. The first rays of the rising sun could now be seen soaking the foot of the distant Govardhan hill too.

It was an ordinary day in Madhavpur.

Krishna raised his hands, shoulder high. They were blue yet again. The voices and imagery still echoed in his brain. He was habitual by now, more or less he had accepted the fact. Whenever he got stuck in his research work, the voices would sneak in, his hands would turn blue and he would have to spend night tossing and turning. He had come to accept it as a part of his solitary life.

As he rose from his bed and stood up, the camera images of

his lab started displaying on the room's entrance wall. The wall had in-built sensors, which could detect Krishna's wake time presence. They were painted with special material on an area of 40x30 inches, which acted as a display for lab visuals in case he wanted to work from his living floor.

There was no sight of Mohan in the lab on those visuals, which bought Krishna some spare time to take a shower and wait for the blue marks to fade away.

As soon as Krishna came out of the shower, he picked up his Mani-Bandh and logged into the Samganak. He was eager to see what was happening on Prithvi. His best guess—the life form should now be in Archean state (Archaea, the unicellular oxygen-shy organisms that closely resembled bacteria and thrived in extreme climates in the young Bhoomi. There was no other explanation for the fact, apart from this, that first citing of life was in and around deep-sea hydrothermal vents).

Things were going great. Given a chance, Krishna would have chosen to stay over on Bhoomi. Why bother with immortality, when you have already been around for so long? Just do what you want to do and then fade into oblivion.

The only bothersome factor with inaction was that things could revert (sooner or later) back to where they were. The threat of people around losing refined cortical capabilities was a real one. Inaction, it seemed, was not an option.

He still remembered the day when Criticality was reached and the age was declared as a Swarnim-Yuga (bringing an end to the then Kali-Yuga), under the Vedic Code. Everyone around, including the whole Council, had cheered for Krishna on fructification of his efforts. He had been under oath to keep the momentum going.

He was now remotely logged onto the system. It was a beautiful morning on Prithvi. Krishna was getting visuals of some ocean with slant sunrays glittering over the wavy surface. Though he wanted to review the vents near which Samganak detected life, but he could not have done that remotely. Then something else caught his eye. The lower right corner of the screen showed a text reading: 'Phase-I Archean State'.

Samganak is sequencing and recognizing the data stream, Mohan needs to see this. Mohan though, was still nowhere to be seen, which made him a bit curious. He almost always used to turn up on the agreed time.

The first thing that came to his mind was a temporary breakdown of MagVahn. He walked towards the balcony. As he slid open the glass door, cool temperate gust of wind flew past his face, ruffling his long flowing hair in the process. He could smell fresh spring flowers in the air. Though it was still too early, people could be seen on the streets of Madhavpur. As he stepped closer to the black wrought iron railing on the edge of the balcony, birds both colourful and dusky flew from the branches of the aragvadha.

He smiled. Something just flashed across his mind. He rushed inside toward the side table, placed next to his bed. From that beautifully carved rectangular teak table with tapered edges, he picked his Venu. He then walked back toward the balcony. Raising the flute to his lips, he closed his eyes and set his mind free to play whatever it felt like to.

His flute was now churning out strings of notes concatenated in a fashion unheard even to him. The pearl like beads, strung on the edge of the saffron-coloured thread tied on to the extremity of the flute, were shining in the sunshine filtering through the thin early morning cover of cotton like blue-greyish clouds on the horizon.

Soon Krishna could listen to chirping of birds intertwining with the melody of his Venu. As he opened his eyes, he saw the small, colourful birds of song, sitting on the wooden top of the balcony railing. They were singing, as if playing their part in the symphony of Nature. More birds started flocking onto that newly found stage.

His balcony railing was now full of small birds of different vibrant colours, outmanoeuvring each other by twittering and chirping. He had never seen anything like that before. He closed his eyes again and kept on playing his flute incessantly.

A few minutes into his song, he heard vigorous flapping of wings, along with a sudden variation in wind force caressing his face. A loud roar of a passing MagVahn pierced through the atmosphere.

He opened his eyes. The MagVahn passing through the tracks, some hundred feet from his balcony, had startled the birds. *The MagVahn is not out of order, what else could be the reason…* he mused. He raised his wrist and dialled for Mohan.

After a long wait, Mohan answered, 'Krishna, I will be right there in a couple of hours or so.'

'You sound agitated, is everything all right?'

'Just having a conversation with Meera. I will be there soon.'

This left Krishna with some more time. He just had to run regular checks down in the lab and then he could plan for the morning. Krishna went downstairs and initiated composition analyser on Prithvi's data.

The tests required at least two hours to complete. He came out of his lab and started for Sarovar Avenue (the last street on eastern boundary of Madhavpur). There was a lake by the side of the Sarovar Avenue, popularly known as—Radha Kund. Just beside the lake there was a café, his favourite one. He always went there on days when he wanted some solitude. Today was one of those.

The sun was now almost at eye-level. Krishna occupied a table in the patio of the café, just next to the lake whose tranquil green water seemed as if it was a sage in a pensive state, only to be perturbed by sporadic gusts of wind. As the day progressed, the winds also grew much balmier and less cooler. One moment the winds seemed non-existent and the next moment, they would start sweeping the length and breadth of the lake. From swinging the kadam trees lining the lake on its eastern end to creating ripples on the lake's surface and disturbing the swans and ducks, the gust was omnipresent.

The old sandstone structure of the ancient origins circling the whole lake except for its western banks could be seen from the patio of the café. Sipping his coffee, Krishna's eyes were fixated upon the swans and the floating weeds in the lake. His favourite blend could be smelled across several tables on the patio. It was neither too bitter nor too strong, mildly flavoured, and sweetened with dried powder of exotic berries.

As he placed his cup down on the paper cut-out, the steam emerged from the hot coffee. Krishna bowed his head down a little. Behind the rising vapours, he could see a pair of swans. The image of the swan couple perforating through the vapours was trembling like a hot noon mirage.

A subtle fragrance of fresh jasmine then overpowered the smell of the berry-laden coffee, as the memories of the bygone years covered the warm sunny day.

He would often teasingly call the place Radhika-Kund. It was their preferred rendezvous spot. They would often meet here in early evenings. The cool breeze, placid water, and the sound of the temple bells in the background—there wasn't a place like that in all of city.

Radhika would often come clad in her favourite churidar suit and dark red wrinkled dupatta with glitters stitched all over it. Her silver earrings, bracelets, and anklets would add to her simplicity. They would often sit on the banks of the Kund and chat for hours at length.

That particular day was a week before Krishna had to leave for the United States. Radhika was sitting beside him on a green patch on the bank, not knowing what to talk about. Dressed in a cream-coloured suit with a churidar and bandhini dupatta, she had jasmine flowers tucked into her hair.

'For how long would you be gone?' she had finally asked.

'Four years for the course work, and then specialization and research.'

'So, you have no definite plan of coming back?'

'Radhika, you know how it is between Uncle Shyam and me. I cannot refuse anything he asks me to do. Not because I am indebted to him or anything even remotely like that, but because he is like my father. I know you are mad at me, but it's my calling, my duty.'

'I never meant it that way. I just want to know when would we finally be together?'

'Once I am done with course work and have gotten into research. What are your plans for now?'

'My parents mean a lot to me, and I am going to assist them here while pursuing my environmental studies,' she declared and stood up to leave.

The sun was now gently touching the horizon, and it was a matter of minutes before it would have gotten completely dark. Radhika's phone rang.

'Yes, I will be there,' replied Radhika tersely to the caller.

'Let me walk you home.'

Those had been the last words they had exchanged face-to-face.

·◆·

They call me the most logical man, and I can't even stop thinking about her. I think I miss her. Krishna slowly pulled himself out of the bag of memories.

Krishna felt a hand on his right shoulder, the aroma emerging from the now lukewarm coffee came back to the foreground, subduing the mild and soothing fragrances of the jasmine emanating from his heart.

'Hi, Vasudevan!'

'Call me Vasu.'

'Vasu, I never knew you came to this café too. Nice place, isn't it?'

'I actually do! In the last rotation, I was given charge of this section of the city,' said Vasudevan as he pulled back a chair for himself. He then kept on talking about his role in the upkeep of the neighbourhood, and what changes were being carried out under his supervision.

How come this person has always been in the background as yet another councillor? All the while involuntarily nodding at Vasudevan's bragging. *How come I missed out on him all along, or is it that this guy has become more vocal, more assertive, and more boisterous of late?*

'Enough about my constituency and my work, how is your project going?' Vasudevan finally said.

'Smoothly sailing on intermittently rocking waves, with a distant and faintly visible shore.'

'I understand, my boy. It's tough.'

'Nah! Not just tough, but mind-draining and boggling too.'

'But you are our best bet.'

'If that is the case, Vasu, what made you so agitated and eager in the Council meet?'

'I am a councillor, Krishna. I have a bunch of people to reply to. I have gone through that report in detail, the one that contained information about depleting Bhoomidium in the crust. I was pretty concerned about the findings of that report. As you would remember, I was on the board supervising Bhoomidium implantation. I know in and out what an imminent deficiency of Bhoomidium bodes for our race. We have been able to keep the report and the ground reality under the rug, but sooner or later people will come to know.'

'I completely understand, sir. But, we have to keep the report under the proverbial rug for an agreed reason. Since any panic or mass hysteria can accelerate the reduction in cellular levels of Bhoomidium. And that is exactly opposite of what we would ever desire.'

Vasudevan nodded. A beep went off on Krishna's Mani-Bandh.

'I will have to make a move. I have some scheduled tests and analysis to run.'

Vasudevan nodded. Both stood up, and Vasudevan extended his arm for a handshake. As their hands met, Krishna's Mani-Bandh beeped twice. Vasudevan didn't fail to notice it, 'Someone's messaging you probably.'

'Just a repeated reminder for the scheduled analysis.'

Krishna turned and started walking towards the nearest MagVahn stop. As he boarded a sparsely occupied coach (and made sure that nobody was around) he checked his Mani-Bandh. It was neither a message nor a reminder. In fact it was displaying some numbers, which left him dumbfounded. He raised his head with his mouth still agape in disbelief. He felt goosebumps out of a sense of amazement. Krishna rolled down his sleeves, thus concealing both his goosebumps and the beeping wrist-phone. Krishna laid his head back on the seat's headrest, and closed his eyes. He deliberately emptied his mind of any thought, and silently waited for his stop to arrive.

The first thing that he looked out for as he entered the lab was that big display. The tests were complete by now and the results were encouraging. The much sought-after separation of bacteria and archaea family had already taken place. The oxygen levels in both the ocean and the atmosphere were now up, though still fairly away from the optimum mark. These were clear indications that photosynthesizing cyanobacteria-like organisms were now evolving. The oxygen liberated in the surroundings by these organisms would oxidize and reduce dissolved iron from the ocean and would create conducive environment for territorial life as well as more complex life in the ocean.

As he was busy running through the nitty-gritty of the test results in detail again, the Mani-Bandh rang. It was Mohan.

'Everything good?'

'Kind of. Meera wants to meet you,' said Mohan.

'Is she around? I will turn on the video,' he then tapped the crystal atop the Mani-Bandh. 'How are you doing, Meera?'

'I am fine. Just wanted to see you,' Meera responded.

'You don't need to ask. Just drop in, any hour of the day.'

'We will be there,' Mohan interrupted.

Krishna nodded and waved his hand across the projection, disconnecting the call. He then stopped any data streaming on all possible screens in the hall and went to his residence on Level One. This way Mohan will have to bring Meera upstairs. Less looking around would mean less suspicion, or so he thought.

He had not met Meera for quite some time now, even though Mohan had been inviting him (for a get-together) for a while. Meera's mention always stirred in him some very old memories. So, he preferred to avoid her. But today was a different day. They both sounded worried, and he could not have sidestepped when they needed him (just to keep himself comfortable under a sheath of evasion).

They arrived. He could see them on the screen in his bedroom. He got up from his bed, and activated the two-way microphone on the screen through a voice-command. 'I am in my living room,' he spoke into the screen, while clearing some articles and papers from the sofa. By the time they both made their way into the room, every bit of paper was either in a neat stack or was behind a piece of furniture.

'Hey, Meera! Come here and sit, I will get you some tea.'

She complied and he brought tea for both of them.

'I have been hearing some rumours, really disturbing ones.' Meera immediately got to the point.

Krishna turned his gaze with narrowed questioning eyes towards Mohan and asked, 'What stories have you been telling Meera?'

'Mohan hasn't told me anything, in fact he is not willing to divulge any information. He won't say a thing, and that is what is bothering me more.' The anguish in Meera's voice was now quite apparent.

'I don't know where she heard all this from,' Mohan said.

'These rumours have been a point of gossip in my office and in a few social gatherings. They are being discussed in our sector, surreptitiously,' she explained.

'And what are these rumours all about?' Krishna asked.

'They all have different versions, but all point towards one thing—the impending end of our civilization.'

'These are baseless rumours,' Krishna stated.

'But Mohan's silence on it has made me a bit paranoid.'

'We both don't know anything about it. Maybe he just didn't want to fuel your suspicions any further,' Krishna replied.

'That would have made some sense, had...' she paused with an undertone of hesitation in her voice.

'Had?'

'Had all the versions, not had one thing in common—your lab.'

'What about the lab?'

'They say that whatever Krishna did to save our civilization at the turn of the Yuga, doesn't work anymore. They say that you are working on some quick fix in your laboratory, but to no avail.'

'But to no avail?'

'They say you are struggling to find any solution.'

'Unbelievable!'

'There is more to it. People gossip that they notice unusual activity in and around your lab. They say they hear noises from machines they have never heard before. And that they sometime see the whole building glowing with strange lights. Is there any trace of truth in all of this?' she asked.

'Do I not look surprised? Do I look like I am concealing anything?' Krishna questioned her.

'My apologies for upsetting you, but you have not given me a comforting answer yet,' Meera said.

'You can stay in our lab for as long as you wish, there are no noises and no special lights. Everything is fine. Someone is playing foul. Someone is out there trying to spread anarchy and fill our hearts with fear. Should we let that happen?'

'No,' she replied with her dove-like eyes, now partially content.

'We are the finest; we are the pinnacle of what a civilization should be like. We do not succumb to fearmongering. All the best efforts are planned pre-emptively to keep our race united and strong. There is no need to panic about anything.'

She nodded as Krishna continued, 'Mohan, we seriously need to raise this with the Council. I have never known such rumours doing rounds. We, Manavas, neither indulged in, nor tolerated such lies and mischiefs.'

'Sure Krishna, I will prepare a detailed note to be presented to the Council.'

'Meera, you both can stay and see for yourselves if anything unusual is being carried out here.'

'No! I didn't come here to spy on you or Mohan,' she said.

'I didn't mean that. But if you hear such dumb rumours again, feel free to call me up.' Krishna stepped forward towards Meera and placed his hand over her head to placate her. But his Mani-Bandh again beeped twice. He pulled his hand back, but before he could begin any small talk to divert everyone's attention from that beep, she asked, 'What was that?'

'Just a reminder of some scheduled test work,' Krishna calmly replied.

Meera nodded and turned to Mohan, 'We should be moving, I guess.'

'Before that, let me fix some lunch for you both.'

'Some other day, Krishna,' she said smilingly.

'Let me accompany Meera home, and I will be back in the lab in an hour or two,' Mohan said.

7

The Elusive Vandal

Krishna was sitting at his study desk, going through some test results, when Mohan returned.

'Phew! That was a task.'

'Why did you let it snowball?'

'I didn't say anything,' Mohan replied earnestly.

'Exactly! You could have soothed her, and calmed her nerves down.'

'I didn't know what to say. I was taken aback when I heard those rumours.'

'Rumours?' his smile was brimming with sarcasm.

'Why, what do you mean?'

'We had this conversation, I guess?' he said. Mohan stood there with a blank look on his face, not able to understand which conversation he was referring to.

'That any stress or panic would erode already threatened levels of Bhoomidium,' Krishna reminded him.

'That's why I brought her here promptly. Only you could have told her a story that made some sense. But, why did you mock the word "rumour"?'

'Because you do understand that it's not a rumour.'

'Not all of it.'

'Come. We have some good progress here.'

Mohan who was still standing quite close to the door of the lab, finally walked towards the desk.

'Look at these reports and pictures. It seems we have some form of territorial life on our new planet,' Krishna said.

Those were the magnified images of microbial life form on Prithvi's dry land surface. Mohan zoomed-in the holographic image till he could see the whole picture of Prithvi as a planet. It was a blue sphere with large patches of dark brown land mass. Mohan kept on staring at the images for a while. 'Those landmasses are expanding, it seems,' Mohan said while still looking pensively at the images.

'They are. The oceans are receding and the new land masses are forming.'

'At this rate, is there any chance that oceans may dry up?'

'They should not. The Samganak ran through all these scenarios, and the calculation says that any new land mass formation would stop at around 30 to 35 per cent of the total surface area of Prithvi.'

'It seems I missed out on a lot of action. The whole morning was consumed in placating Meera.'

'Are you kidding? We are lucky that we did come to know about those stories going around, through Meera.'

He nodded in agreement and then said, 'I am not sure what is happening as I have not seen Meera so emotional before, not at least in this Yuga.'

'You are right; we have evolved beyond fear and suspicion. We know how to keep our emotions in check.'

'Then why are people propagating such stories and why such emotional outbursts?' Mohan asked.

'You remember that beep on my Mani-Bandh?'

Mohan nodded. 'I have added a Bhoomidium-level detector into it,' Krishna informed him.

'You mean…'

'Yes, her Bhoomidium levels are already down.'

'Tell me, how low are they?' he asked.

'She is fine for now. They have dipped, but yet significantly above the differentiating mark.'

Mohan sighed with relief initially, but then asked, 'Why she? Maybe these rumours made her panic and she stressed herself way too much, and burned her Bhoomidium levels low.'

'You got the causal relationship wrong. You are citing cause as an effect and effect as a cause.'

'You mean she is panicking because her levels were already down? But then why just her?'

'She is not alone. I met your old boss, Vasudevan, this morning. He also ticked off the metre.'

'Vasu?'

'And also another guy who boarded the MagVahn and sat beside me today morning.'

'The whole race of Manavas is succumbing? Is it so?' Mohan was now more perturbed than ever before.

'Here is the catch: That guy boarded from your sector. The levels are dipping only in your sector of the city.'

'That's what Meera has been saying over and over again about those rumours. That they are virtually non-existent outside our sector.'

'Someone was able to propagate those rumours only because, the levels were already down and people were ready to believe them,' Krishna told him.

'Is it a systematic campaign?'

'Could be.'

'We will bring this up with the Council. This is serious stuff, we will prepare a detailed note and present to the Council at the earliest.'

'You want it to be reported it to the Council?'

'Why? What's wrong with that?'

'Nothing in Jambhu-Dweep and particularly in Madhavpur ever happens without the Council already aware of it,' Krishna stated.

Mohan pulled a chair and sank in it, 'I think I need to slow down a bit.'

He then grabbed Krishna's hand by the wrist and said, 'Do I make it beep too?'

They both waited for the sound, but there was none.

'Now, tell me what should we be doing?'

'It's an insider's job,' Krishna declared.

'Vasu? I heard he was the one, making a huge issue out of the project's progress in the last Council meet.'

'Cannot be, he beeped on Bhoomidium counter indicating a dip in his own Bhoomidium levels. This could be a rivalry or a well-thought-out plan to hit two birds with one stone.'

'Us and Vasu?' asked Mohan.

Krishna nodded, while walking towards the screen. 'We have reached Stage Two. Prithvi's atmosphere has more or less settled around 20–22 per cent oxygen, and simple life in form of microorganisms has started appearing. This is our brainchild. We not only have to take it forward, but will also have to protect it. Even if there is any attempt of sabotage, we must guard our project. In the coming months our focus will solely be this,' he said pointing towards the screen.

'It is our hope, our tomorrow,' Mohan agreed with him.

Krishna nodded and said, 'I will run some more simulations. I suggest you go upstairs, and take some rest.'

Mohan smiled, the suggestion resonated with him very well.

Krishna began running some additional tests to generate a

composition analysis of the territorial life and some other important markers. His plans for the rest of the day were already set. *Two hours to go before I get this report in hand, until then I should rote the layout.* And he began looking for the detailed layout of sector-108 on his Mani-Bandh.

It was five in the evening and with each passing minute the sun was growing old and pale. While still sitting by his desk, Krishna raised his head and looked out. He could not help but notice the similarity between the ebb and flow of life and a typical summer day.

Just like a rising sun, a child would be born—soft and soothing. He would learn to leave behind the horizon and leap into the unimaginably limitless sky. After making a mark on otherwise unconquerable vast sky, he would blossom into a ball of passion, hot and ever-ready for any challenge that would dare meet him eye in eye. The pace with which nature brings that passion onto the summer sun, with the same pace and surety it dissipates the very passion and heat. And into that calmness of time, the sun sets after again being reduced to a soft spot on the horizon.

That had been the normal course of life on Bhoomi. But then Manavas made a conscious choice to not set into the oblivion. They were happy to be stuck on the zenith, till nature chose an excuse to bring about a plausible day-end for them.

Am I playing against the will of the nature itself? But Krishna couldn't complain about an uneven playing field now, when on that eventful evening in his lab back in NYCAR he did just that and happily gloated over his victory. That evening when he finally created carrier's backbone and fixed all jigsaw pieces to eventually create Bhoomidium.

But this time it was not as simple as that. The task now was more complex, intensely procedural and seemingly megalomaniacal.

Krishna cleared his mind of all the tussles and reclined back on his chair. He was pondering on where to look for plausible reasons for plummeting levels of Bhoomidium in Mohan's sector, when he dozed off. Within a few moments his eyeballs beneath his eyelids started moving randomly and his fingernails turned blue.

It was 6 p.m. when the Mani-Bandh started chiming. Krishna woke up and snoozed his alarm. He was trying to recall as well as decipher his dream. Re-running the whole sequence in his mind, he smiled. His task for the evening was now a lot easier.

He rose from his chair, and opened a drawer on his work desk and pulled out a pair of gloves. He had to conceal his blue fingertips before Mohan showed up.

As he slid his hand in those gloves, he heard Mohan's footsteps. He turned and said, 'You look better now.'

'A lot better,' Mohan replied.

'Eat something, we will be out partying till late tonight,' Krishna said.

'Awesome!' Mohan said and then noticed Krishna's glove-clad hands. 'Tingling again?'

Krishna nodded, 'I feel better with these on. I am going into the server room, meet me there after your dinner.'

He went into the room, and in another twenty minutes Mohan also joined him there. As Mohan entered the room, he saw Krishna stroking his hands supposedly against something beneath a hanger on the wall. It seemed as if he was looking for something, maybe the source of some field or radiation.

'What is it?' Mohan asked.

Krishna turned back and smiled, he then closed his eyes for a moment.

A pair of robes appeared hanging from that rod. 'This is an updated pair of the Yocto-Suit for our mission tonight.'

'This is beyond belief!' Mohan exclaimed.

'I have redesigned the Yocto particles to refract light around them to make it and anyone inside the suit invisible.'

'And it runs on thought command?'

'Yes it does, but only through the wrist-phone. Now pick up your robe, wear it and I will update your wrist-phone too. We will make a move at eight, once it is dark. Till then get conversant with your new gadgets. And yes, we will leave the lab with stealth on. Lest we are being spied upon.'

At eight sharp, both slipped outside the lab as nimble as possible. They had to avoid walking on grass or on dry fallen leaves, as to not make any hustling sound. Krishna pointed towards the sidewalk, and asked Mohan to keep to it. Both were wearing earpieces to talk to each other. They were both able to see each other's location on an interactive map on their wrist-phones.

'Why walk all the way when we can board the MagVahn?'

'We need to avoid strong magnetic fields; it can disrupt the Yocto-particles of the suit. Now listen, we have to reach the supplies on the second level. The entry to the underground is some two kilometres from here, shouldn't take us more than ten minutes of walking to reach there,' Krishna stated.

'What about the access codes?'

'I have enabled the parallel security system which is covered under authority bestowed upon me, and it would not be logged. No security breaches,' Krishna replied.

Both reached the entrance to the underground. Krishna stepped forward and started punching some codes into the Access Box installed just next to the door. It took well over a couple of minutes before he could unlock the door. He then slid open the door only slightly, and jammed the surveillance device installed on the head of the entrance using EM pulses from his Mani-Bandh. He then squeezed his way inside and Mohan followed suit.

The place was warm and moist, with a buzzing sound in the background. They had to use staircases to reach the second level, because using the elevator would have triggered in-house surveillance alarms.

Krishna's best guess was that water supply of the sector was tampered with. 'We need to reach to the water supply chamber. It will be on your right, as we reach the Level Two aisle,' he said.

After a tedious walk down the spiral staircase, they reached the Level Two aisle. Krishna jammed all the surveillance devices in the aisle, and quietly unlocked the supply chamber door. They were now both inside the chamber. It was completely dark and full of noise from the machines. He pulled out two pairs of glasses from his pocket, and tapped Mohan on his shoulder. 'Wear these glasses and turn on the night-vision.' He then walked towards the main control panel of the chamber and thoroughly queried the system for a few minutes and then paused.

'Did you find anything?' Mohan quipped.

'The systems are fine, nothing in here. But let me think, I have a strong feeling something is still going on here.'

Mohan was standing next to a big vertical pipe, without realizing it he placed his hand on it for support. As his hand made contact with the big pipe, it made a metallic sound, and drew Krishna's attention.

'The main supply pipe!' Krishna said in a buoyant tone.

'What?'

'Just stand there and I will show you what.'

The pipe had a big joint some three feet from the ground. The joint housed the final filtering devices. Krishna started sweeping his Mani-Bandh across the pipe from bottom to top. The readings on his device changed.

'So, Bhoomidium levels are changing after passing through this filtering stage?' a bewildered Mohan looked on. Krishna nodded and started looking for the seal around the box.

'We probably shouldn't unbox this filter,' Mohan said, as Krishna was about to reach for the seal.

'Of course not! That would set off the alarms. I will map it onto my device.'

He pointed the front of his Mani-Bandh towards the joint and it drew a three-dimensional image of the filter joint. There was an unusually small hemispherical structure attached to the upper part of the joint. 'Here it is, I will map this object too and will study it back in the lab.'

'Do we try and detach it?' Mohan asked.

'If we do, whosoever planted it would know. Let's move back.'

He then beamed images and data back to the Samganak for analysis.

On reaching the lab, Krishna approached the screen. On the display he could see weeds and low-lying plants covering vast tracts of Prithvi's land. The green patches were now more visible on Prithvi.

He then pulled up a detailed report on the composition of the mystery object on the supply line. 'I have never seen anything like that. All it does is release different waves and particles in a synchronized manner,' Krishna concluded.

Mohan suggested, 'Try making a 3D model from the images. Maybe we can pass some water through the model.'

With an exact replica in his hand, he then fetched a foot-long pipe and placed the object right in the middle of it. Mohan took some supply water and passed it through one end of the hollow pipe. The water from the other end was collected into a jar. Krishna then took the collected sample water and placed a few drops of it on a fluid-composition analyser on the control panel.

Krishna raised the replica to his eye-level, holding it between his thumb and index finger. He narrowed his left eye and examined it with his right, as if inspecting a diamond. As the screen's colours changed, his focus shifted to the screen. The analysis was complete.

Krishna stood there with his mouth agape and kept staring onto the screen with his eyes wide open. It was as if he had painted a masterpiece and somebody just walked in and vandalized his proud creation.

As Krishna stood there amazed and in utter disbelief, Mohan spoke up, 'The backbone...'

Krishna heard him but didn't turn and was now clinching his fist, on seeing his work of art demolished. 'Yes! The backbone. This device is separating backbone from the rest of the structure.' Krishna said as he loosened his tightened fist and regained his calm.

'It can disintegrate Bhoomidium! This is a weapon in itself, if it can do so with such ease,' Mohan said.

'The bigger question is who made this?'

'Someone who is an enemy of our civilization, our society.'

'To undo what I have designed, means someone on Bhoomi either equals or surpasses the lab's capabilities.'

Mohan nodded. 'If we try removing this implant, we raise alarms. How do we then solve my sector's problem?'

'The fuel supply line! The intruder has taken over the water supply line, so we will use the fuel supply. I would add Bhoomidium-1008 to the supply for the sector. It is highly stable and won't burn. It would diffuse in households from there on.'

Mohan nodded in agreement.

'I can keep on stabilizing the compound and can make it more hack-proof. But eventually whosoever is doing this would catch up and find new ways to disrupt the levels.'

'We need to zero in upon that person. If required we must call an Empowered Group meeting,' Mohan suggested. Only five of the most senior councillors had the authority to chair the Empowered Group meeting. And apart from the top five, only Krishna had the authority to call or attend one.

'Let's think over it. What if the designer of this is an Empowered Councillor?' Krishna said with the mysterious object still in his hand.

'Are we trapped here? If we stay quiet, we risk much bolder attacks. If we go to the Council, we would make it apparent to the perpetrator that we are scared. The Manavas think twice before treating someone unjustly even once, and this person, is actually trying to harm innocent people. What kind of a war is this? How do we tackle this?'

'Calm down, we will figure something out.'

Mohan nodded and picked up his stuff and said, 'Will see you at eight tomorrow morning.'

It was a long and exhausting day for Krishna. He was now alone and had to clear his mind before he could think of anything. He took a deep breath trying to assimilate all the information, which seemed to have inundated him.

Firstly, few of his close acquaintances were now already hovering near the Criticality mark. Secondly, this was all planned and engineered.

The device could have been made only in two ways, either someone knew how to fabricate Bhoomidium, or someone had access to large computation facilities. Outside his facility, such computational powers were non-existent because of the moratorium. And even if the other guy did hack into each handheld device in Madhavpur, still the computational power required for such a feat won't sum up. There was a moratorium on holding big computational facilities in Madhavpur, apart from the Council sanctioned Samganak.

If indeed it was an insider's job, confrontation will be inevitable. What Krishna feared was that such an act of audacity would be backed with a strong plan. He was now left with only one choice. He needed to act, and act decisively.

8

The Berry Affair

He was standing beside his building, when in the nearby lamppost's feeble light he saw someone moving down the street. The otherwise deserted look of the street was now being defied by that very man, walking briskly past the row of houses.

Not only his fast and surreptitious gait but also his ankle-length black overcoat caught Krishna's attention. He looked around (and noticing no one watching him), turned on his Yocto-Suit and started following the person.

With distance growing between both, the person in the overcoat was now appearing like a dark shadow under streetlights. He had to pick pace to keep up with that person. Some hundred metres ahead, there was a left and a right turn on the street end. He could not risk losing the chase; he had to catch up before that person could take a turn.

He was now half-walking and half-running. He wanted to run fast but his feet and arms seemed stiff. *Could be an effect of the Yocto-Suit.* He kept on trying, but his pace seemed unusually slow, by any standards.

When the person in the overcoat was passing in front of the last but one house, its lights went on—this startled the mystery man and he paused. Now instead of pacing his way to the street end, he started crouching. This further deepened Krishna's doubts.

Something is fishy, is this man the intruder? He could not let this man go.

He was now barely some ten steps behind the person. He had to be careful, and not give that mystery man the sense of being chased. He waited till the person passed the house, and regained his pace.

The mystery man took a left and crossed into the intersecting street. He was headed towards sector-108. Krishna followed him with whatever pace he could muster out of his stiff legs. The man missed the first two turns on the street and kept on striding towards the end of the road.

A thought struck Krishna. *Is he headed towards the supply facility of the sector?* If he was the same person who implanted the device on the water pipe, he could now very well do anything obnoxious.

I should probably hack into the central facility servers and change the access code to the supply chambers!

He was now breathing heavily and perspiring profusely. His legs and arms were now heavier and stiffer than before. This could very well have been a lactic acid build-up in his muscles, from lack of rest. He tried raising his arm to access his Mani-Bandh, but they were rigid from the elbow joints. He was tired and was out of breath, but could not have given up on the chase.

He finally raised his hand. To his wonder, he could see the display of his wrist-device but could not decipher what was written on it. The symbols on the display didn't make any sense to him. A drop of his sweat fell on the display. It became blurred. He gave up on the idea of changing the access codes.

The mystery man took the last left turn on the street, making it quite clear that he was headed towards the facility. Krishna was now some twenty steps behind him, the man then reached the door of the facility. Krishna stopped some 15–20 steps from the door.

His vision was now blurry at best and the low light was not

helping either. He could not make out what the man in the long coat was up to. All he could see was, him fixing something adjacent to the access control box. Krishna stood there steadfast and kept on noticing. He could have moved in and tried accosting the person. But somehow he could not find the will to do so, as if his mind had already made a choice—to not to. He then from the comfort of the stealth of his Yocto-Suit, was trying to figure out the plans of the man in the overcoat.

Unaware of the onlooker, the mystery man kept on to his work with a razor sharp focus. *What kind of new trouble is this?* Krishna could not decide what he was more eager to know about, the trouble or the trouble-brewer.

Meanwhile, the mystery man pressed a button on the hemispherical object that he had affixed just next to the panel. A bright glittering ring of cyan-coloured lights circumferencing the hemisphere started glowing. The overcoat-clad man then checked his wrist-device. He now turned back and started walking away from the door.

Mystery man probably had no access to door combinations and was trying to dismantle the door using a controlled explosion. He stood there silently watching the door. After few seconds the flashing lights turned red. The man ducked and was now lying flat on the ground with his hands over the back of his head.

Krishna was too stiff and startled to react. Before he could blink another eye, a shrill sound and a neon blue shock wave emanated from that device. The shock wave was followed by a heat wave and balls of fire. Krishna fell down and rolled over his belly.

He could feel the heat all around him. The radiation detector on his Mani-Bandh went off. It started chiming. His cover was now blown; no way could the suit have withstood such a strong radiation.

What was it? Did that freak just set off a nuclear device? But the heat wave subsided. *Or was it a miniature Electro-Magnetic Pulse (EMP) device.*

As Krishna raised his head to look up, he saw the man standing right in front of him. He pulled out a gun from underneath his coat, and pointed it at Krishna. *Who is he? And how on Bhoomi did he get access to such weaponries?* With big fireballs rising from the facility building, he could only see the silhouette of the person. The face was still not visible to him.

Even before the bright light in the background could subside and Krishna could see who he was, the man pulled the trigger.

A bright spark flashed from the barrel and everything started growing faint and fuzzy for Krishna. His visuals were now filled with bright lights. The shrill sound faded into the background and he could now hear some soothing flute and bird chime in the distance.

Have I been shot? All these pleasant lights and sounds, is this my oxygen-starved languishing brain's hallucination? After that his consciousness was filled with even brighter lights and louder notes of flutes and chimes.

•◆

He woke up breathing heavily and sweating profusely. It was his 6 a.m. alarm.

It took him a while to normalize his breath and pull himself out of the clutches of that life-like dream. He changed his robe and dashed out of the lab. After ten minute of jogging, he could see Mount Govardhan glittering in the morning sunshine. With his Venu tucked in his waistband, he headed towards west.

He wanted to feel the cool morning breeze in his face. He remembered the dream vividly, and just wanted to shake off the emotional grip of it. Reaching the base of the Mount Govardhan, he raised his head and saw the peak. Pulled in a long puff of morning air and started his ascent.

Reaching the top he sat down on the grass facing the sunrise, with his arms embracing his folded legs. The sun was now over the horizon and was surrounded by thin grey clouds. He pulled out his Venu and placed it beside himself on the grass. It was a gift from Radhika, after she had heard him play a flute in his college fest.

Krishna was still perturbed with all the happenings. *Is quantity more pressing than quality?* Humans always had their chance. They had a fully functional brain for rational choices. Still things went so far, that they had to take help of scientific intervention to undo the damage. Bhoomidium metamorphosed the then humans into a refined race of Manavas. But was it worthwhile, who knows?

The sacrifices were too many to recall. Though he has been young, vital, and healthy for almost two million years. But his beloved was now nowhere to be seen; it was a separation till eternity.

There were mornings when he used to wake, looking forward to seeing that beautiful face and that mellowing voice. Now what does he have to wake up to? Buying eternity for Manavas, till eternity? When the sole purpose of existence becomes existence itself, does it not defy the very purpose of higher living?

Krishna now reclined and lied down on the grass, gazing at the early morning blue sky. He cleared his mind, and recalled the day when the foundation of the modern Manava society was laid. The oath of allegiance and dedication to the mission he undertook. He recalled it all. Serving the cause was his mission. It was not mere existence he was fighting for. There was the cause, a basis on which foundation of a just and rational society was laid. He had unwavering support of Mohan, Shyam, Vasu, and many more who understood the cause.

Krishna got up, sat in lotus position, and picked up his flute. He closed his eyes and imagined the soft and radiant face of Radhika.

He then started playing. His notes were not only as melodious as earlier, but also had a hint of softness, that only a true love could have brought along. As he kept on playing, birds of songs and colourful butterflies began surrounding him.

They followed the music of Krishna, from all directions. He could feel the little ones around him flapping wings, hopping on tiny feet, twittering through small yet strong beaks and echoing his notes. He was now beyond the point of discerning, if whether he was driving those notes down the lane of a symphony or was it the other way around.

The cool gust of air blowing from the west was now ruffling his hair. As the air blew between the strands of his hair and untangled them, he felt a disentangling of his own self too. He could feel his consciousness, getting untied from the material realms of worldly perception. As if the music emanating from the flute was pulling him from the shores, into the ever-flowing ocean of universal consciousness. Where the isolated strands of his perceptions began matting into a single string, floating on the surface of the ever-conscious ocean of oneness.

A small dusky feathered bird, hopped onto Krishna's lap. Krishna opened his eyes and could not help but smile, parting the Venu from his lips. As the music halted, the small bird atop his lap started looking into his eye.

Almost baffled by such behaviour of the bird, he raised his hand with his index finger extended out. He wanted to pat the wings of the bold one. But before he could extend his arm any further, the bird flew. The sound of wings flapping made all others birds take flight too.

As the flock of birds took to the sky, so did hundreds of butterflies. They rose from the grass cover, where up until now they had gone mostly unnoticed by Krishna. The colourful-winged creatures of flight now surrounded him. No matter in what direction he turned it was an all-surrounding canvas, full of countless colours.

The sun was now already up to the eye-level. *I must race back to the lab, Mohan could turn up any moment now.*

As Krishna neared the lab, he saw Mohan sitting on the bench on the grass patch, behind the sidewalk. With both his arms spread out and resting on the top of the backrest of the bench, he was busy soaking sunlight.

'I saw you coming and thought would wait for you. Nice sunny day, isn't it?'

'That's what prompted me for a run. Let's go inside. Let's see what new we got today,' Krishna said enthusiastically. 'We are in early Terra Life form stage,' Mohan said.

'Any sign of vertebrate life on land?'

'We should feel lucky if we find some arthropods or some sort of bugs. Though the plant life has prospered well on surface,' Mohan said.

'And the aquatic?'

'The aquatic has been doing well, too. They have diversified into various species,' Mohan replied.

Krishna nodded. Both entered the lab. The giant screen was on, displaying various imageries of Prithvi. A place so serene yet so full of life, it could have been confused with an uninhabited land on Bhoomi, by an untrained eye. The vast terrain of land was covered with volcanic soil, neighboured by patchy tracts of green. And those terrains then either culminated into still further ranges of volcanoes and mountains or into rivers and oceans. Their task now was to find needle in a haystack.

'I have ran a module to back up the latest data feed to your terminal. I am in no imminent mood to work. So, my dear...'

'Consider it done,' Mohan stated.

'Look out for arthropods in green tracts and for any amphibian life along coasts. I also want an elaborate report on the diversification factor.'

Mohan nodded.

'I will be on the terrace for a while. Just buzz me if you want me here.'

Mohan smiled, he could sense that something was going on with Krishna.

•◆

It was now a pre-midday sun, bright enough. Krishna walked up to the backside of the terrace. He could see the Radha-Kund from there. The emerald green water and the flocks of birds in and around it could be seen even from that distance. It was a pleasing, picture-perfect landscape.

Krishna, during his university days, had always fancied settling there, besides the lake, in a nice small cottage with Radhika. His plan was to work in United States until the completion of Project Amrit. He always wanted to come back to Madhavpur. The turn of events did make his project bring him back to the city he always desired. But still couldn't vouch him his dreams. Radhika had stuck to her decision and he to his.

I have never missed her like this before. Or maybe he was too busy to think about her, up until now. And now when things were again scheduled for a change, he was getting nostalgic.

The foregone is foregone, no use ruminating the past. I have a big fight ahead, with an enemy whose capabilities I am still not aware of.

Krishna stood there in peace for almost thirty minutes or so. Then it got too hot for him to stand under the sun, he made his way back to the lab. On his way, he prepared two cups of coffee from the brewer in his living room, the one that had aromatic berry sugar in it.

'Coffee.' Krishna placed the mug on a small table next to the panel.

'I was going over this data, and there is good news,' Mohan said.

'Keep it coming.'

'The arthropods, they are all around the vegetation. They have diversified to such a large extent, that now there is a definitive food chain hierarchy.'

'Aha! The smart carnivore bugs are now living off the innocuous plant-eating bugs. Sounds like Nature at work.'

Mohan smiled, acknowledging the sarcasm and then said, 'The aquatic life, the plant life, and invertebrate life is now quite diversified. We stand quite a fair chance in case of any glitch, for now.'

'Just waiting for vertebrate life to move towards the land.'

'I have some more surprises in store for you,' Mohan added.

'Then just shoot.'

'I have detected the metabolite by-product of the genes which are quintessential to the vertebrates. And I have detected them on land,' Mohan stated.

'Excellent. Did we get to locate any per-se?'

'Not yet, but we can. We need to train Samganak to calculate the locations with maximum probability,' he replied.

'That should work,' Krishna said as he moved towards the control panel.

He pulled up the map of Prithvi on the screen. The landmasses were now visibly demarcated at many places. The gaps between the newly separating continents were still no bigger than creeks filled with ocean water. The continents were shifting along a common land mass as a fulcrum. The idea was to have life forms diversified and uniformly spread out, before these continents totally drifted away from each other. So that with basic root species present on all separated continents, they could thereon evolve according to the changing topography and climate.

While Krishna was busy working on the control panel, Mohan was sitting back comfortably sipping on to his coffee. 'I could actually never appreciate this coffee more than the other varieties. But yes you were right; it does help soothe your nerves better than those. Not to mention its wonderful aroma.'

Krishna turned back and flashed a big smile, making his sense of vindication ostensible. He and Mohan had always differed on this one. Krishna from his childhood would go out to nearby woods and collect edible berries of all kind, which he would then dry in the sun and ground. As he grew, the forest cover shrank and the berries grew rare. He then started planting them in his backyard. Mohan could never understand this, and considered it a superfluous ritual.

Mohan rose from his seat and walked toward the panel. 'Krishna, you were right about many things. But people around you chose to ignore all that all along. They just cherry-picked what they wanted to hear.'

'It's called power dynamics, Mohan. You cannot just wish it away. You can flow along with it, but can never oppose.'

'Had they heeded your advice on 1007, and instead given you a free hand and time to work on it, this would not have happened. They all so innocently believed that science could be built to order. Just build spaceships, find another suitable planet on some other galaxy and march to it.'

Krishna smiled in response, while still working on the panel.

'You never take it personally, do you?' Mohan asked.

'No, I never let myself take it personally, ever.'

'Why?'

'I am here for the oath. The oath we all took for the continuity of our civilization. It matters least to me, who says what or who holds how much power in here. I have always suggested, in my capacity as the Chief Scientific Advisor, what was best for the Manavas and Madhavpur. Then it's up to the discretion of the Council to accept them or not. Let's face it Mohan, sitting in a laboratory and coming up with scenarios is relatively easier than governing and determining what is best for your people. They have done well in their job, as much as we have in ours. We all are here to play our part and not to make others play their part as per our whims.'

'Then why did you conceal the project from the Council?'

'I did not.'

'You didn't?' Mohan was a little confused.

'As per the governing constitution, in case of an imminent and severe danger to the civilization, required measures can be taken by Chief Scientific Advisor with the consent of the Head of the Council; without going to the entire Council or seeking their consent. And the danger, as I might well remind you, is that to our very existence.'

'So Shyam knows, which further bolsters my point that we should go to the Empowered Group to raise our concerns regarding the sector-108 incident,' Mohan stated.

'Let me complete instructing the Samganak,' Krishna then said.

Mohan walked back to his chair, placing his now empty coffee mug on the side desk.

After a prolonged gap interwoven with sound of his fingers tapping on the touch panel, Krishna said, 'It's ready. I have fed in all the details required to carry out the search.'

Both now stood by the screen, waiting for the Samganak to begin search for the coveted beings, which could manoeuvre both land and sea alike.

The Samganak started pitching some breathtaking visuals. It was some coast on the easternmost border of the landmass.

Samganak then started searching down the coastline. The ocean water was translucent towards the beach. As the distance from the shore increased it was changing its colour from light emerald to light blue, and then dark blue further into the ocean. The narrow but long strip of beach was made up of golden gravel and sand. The incessant waves, over the period of time were crushing those rough gravels into fine sand. The high cliffs, standing guard to the serene coastline, were shining in the bourgeoning morning sunlight.

Amid those colourful and mesmerizing visuals, Krishna noticed some movement in the sand at one place. He stepped forward and instructed Samganak to concentrate on that particular area. It was a breeding ground. This was what he was looking for, creatures that could live in oceans and lay eggs on the ground. He started analysing the new discovery.

'They are coming out of the oceans,' Mohan observed.

'In search of food and safe grounds for laying eggs—yes, they are.'

The analysis report started appearing on the screen in an inset. The creature had the features of proto-amphibians. They were quite capable of dividing their time between the land and the sea.

'Do we go and analyse the data stream in the server room?' Mohan asked.

'The reports are pretty conclusive, so we can skip that.'

He then pushed the report onto his hand device, and projected the same for Mohan to see. 'They are already there in numbers and have differentiated into many species. The biomarkers suggest that they are already feeding on territorial plants and bugs. This is a fine progress,' Krishna said with a smile.

9

The Dance of the Cosmos

It was almost evening, and Mohan was still sitting there analysing data. He found it hard to understand why he could not get access to programming the actual Café Evolution project on Samganak.

Will he or will he not get annoyed if I ask him so? But with Mohan's personal office space converted into some slow-motion movie theatre and with all the work being of either post-analysis or being auxiliary, he probably knew the answer.

He then heard Krishna coming downstairs, and promptly asked him, 'When can I get access to the Main Control Panel?'

'Not in the near future,' Krishna said, as if reciting a prepared answer.

'And the reason would be?'

'Put on your best, it's almost time,' Krishna instead said.

'I would like an answer to my query with reasons, please.'

'I do not want to share the burden. If the project doesn't materialize, I alone take the responsibility,' Krishna said matter-of-factly.

'Well, that makes partial sense.'

'Let it be, for now. Now get up and dress up in your best.'

'For? And why are you so dressed up?'

Krishna was dressed in a saffron-coloured robe with handcrafted lotuses and peacocks all over the upper-left corner (across his shoulder and heart). The accompanying waistband was a contrasting yellow with a small buckle on it, crusted with gems.

'For the Bharatnatayam show, tonight,' Krishna replied.

'Oh gosh! I had to pick my wife to be there by seven for the show!' Mohan panicked a bit.

'I called Meera. I told her that you were busy with me on something significant. She must have reached there by now.'

'I have no time to go home and change. I will have to borrow something from you.'

'Help yourself,' Krishna offered, and pointed towards the staircase leading to his living room.

The show was being held in the Art and Culture Centre of the Council Building. Bharatnatayam was one of the art legacies that the Manavas had inherited. The most ancient documented dance form, which emerged from India in distant antiquity. It was an amalgam of dance and expression of emotions. The dance form was a creative means of worshipping the Lord of the Cosmos—Natraj (the God with matted hair).

As they entered the hall, it was already dark and the spotlights were on. Though the first performance was yet to start but the stage was all set. 'Let's sit in the front, there are still some vacant seats,' Mohan whispered.

'We will sit here, at the back of the hall.'

He followed Krishna and sat two rows behind the last occupied row.

The show started and the classical dancers draped in beautiful sarees, gave some breathtaking performances one after another. Each performance was followed by heartiest round of applauses from the audience.

'I wanted to keep a low profile. The front rows would be full of councillors and other prominent people.'

Mohan nodded in concurrence. After some good twenty minutes into the show, Krishna asked, 'When will Meera perform?'

'Hers is the last performance of the evening. She is leading a group of performers.' Meanwhile Vallabha, the childhood friend of Meera, appeared on stage for the last solo performance of the evening.

'Are you enjoying? Or are just here to pick up Meera?'

'Come on, Krishna. I was busy. I would never have missed out on our annual cultural show.'

'So, you are enjoying the show. Good, you should.'

'Should?' Mohan was a little baffled and impatient.

'This could be the last show which we might be enjoying here in this hall,' Krishna said.

A shadow fell on Mohan's face. 'But I actually doubt that we might have to move in less than a year's time. The whole process will still take longer, right?'

'The Vedic Code is under threat,' Krishna explained.

Mohan grew pale. The first coherent thought he could assemble together was that Krishna was pulling a prank. Because if it were true, it would be a catastrophe.

'What prompted you to say so? How could you be so sure?' Mohan asked.

'Trust me, no sane person on Bhoomi would ever want this but I fear this might happen. And, I say so with a good degree of surety.'

'We would lose moral right to continue on Bhoomi as a civilization. And more than that, wars may ensue,' Mohan explained.

'We will have to eventually vacate Bhoomi, in any scenario. It is the war bit which I am more worried about.'

The sombre mood of the conversation was broken by an uproar of applause. The curtains drew close, as the stage was being redone for the mega performance.

'Do we have a plan to deal with such a likelihood?' Mohan asked.

'The code is not a coercively enforceable law. It's an understanding, a wilful way of paying respect and being grateful.'

The curtains started rising, the conversation lulled. The stage was profoundly decorated with lights in a very thoughtful manner. It was draped with silken fabric in vivid colours on the edges and the background. A low-lying smoke filled the stage. The static smoke suffused in vibrant lights of different colours, was setting the mood for the much-anticipated performance.

A powerful electromagnet then pulled the low-lying smoke up till the roof above the stage, forming a thick curtain of smoke of a sort. After a short interval, the speed with which the smoke curtain went up, it came down. Revealing the troupe of dancers on the stage.

Finally, Meera appeared on the stage, draped in a cream-coloured saree lined with golden embroidery and with her hair-bun wrapped around in jasmine garlands. She was looking the most charming of all. She moved on to the centre stage, with four artistes from each preceding solo performances on both sides. She then folded her hands in a Vedic gesture of 'Namaskaram'. With her knees bent a little and her feet touching each other forming a 'V', she started wobbling her fingers as if a lotus was blossoming.

The whole performance was a flawless coordination of feet movement and portrayal of emotions through facial expressions. Krishna turned towards Mohan, while he was still absorbed in the performance. He could see that gleam of happiness in his eyes; the contentment, which emerges from seeing someone you love and care for. He was now missing companionship more than ever before, and the fact that Meera, all bejeweled at the moment, resembled Radhika, was not helping either. The whole auditorium was filled with divine concoction of Vedic chants, beats, and synchronized tapping of feet.

Meera and her group ended the show, again with a namaskaram and the whole auditorium gave a standing ovation to the group.

They both started moving, as Mohan was to meet Meera near the main exit. 'I will have to go to the lab. You catch up with Meera and I will see you tomorrow,' Krishna said.

'How about dinner at our place?'

'Some other day, Mohan.'

Krishna had to rush back to the lab; his Mani-Bandh had received a distress signal from the Samganak, some ten minutes back. And now he was not able to make contact with the lab's computers.

―•―

He was standing near the control panel, all sweaty and still wheezing from the dash he had made to the lab. The controls were now up and running and Krishna was able to access the main computer.

Despite the climate controls inside the lab, it was uncomfortably hot and humid. His main task was now to revive the cooling units of the system. *What could have been more malicious than this?* The only point of respite was that everything functioned as planned and Samganak handled it all very well by itself.

There was a loud clacking sound at the main door of the lab. It was Mohan. 'What's the matter, Krishna?'

'You should have been at home.'

'We saw you running in a haste. Meera was worried, so she asked me to go to the lab instead.'

'All is fine, Mohan, go back home. It's a big day for you and Meera, work can wait.'

'What is it?' Mohan insisted.

After a subsequent pause, he said, 'There was a cyberattack on Samganak while we were at the cultural centre.'

'Is our data and work fine?'

'Yes, it is. Café Evolution is fine and safe. Samganak sent me a distress signal and then went offline from all networks to protect itself. The data lines to the server room and De-Accelerator chamber were snapped voluntarily by Samganak.'

'It did all this by itself?'

'There are very precise mechanisms to protect Samganak from any such cyberattacks.'

Mohan still looked puzzled, to which Krishna said, 'There is a standby Artificial Intelligence programme. It usually doesn't reside in the system.'

'What about the moratorium?'

'You mean that on Artificial Intelligence? As per the norms Samganak does not display any Artificial Intelligence under normal circumstances. But for situation like these, Samganak is well programmed to load on the AI programme module. This enables the system to take any decision required to fend off any sort of intrusion. I developed the AI module at the beginning of the project, as a precautionary measure. I wanted to make sure that our system had considerable hack resistance, in case we encountered any intelligent but belligerent life form.'

'I am glad we have such a defence mechanism, now the question is who engineered this attack? Any trails left behind?' Mohan asked.

'None. It was a sequential attempt at destroying the Samganak. The hacker first tried gaining administrative controls; it could not go past our first tier of security. Then went for controlling all the data servers, but second tier of security kicked in and blew wires connecting servers to the system. At this point Samganak went offline, and loaded the AI module. Only then it could root out the attack. The hacker still managed to delete all the trails and was able to shut down the cooling units of the processor.'

'No wonder it is roasting hot in here,' Mohan remarked.

'I want you to go home and stay with Meera; I will have to repair the systems. I want it fully functional by morning.'

'Why would I leave you now? We will both fix it. This definitely is going to take much time and effort.'

'Our lab was targeted, when we were out. I do not want you to leave Meera alone.'

'I will call and ask Vallabha to pick up Meera. She will stay at her place.'

Mohan was adamant about being there with Krishna, and Krishna knew this. He relented. He asked Mohan to mend all the data connections and bring back the server room and De-Accelerator on to the Samganak network. While he himself started reinitiating all the sequences on Samganak and made sure that no necessary software module was amiss.

It took more than two hours to get the server room and De-Accelerator online, while software re-initiation was taking a little longer. Mohan came back and quietly sat on his chair beside his desk. 'The person or the group who targeted Samganak is the same that tampered with 108's water supply.'

'What makes you think it's a group?'

'No individual can single-handedly carry out such operations alone. These people have expertise, know our systems, have resources, and probably know about our movements too. replied Mohan.

Krishna just nodded, while still working.

'What conclusive surety were you talking about at the art centre?' Mohan asked.

'You mean the Vedic Code,' he took a pause and smiled, 'it's hard to explain, a sort of hunch.'

'I know you very well Krishna, you do not make such serious statements based on just a hunch.'

'I have guarded this secret for quite long now. There are times when I hear voices in my sleep. Voices, which I suppose, are from the core. Sounds like wild imagination, but it is true.'

'I believe you. Quite strange though.'

'As a matter of fact I did not discover the backbone of Bhoomidium, but I was guided by these very voices.'

'Krishna! Even Benzene ring's structure was discovered in a dream. Remember the Ouroboros dreams? These are voices from within; your inner intellect is guiding you through. The core with uniform and ever-pervading consciousness is just a postulated theory.'

Nonetheless, it was Krishna's favourite theory.

The theory was suggested by a group of researchers at NYCAR. Before they could move onto advancing their theories and backing it with data, funds were frozen. Works with long-term implications, bordering on elements of spirituality was beginning to be considered luxury. As resources grew scarce, many such projects were reduced to being just books to be shovelled away into shelves, never to be dusted again.

On one idle evening, long after Criticality was reached, Krishna came across one such book, which talked about parallel universes and a core full of energy around which these universes revolved. By that time he already knew about the probable problem that could arise with 1007 isotope. He was searching for solutions and the theory seemed to make some sense to him.

'I will let you in on a secret—it isn't just a postulated theory. Moreover, you yourself have seen the payloads reaching those different universes.'

'It is not widely accepted, was what I meant. And it reached a faraway planet, which might be in some far-fetched corner of our own universe. I thought we were working on presumptive models, how do we explain these other universes to everyone else?' Mohan wondered.

'If we base validity on the level of acceptance, I am not sure I would still call it evolution into a finer race. A widely popular myth is still a myth and a truth ignored will still qualify as a truth.'

'Krishna, all I meant was you cannot credit all your achievement to some voices. I want to know more about the core, everybody would like to, just that nobody ever studied about it.'

'I was the first person who got exposed to Bhoomidium. Now I am not sure whether it was just prolonged exposure or some other factors that also played role, but it did to me something beyond what it did to others. On the surface I am similar to the other Manavas, but my brain has evolved to another level. I myself once believed that my pre-Bhoomidium intelligence had a major role in me being CD1++, but this goes beyond that. This just goes beyond science and numbers. When I came across this very theory in National Archives, my brain started running scenarios and they all fitted well into telling a tale; a tale of parallel universes. There was a point in time, when it was euphoric. Bhoomi and especially Madhavpur were all about fun, frolic, and sunshine. Almost utopia! But my brain was looking forward, it knew that Nature supports anarchy and utopia in this ephemeral world is often an illusion or a transitory and fleeting reality. I had so much free time at hand and the solitude at lab made me venture out of the settlement. I started going to the hills and stayed there all day long. Had it been all about theories, research, and numbers it won't have been a lore worth narrating. But my mind…it started connecting. It began to connect into the infinite energy pool we know as Nature or universe. I could feel it. It could have been either way. Either the theory about the core was making impressions on my mind or it was for real, and my mind was using that theory as a manual to connect. I could sense the unified consciousness pervading through me. The roadmaps started appearing on the horizon of my mind. I started work on creating 1008 and on developing methods to initiate the sequences that could evolve life on newer planets and in newer universes from scratch. So that, when the time came we could either march, or could pass on the baton,' Krishna concluded.

'I always had this in the back of my mind. On the day of the launch, I saw and understood it. Just that I never wanted to believe in your theory. When my wife discusses plans for next summer or a new dining-set or home renovation, I just feign a smile and nod in agreement. When you have to shift from one house to another it takes a while to settle and adjust, we might have to leap across time and space. The brain still acknowledges it, but the mind grows adamant in disbelief. How convenient it was in earlier days, live along a cosy river basin, deplete all resources, and then move onto other greener pastures. Why now do we have to move in such an unprecedented manner?' Mohan said.

'We have already exhausted all our cosy green pastures. We have sucked Bhoomi dry of all her resources two million years ago. She nurtured us, and we poisoned her. We, the Manavas, were living off borrowed time.'

Mohan nodded in agreement. 'Vallabha saw you in the hills, especially on Mount Meru. During her morning runs.'

'Those hills are not ordinary, they echo of antiquity. There is some tale, some epic engrained there, which we know not of,' Krishna replied.

'I somehow have a feeling that all these events are not isolated,' Mohan said.

By now Krishna was done preparing the Samganak for a fresh start. And it was back online. He then turned on the datastream. Samganak started generating report on the progress of Café Evolution.

'Mohan, the life form has progressed. The amphibians have adapted to a full-time land life,' Krishna declared.

The amphibians had evolved into proto-reptiles and were feeding off bugs and insects. The climate on Prithvi was still harsh. But life had evolved to such an extent that it was safe to say that they were there to stay. The major objective of the early life form was to survive, breed, and diversify.

It was now well past midnight, and on Krishna's advice Mohan left for Vallabha's place to join Meera. As the night grew darker, 'Who is behind these attacks?' was the predominant question engulfing Krishna's mind.

10

A Foe among Friends

'No one is allowed to question the soundness of the project. No one.'

'Calm down, Vasu! No one here is questioning the sanctity of the project. Don't get worked up,' Vitthal said as he rolled towards his left in his huge wooden chair with generously wide armrests.

'Vasu is right; we should steer clear from sounding as if we are inquiring into the fundamentals of the project. This is a brainstorming session, and we need to hear out each other's arguments without being judgemental,' Narayan said.

'And I would reiterate my point that more computational power be sanctioned for calculating the exact timeline. We must strive for a scenario where we have ample buffer time between dropping Bhoomidium levels and a new habitat. I would also like us to chalk out a plan as to what percentage of resources are we willing to consider again for searching the already habitable new planet, somewhere near to home,' Gopal said.

Shyam was standing by the side of a table. He was more comfortable standing, this way he was able to get a psychologically holistic perspective of the discussion. He wanted to reserve his words and listen to what other Empowered Councillors had to say. He knew they were suppressing some sudden emotions, probably a mix of surprise and betrayal—one that emerges from being bypassed.

Shyam had no qualms about using his discretionary powers. The whole changed course of the project was Krishna's brainchild, and after a three-hour presentation, Shyam didn't blink an eye before according his nod. He still remembered the last page of the presentation—'Approval of Head of the Council for the proposed modification in project, under discretionary power accorded by the Constitution, requested.'

'We cannot split our focus at this critical juncture. It's not about our convenience anymore; it's about our survival. And in such cases, I prefer leaving the subject matter to the subject matter expert,' Vasu spoke in a gentle but firm tone.

Vitthal stood up from his chair and, leaning forward with his palms placed on the table's edge, said, 'Help me understand the whole thing.' He then moved towards a touch-sensitive whiteboard in the room, a few steps away from the conference table.

'We had a general consensus that Krishna would work towards stabilizing the Bhoomidium levels on Bhoomi, which he did. And we had a consensus on going out in quest of an inhabitable planet for migration, if need be. Now that he isn't looking out for any readily inhabitable planet but is instead preparing a new one, he must have some good reasons for it.' Vitthal said as he jotted down all the points on the boards with his finger impressions.

'Reasons please, Krishna,' Gopal prompted.

Gopal, Vitthal, and Narayan used to be the Heads of the three biggest research universities of India in Kali-Yuga. They were all good acquaintances and used to meet each other in academic seminars, apart from being alumni of the same college—Indian Institute of Research Sciences. The trio was also part of the Advisory Committee set-up by the Government of India to counter climate change and degradation of environment.

Though the genius of the three was unsurpassed by anybody of their batch, yet Gopal was the most ambitious of them all. He was a child prodigy too. He was a champion throughout and achieved whatever he used to set his aim at; until he grew so indispensable and crucial to the government projects that his clearances for deputation abroad, never went through. His boon became his bane.

When all the nations were facing trouble combating climate change, European Union and Japan asked for Indian assistance. Indian authorities chose Vitthal for deputation to the German research institute in Berlin and Narayan for the Japanese research institute in Tokyo. The indispensable cream of the talent—Gopal—was retained in India by the government.

Gopal had been left seething. His dedication, intelligence, and hard work were now presumably working against his ambitions and desires. And this was not even the first time he had to lick his wounds.

When a dearth of skill pool and shrinking population base compelled the apex research body constituted by the Government of United States to invite applications from world over, Gopal's hopes had been high and fingers crossed.

But it was Shyam who had been selected, on the basis of his experience and administrative skills. Gopal did not frown and kept to his lab and university. He toiled endlessly, and in return he just wanted to be known worldwide. But when after five years he saw himself missing the party again, over the European and Japanese saga, his ego was scathed. He withdrew from all governmental advisory bodies and committees, and confided himself to his university.

After two years of the self-imposed exile, the ministry contacted him again. He was pleasantly unaffected and unmoved. They wanted him to head the Indian operations of the biggest 'Conservation and Coordination' project. It took him less than ten seconds to refuse with a cold 'No'. The government had to rope in Shyam to convince Gopal, after which he had finally given in.

But that was then. After the beginning of the 'Swarnim-Yuga', he was a changed man. He was much calmer and his wisdom had replaced his ego and his perception had matured.

'I am in service of the Empowered Council, and bound to answer any query. But before I proceed to that, I would just like to put forward a humble request. None of the matters discussed here, must go out. The Bhoomidium levels are dropping and any panic or even a hint of it can be contagious. And nothing accelerates the decline of cellular levels of Bhoomidium faster than panic and stress,' Krishna said.

'Any information put forward to the Council is confidential and we all are under oath to maintain required secrecy. Worry not,' Gopal stated in an affirming tone.

'The quest for a new inhabitable planet was leading us nowhere. It was my call to build a more conducive planet for our movement. I am not at all averse to allocating resources for continuing the quest for a new abode nearby, but I would recommend that additional resources be sanctioned,' Krishna said.

'We would like to hear more about what made you think so?' Gopal prompted.

'Gopal, I have been working my days and nights off on this project. If the biggest take-home I have to pick from my work, it would inevitably be the Laws of Nature—the laws we know not much of. They are not to be confused with the laws of physics that we encounter every day of our lives. The laws of Nature I am talking about have more to do with the Orderliness of the Universe. There exist no schools of thought among the Manavas to study such laws. They can only be sensed by the intuitive mind and cannot, as of now, be formulated by the analytical mind. With whatever limited understanding I have of these laws, it seems, the universe was not designed to support intelligent life on multiple locations. And with no need for life, none of the planets, barring Bhoomi, had environments conducive for life. We can still go out and search for an exception, but do we really want to focus on looking for the proverbial needle in the haystack?' Krishna said.

'No, we don't. What we are suggesting is keeping enough options open,' Gopal stated.

Narayan got up from his seat and wrote 'Option not feasible' on the white board. Gopal raised a brow, but said nothing.

'So what's the game plan, Krishna. Are we looking at changing chemical composition of the newly found planet? What was its name by the way?' Narayan asked.

'Prithvi. And, yes eventually we will have to manoeuvre its environment.'

'Did we breach any moratoriums?' Gopal asked in a subtle but steady tone.

'Moratorium was set by us to stop any wasteful and/or perilous toying around with technology, to protect us from the unforeseen. If the turns of events pose a threat to our existence and we need to bend some rules to get by, so be it,' Vasu said.

'Quite a lot, as a matter of fact,' Krishna continued with his reply.

'How did you start the sequence, Krishna?' asked Vitthal.

'I studied all the evolutionary history of pre-Manavas era. There was a clear pattern of proliferation of species and then natural selection. I then distilled the whole process into a mathematical sequence, an outright manifestation of beauty and symmetry. The real challenge though was to encode the sequence into a primordial super cell.'

'And you then teleported the cell to Prithvi,' Vitthal finished for Krishna. Krishna smiled and nodded in affirmation.

Krishna had no motivation to divulge exact project details to the Empowered Group, he had Shyam's support and it was all he cared about. The people he was dealing with were eminent scientists of their time, the sheer result of their hard work and dedication. But they were now out of the lab for a considerable time, looking into the administration of Madhavpur. Krishna was never in favour of going to the Empowered Group, but Mohan had convinced him. Mohan, though, did have a point. Moreover, he had known that the element of surprise would be in Krishna's favour and he would be the one driving the conversation.

'Was this ever tested? Do we have empirical or anecdotal data to back the experiment?' Gopal asked. At this point, Narayan and Vasu sighed in disapproval.

'Stop being hyper-sceptical, Gopal,' Vasu said.

Krishna then hesitatingly said, 'I have something more here to add, about which even Shyam doesn't know of. And it won't be music to anyone's ears in the room.' No one in the room said a word. 'Our facilities are under attack.'

'What kind of an attack?' Shyam asked, he was clearly perturbed.

'A massive cyberattack was launched on Samganak. We were able to bring it back online there and then, but the point of concern is that a computer large enough for such kind of operations does exist,' Krishna replied.

'No Krishna, this is much more serious than that. The state of Madhavpur has no enemy. So, who can it be? Was it traced?' Shyam inquired.

'No. But I think this could very well have been an inside job.'

'What do you mean by an inside job?' Gopal asked.

'Someone who knows Madhavpur inside-out and has resources.' Krishna explained.

'You sir, without any evidence, are trying to fix blames? I don't buy into your logic,' Gopal shot back at Krishna.

'A committee comprising Narayan, Vitthal, and Gopal will look into the matter. And it very well might be a mischief, we need not worry so much,' Shyam stated.

Krishna nodded in agreement. Gopal rose from his seat, despite the tepid argument he looked calm and composed. He walked right up to the place where Krishna stood, and placed his right arm on his shoulder. With his narrow moustache and hair brushed back, he looked more like a retired general of some imperial army. At times, his tall and broad stature did come around as intimidating. But today was not that day, as Krishna stood firmly before him.

'None of us here wish ill for you. My criticism springs out of worry—worry for you, Krishna. You have a young mind, and we here have fought countless scathing battles. We have fallen numerous times, and have risen. Risen with lessons learnt. We do not want you to learn those lessons the hard way. You have always led from the front, and we appreciate that. You were given the onus of the project, as your chance discovery lead us to Bhoomidium. It was a job well done. That's why I played an instrumental role in securing you the Café Evolution, having faith in your reports and opinion, despite the moratorium. You exuded confidence, and you were given the duty and high office of the Chief Advisor. But my dear son, things have come too far. We as a civilization need a new abode. It's a make-or-break situation for us. My only suggestion for you would be to take everybody in confidence. And share facts and seek support as much as possible, covert operations won't help,' Gopal said to him.

'Here I would like to differ, Gopal,' Vasudevan interrupted. 'I have seen his style of working from the time he barely came out of his teens. Even if Krishna is putting forward an opinion, rest assured it must be amply backed by facts. As I said earlier, in the hour of need, leave the subject to the subject matter expert. Be his guiding light, Gopal. The rest he will manage.'

Gopal turned toward Vasudevan and said, 'That's what I am trying to do.' His words were like as if a heavy metal ball has hit a freshly laid concrete floor. No one had any comeback answer for him now.

'I do understand, sir. I was just wary of too many cooks spoiling the broth,' Krishna said.

'Now that we all agree, that Krishna is taking all the requisite steps towards what's best for us. We need to offer him our unconditional support,' Narayan said.

'Krishna will now have to work on replenishing the Bhoomidium levels here, keep working on Prithvi as well as search for plausible planets in the vicinity,' Shyam announced. Everybody nodded in accordance.

'Then let's call it a day,' Vasu said.

'Enough of work; lets meet outside for tea and snacks,' Vitthal said.

Some 200 metres from the Council building was the most famous cafeteria of Central Madhavpur. Everybody walked to Café Moksha, down the lane. It was a nice, grand café with spacious outside seating.

The Café's patio, cobblestone-laid, was an excellent place to sit and watch the sunset. The 53rd Avenue, on which Moksha was located, passed through a sloping terrain from east to west. Sitting in its patio one could see the glittering asphalt road diving down the slope, giving way to the visuals of clear blue evening sky. The play of Nature became more profound during summer evenings. The sun would appear to set down the 53rd Avenue, leaving behind an excellent trail of reddish-orange hues unto the late summer dusks.

Sitting on the chair closest to the patio fencing, Krishna could see the sun slipping down the street. On his left he could see the Council building, glowing reddish-orange in the slant early evening sunlight. A very prominent symbol engraved on top of the building's wall attracted his attention. It was not for the first time he had seen that legendary symbol, which was embossed on all the four sides of the building and could be seen from a distance. But the Council symbol was now inundated in evening lights, and looked even more pleasing to the eye and the mind. It was called 'Om'. A symbol you would get if you held a hand-drawn outline sketch of a lotus, horizontally. It was the symbol of eternal truth and purity.

'What will you have, Krishna?' Vasu asked.

'Nothing. I am pretty much packed.'

'Now, do not take anything personally. Behind those walls of Council we need to fulfil our duties. Mere questioning you or demoralizing you has never been my intention,' Gopal said.

'I am not one of those who gets demoralized by anyone's words or actions. I carry a clear sense of conscience, and do what I believe in.' Krishna spoke in a flat tone with an ice-cold look on his face.

'You might be very conversant with gadgets and gizmos, but let me tell you something—you have the heart of a child. No pretending, whatsoever.' Gopal said as he broke into a hysteria of laughter. Everybody else joined in, and that made nonchalant Krishna break a smile too. They all raised their coffee mugs in a toast, and Krishna raised his glass of water.

•◆•

Shyam lived on the 101st lane, a couple of kilometres from Krishna's lab. His conch-shaped house was made of chrome-plated shield, just like every other house in Madhavpur. Still, what would set it apart from all other houses was a big saffron-coloured Vedic Swastika adorning the roof. It was a symbol of trust, faith, and security and was always awarded to the Chief of Manavas.

'Uncle, can I get some coffee please?'

'I still have the berry mix you gifted me.'

'A scoop of that would do,' he said.

'Why, you were full an hour ago?' Shyam asked.

'My coffee is for that time of the day when I clear my mind of all thoughts. I just need to relax. And the famous five wouldn't have allowed that,' he said.

'I agree with you, but then no denying to what Gopal said. Pulling up the Chief Scientific Advisor is a day's job for an Empowered Councillor,' Shyam said and laughed at his own joke.

Shyam had always been by Krishna's side, right from his childhood. As a young child, Krishna had always sat next to his favourite Uncle to ask questions about stars, galaxies, farm animals, computers, and whatever else came to his inquisitive little mind. Shyam would always make sure he answered all his queries to his satisfaction. And when Krishna's queries started wearing him down, he surreptitiously would signal Rukmani to fetch Krishna his favourite payasam and other sweets. The treat (so very lovingly) prepared by Aunt Rukmani, would always distract little Krishna. Gorging into those homemade delicacies, he would eat till his belly ached.

'You didn't ask again?' Krishna said.

'I trust you; it very well could be an inside job. The way these people are now behaving, I wonder if they were ever evolved.'

'I couldn't agree more with you. What are they more worried about, than the problem at hand? Why would they, especially Gopal, act up like that?' said Krishna.

'More than they, it's Gopal who worries me. Who knows, what he or they are up to?'

'Still, what's up with Gopal?' Krishna persisted.

'Gopal always had an eye on whatever I achieved. Now he sees me in you. And envies you too.'

'But if the Bhoomidium levels have not dropped, which I presume have not, he or anybody else shouldn't be behaving out of so much ego and so irrationally,' Krishna said.

'I now doubt if he ever changed.' Shyam wondered.

Krishna placed his coffee mug on the side table, and stood up to leave. 'Why don't you stay over Krishna?' Shyam suggested.

'I need to get back to the lab for some work.'

'You didn't tell me where has it reached?'

'You need to see it for yourself.'

'And when would that be?'

'Pretty soon.'

11

The Jurassic Summer

'He actually said that?'

'It doesn't matter, he is a non-issue and a non-player.'

'The very conviction in his voice gets him his ways. We must be wary of him.'

Krishna nodded in response.

Even though it had been a few days since the big-five had met, Krishna refrained from talking about the meeting. But today he had let Mohan in into some details of the meet.

Apart from the intermittent chat, it was otherwise quite a busy day for both of them. The Bhoomidium circulation pipes were to be reconnected with the fuel pipelines. Similar devices were found on more treatment plants of almost 40 per cent of the town. Krishna had sneaked in a stealth code into the control systems of all the plants, for monitoring Bhoomidium levels in water passing through the output pipes. They were low at many places. The Bhoomidium supply pipes which emerged from deep inside the core of the Bhoomi passed through the lower basement of Café Evolution, before entering Madhavpur. They were meant to circulate Bhoomidium from the core to the water supply of the city. The spent water would then (after treatment) be allowed to mix with soil and then seep back into the core. Thus completing the cycle.

While routing Bhoomidium through the fuel line was a quick fix for the problem at hand, it prolonged the recycling path of Bhoomidium. But then, Krishna was more worried about fixing the current crisis.

'What if it's not an inside job?'

Krishna stopped and while still looking at the control panel of the Samganak asked, 'Then?'

'What if it's them?' Mohan suggested.

Now he turned and gave Mohan an icy look with narrowed eyes. Usually, people would refrain from raising such topics in his presence. But Mohan enjoyed the liberty to do so, although not without irking him.

Mohan was quick enough to realize his folly. Tomfoolery was one thing, but upsetting Krishna? Mohan valued his friendship too much to do that. He now knew that only a stretch of silence would undo the harm caused. An uneasy calm followed.

Meanwhile, a humid and warm gust of air ruffled some papers lying on Krishna's desk. Mohan walked towards the open window on the backside of the hall. He could see the summer moon near the daylit horizon. It was very bright.

The moon, which looked so calm and serene, too had a turbulent history. Hit, hurt, and fragmented it was almost coming down tumbling towards Bhoomi.

After the last asteroid impact, when everybody was acting trigger-happy to evaporate the moon, Krishna stood by Mohan. He as a citizen of Madhavpur raised his voice, and Krishna had backed him. His long-standing expertise in geo-sciences helped him see what others couldn't. No moon would have meant no tides over the oceans of Bhoomi, and could have altered the climate.

That is what friends are for. These were testing times for Krishna, and he had to stand by him.

'Maybe you are right. Gopal could be the one,' Mohan said.

'Not again, it is a non-issue. Now, will you come over here?'

'Sure, but we almost lost our servers and the Bhoomidium supply line had to be redone. Is it still a non-issue then?'

'Can't you see through? This is being done to spread panic and anarchy. And we under no circumstances would succumb to such pressure tactics. Now, come here. Will you?'

Mohan nodded and walked up to the screen. 'I have got some very interesting finds here. The concentration of this particular amino acid, which promotes muscle growth in animals, is increasing in some species of the vegetation. This means the most marvellous work of evolution is about to show up,' Krishna then said.

'Why don't we just bypass them? Wouldn't it take more time and effort to go through the whole process?' Mohan asked.

'You are always better off by not challenging the path set by the Nature, moreover, it is utterly important. The Nature would unfurl its wings of creative flight to the fullest. And will test its own skills of begetting bioengineering marvels. We just need to confirm their presence first, then will discuss the future course of action,' Krishna said.

'Why are they important in our sequence? They were sitting ducks when it came to sustenance on a turbulent planet, had no advance brain capabilities either and were heavy on resources.' Mohan said.

'Life, even on Bhoomi, from the beginning had two parallel strategies for survival. The fear or the survival instinct as we better know it as, and the learning and thinking skills. In lower animal kingdom like reptiles and amphibians, the instinct of survival rules the roost. While in upper or more advanced animal kingdom the instinct of survival and learning-thinking capabilities work in tandem. Mother Nature never keeps all its eggs in one basket.

Diversification is the key to survival. And before life propagates to higher levels of learning and thinking, let it first test out the upper limits of mean machines powered by sheer energy and sustained by the instincts alone.' Krishna concluded.

Mohan nodded and said, 'I will get the data room ready.'

They both now moved to the data room. Krishna stood in the corner of the room with his Yocto-Suit turned on, while Mohan prepared the data servers.

They both were now wired to the Bionic Data Analyser. *Where do you want to look out first?* Krishna thought, which Mohan could hear over his earpiece.

'I think I heard you.' Mohan replied.

'I have incorporated a two-way thought sharer between both the Interfaces. So whatever I think you will be able to hear, and vice-versa.' he said.

'Okay then! I think I want to first look somewhere along freshwater streams in a dense forest having tall trees,' Mohan said. Krishna then issued a thought command for Samganak to play data accordingly.

For quite some time, they kept on looking with no luck. *You have to bear in mind that a mass extinction has occurred on Prithvi, wiping out around 70 per cent of both marine and terrestrial population. We have to be patient*, Krishna thought.

The Permian-Triassic[2] one? Mohan thought.

It basically made more resources available for their arrival.

Let's skip forward then, thought Mohan.

They were still interested in looking around the streams. The dense vegetation cover made the search a tiring affair. As they were scanning around a winding creek, Krishna noticed something. It

---

[2] Pre-Dinosaur era on Earth/Prithvi.

was a nest. There were unhatched eggs in it, at least four. They were huge, light brown in colour with an undertone of bluish tinge and with dark blue spots all over. The nest itself was made out of wooden sticks, and was perched in between branched out tree trunk (some 50 feet above the ground). The nest was intelligently designed to support the weight of the eggs and was at a safe height from all plausible predators.

They are really huge! Will the mother be around? Mohan thought.

Seems so. They are freshly laid. Krishna could now hear some rustling around the nest. His heart was now racing in anticipation, eager to know who was lurking around the bushes.

There is something out there, probably well camouflaged amidst the vegetation, Mohan thought. The noise was now growing louder and was fast approaching the nest. They were still not able to figure out any distinct object amid the low-lying bushes. The ground around the tree trunk, though, was clear of any undergrowth. The creature now moved forward and as it came out of the green cover into the mud surrounding the tree, they both saw the surreal.

'Welcome to the Jurassic Age!' exclaimed Krishna aloud, clasping his hand in excitement and then clinching his fists with a sense of accomplishment.

It was a Eoraptor.

These must be the first-ever actual visuals of a dinosaur ever seen by a Manava, Mohan thought. The Eoraptor was a sleek and agile creature almost three-and-half-feet-long and dark-green in colour. It leaped and climbed onto the tree trunk and perched beside the nest. The creature was anxious and looking around.

There always have been two schools of thought, which argued whether dinosaurs were dumb as other reptiles or had a fair amount of cognitive skills, Krishna thought.

What do you think?

I think they were smart and cared for their young ones. Look at this Eoraptor, she is standing guard, constantly looking around, as Krishna completed his thought, something happened. The Eoraptor grew more attentive and after few ritualistic rounds of looking around, stepped close to the nest.

After a few moments of standing frozen, the bipedal dug its slender jaw into the nest and seized an egg. After smashing and swallowing the egg, the raptor jumped from the tree and dashed into the woods again.

It was a male predating Eoraptor. And those were helpless eggs of another dinosaur. Krishna halted the Bionic analysis and removed his Interface. 'We have enough data for analysis now,' he said.

'And that was not a caring mother,' Mohan said.

•◆

Krishna now punched in customized parameters for analysis of the collected data. Mohan went into the De-Accelerator chamber for final checks and preparations.

'Why are there three terminals in the chamber?' Mohan asked upon entering the chamber.

'I did some tweaking, have added some new features and we are expecting a guest.'

As they spoke, the doorbell rang. Mohan was standing near the entry of the chamber and was thus a little out of range from the voice command receptors in the halls. As he was about to move toward the hall to issue command for opening the door, Krishna signalled him to stop. He closed his eyes and the door unlocked.

'This is starting to freak me out Krishna—now you control lab doors with your thoughts?'

The guest for the day was Shyam. 'A pleasant surprise, Uncle!

Has been a long time since we all sat down and chatted.' Mohan was brimming with joy.

'Nice to see you too! We will have a heart-to-heart soon, but today I have turned up for the movie screening.'

'You are on time, Uncle; the show is about to begin. But before that you both will have to go through a very brief training session.' Krishna spoke as he pulled out two goggle-like devices from a chest of his work desk. Shyam was now looking at Mohan with curiosity. Mohan shrugged with his arms extended and palms facing up.

'Well! Well! Don't be taken aback. I just want you people to go through a simulation training to get accustomed to the upgraded De-Accelerator.' He then handed them both the devices. They wore the device and for some fifteen minutes sat through the simulation.

'How did you manage to do that?' Shyam asked.

'We are now able to sneak in data from Bhoomi to Universe-1408. Plus this is easier than that, simple super-positioning of two alternate realities, just an illusion. The simulation would have helped you both in getting familiar with the De-Accelerator. Still here is a pill, to reduce uneasiness or nausea.' Krishna pulled out a transparent pack of pills from his pocket.

'Nah! I am good to go,' Shyam said.

'I will definitely be needing that.' Mohan grabbed the pill from Krishna's hand. The chamber was maintained a tad below the normal room temperature. The extra chair had now sneaked in between the already two present in the globe.

'On my count of five! One, two, three, four, and five!' Krishna started the De-Accelerator. The fast-paced images started slowing down, with mindless background humming becoming intelligible. As the frequency metre on the control panel started inching towards the 4,000,000,000 Hz mark, they could feel their body becoming lighter.

At 1,000,000,000 Hz they started having a simultaneous out-of-body experience. They could see themselves sitting on the chair, and could also see each other. At around 2,000,000,000 Hz a sudden blackout occurred, as if there was a lapse in the consciousness.

When the consciousness phased in, they were standing besides each other in a lush green jungle. It took a few seconds for them to make sense out of the audio-visual sensory inputs. They looked around. As far as they could see there was undergrowth, bushes, and huge trees.

'We are in a Jurassic-Age forest now,' Krishna explained.

'This stuff is amazing. Haven't been on a jungle safari in a while,' Mohan said.

'There are no animals on Jambhu-Dweep; we haven't encountered one in ages. Be on your guards and tread carefully.' Shyam warned them.

'This is just a simulation, Uncle. An interlacing of our perception with data received from Prithvi. We are safe. Just do not bump into things or come into any harm's way. Anything which frightens your brain will throw it into fight or flight mode, and will wake you up. And sudden changes in brain operating frequencies will leave you uneasy for a day or two,' Krishna said.

'We need to find the closest stream, Krishna. Our best bet,' Shyam said.

They could hear gushing of a stream on their left, Krishna signalled and the trio started moving leftwards. They had to walk carefully, as the undergrowth was entangling their feet. Krishna stepped forward and with a machete drawn out of his robe, started clearing the vegetation to make way for all.

'Why would you carry that?' Mohan asked.

'After the full simulation training programme, you still think I am carrying this?' Krishna said while laughing.

'It's simply not there. This is just a mental picture of 1408, Mohan. Be calm.' Shyam said in a reassuring tone.

Krishna was now looking out for possible ditches, while clearing the path for a trail. As he was swinging his arm he could see the bright midday sunlight grow feeble. It took him a while before noticing that it was not a passing cloud cover but a hovering shadow. He looked up and noticed a large winged creature hovering.

It was a giant Pterosaur. The avian dinosaur was circling right above their head. Krishna froze and said, 'This flying dino cannot see us. It probably has sited his prey and very well might nose-dive on or around us. We will have to maintain steel nerves and not let even an iota of fear in our minds.'

'Keep moving, and do not get freaked out,' Shyam suggested.

'I had my nerve soothing pill,' said Mohan with a grin on his face. They then started moving again. The winged raptor flew away after few more circles, into the horizon streaked with grey clouds. It was a sunny mid-afternoon. Sun had started its descent after attaining the zenith on the dark blue summer sky. The day and night of the Jurassic era were much warmer, due to higher carbon dioxide levels.

The group ducked in amazement as they heard the sound of a big explosion to their right. It was a volcano, an active one. With the burst, a fresh big cloud of ash has just risen out of the volcano's peak. 'These volcanic eruptions have been releasing greenhouse gases to the atmosphere for millions of years now. They keep the earth warm enough for these cold-blooded dinos,' Krishna explained.

While Krishna was still explaining, Shyam noticed something. It was the footprint of a raptor. 'We should be following those footprints, Krishna. And what did you say our mission of this whole psychedelic trip is?'

'Absolutely nothing! We are here on a vacation. I wanted us

to see what a Manava eye has never seen before—these dinosaurs. No motive, no mission.'

'It better only be a vacation, I have a meeting to attend tomorrow morning,' Shyam said.

'We are operating at super-scaled up timescales. We can spend a year here and still it won't be an hour on Bhoomi. Don't you enjoy a leisurely hiking on a sunny day?' Krishna joked.

'It's an absolute pleasure to be with you boys again. A much-needed vacation indeed,' Shyam replied. The trio then started following the footprints leading them to the nearby freshwater stream. As they approached the stream the first thing they could notice was a herd of herbivores, drinking water on the other side of the stream.

It was a group of Brachiosauruses, one of the largest herbivores of the Jurassic era. They were around 80 to 90 feet in length and when standing on all four legs were almost 50 feet high. They were huge dinos, as if a creatively styled building had started moving around on four legs. Gigantic.

They were drinking water along the bend of the river, and only two would come forward to guzzle down water at a time. The rest either munched on soft leaves from treetops or stood guard for the herd. They were predominantly dark green in colour with tinges of blue and purple along the length of their body from neck to tail.

Then there was an array of hardened feather along their spine, which helped them detect change in the direction of air and its atmospheric pressure. The sense of wind direction helped them align themselves with the flow of it, at times to get smells and at other times to avoid opening their cross section to strong winds. The change in wind pressure worked as a mechanism to detect any big fast moving being approaching them, big predating dinos mostly.

As Krishna tried absorbing such a rare and beautiful sight, a sheer fascinating and natural law defying thing occurred. A fully grown 50 metric ton brachiosaurus located at the right end of the group stood on his hind legs, with his fore legs curled inside towards his chest. He could now graze the tallest tree on the stream bank. The trio stood there watching the work of Nature in complete silence, awestruck.

'They are beautiful and unbelievably gigantic,' Mohan said in awe of them.

'Yes, they are,' Shyam agreed. 'How about we cross the stream and see them up close?' They started moving towards the stream. The bank and the riverbed were full of small pebbles and gravels. They had to tread carefully as the pebbles that had come rolling down the hills along with the stream, had made it slippery. The stream was some 50-feet wide at the bend, and was half to a full foot deep in many places. The water was cooler than the surrounding atmosphere. There was uncanny buoyancy in the atmosphere, which the trio now noticed, as they dipped their feet in water and subsequently lifted them to move forward.

'My feet feel lighter, Krishna. How big and dense is this planet?' Shyam asked.

'Exactly the same size as Bhoomi, the elevated level of greenhouse gases makes you feel lighter. This not only helps these giant raptors to move around easily but also would help them survive, later on.' Krishna replied.

'Now what would that mean?' Mohan asked.

'They will grow air-borne, those that will not perish. They will have to gradually adopt to flying by reducing their weight, while the buoyant force is still there.'

Shyam nodded. As they were crossing the stream, the ground beneath them shook, as if something huge had thumped the ground. Outward circular ripples started appearing on the water surrounding their feet.

'Wait!' Krishna said immediately.

Before they could make sense of the situation, the group of brachiosauruses halted and turned. Something was approaching them. As the trees blocking the view started falling after getting trampled under the feet of the approaching being, the group of dinos started giving out shrill distress calls. They were now able to see from their eye-level of 50 feet what Krishna and the others couldn't. They rearranged themselves in a formation, with younger dinosaurs in the middle of the group and the bigger intimidating adults on the periphery.

As the deafening, rumbling sounds filling the air grew closer; they could now see the uninvited party crasher. It was a T-Rex. Barely 25–35 feet in height in comparison to the giant 50-feet stature of the brachiosauruses, it was nonetheless a brutal killing machine. There was no way that a single T-Rex could have preyed upon a herd of brachiosaurus. It was either a desperate starved dino or was trying to protect its territory.

The brachiosaurus herd was still shrieking, either trying to intimidate the T-Rex or calling for any nearby reinforcement. The whole atmosphere was now filled with a mixture of shrill and deep clarion calls.

The adult-most brachiosaurus stood on their hind limbs, towering over 50 feet. The T-Rex was ostensibly intimidated by this war readiness of the herd. It started moving from his left to right in a desperate attempt to find chink in the armour of the herd, to reach the younger herbivores standing inside the formation.

The young dinos measured some 20 feet and were vulnerable to the T-Rex. They were scared and they too were yelling at the peak of their voices. The herd was willing to go to any length to save the two young dinos.

The T-Rex was now moving more swiftly from one position of vantage to another. The biggest dino, who was already on his hind limbs, came back thumping on the ground with full force quite close to the Rex. The Rex could barely save himself from being trampled.

The Rex was now scared and it's deep voiced rumbling grew shriller. In a fit of frenzy it made a final attempt at assault and did manage to impinge some deep scathing with its razor sharp fore limb claws. The alpha dino of the herd was now wounded and bleeding.

'That's not a good sign for the herd,' Mohan observed. Shyam turned and looked towards him, giving him a puzzled look. 'This will attract small predators and scavengers—the smell of the blood. I have read about this. This wounding will signal others that a hunt has been won, when it is not the case.'

As Mohan spoke, a group of eoraptors was on its way out of their safe ambush. The group started hopping and running towards the herd. They finally emerged into the scene from behind the trio's back, zooming past Krishna (standing mid-stream). Shyam and Mohan ducked a little until Krishna reassured them. The eoraptors were fast and crossed the stream in jiffy, but for one. The last raptor of the group slowed down a little midway in the stream and started staring in the direction of the trio. 'What is this creature up to?' said Shyam.

'I too am not sure,' replied Krishna, and then he turned back to see if there was something else of interest there. There was nothing.

After a brief pause the eoraptor regained his speed and leaped forward to regroup. A frenzied T-Rex and a group of eoraptors now surrounded the herd.

The herd went all out and the shrieks were now growing thicker and deeper. The balance of the game was shifting, eventually. The herd became aggressive and gave up the hitherto defensive stance. The outer line of defence now mounted an assault on the T-Rex, by trying to trample it with their forelimbs.

The Rex got hurt as its tail got trapped under the feet of the wounded alpha. It gave up. Wounded and its spirit broken, it mustered all its courage to escape the herd.

As the Rex dashed towards the forest away from the stream, the herd now had other challenges. The eoraptors had smelled the blood and were in no mood to give up on the feast. They depended on number and their small size to overwhelm the prey. One after another, the eoraptor stuck to the feet of the brachiosaurus and started delivering scathes. The herd fought back, reaching out to their feet with their long neck, and also thumping their feet to get them off. The majority of the eoraptors were squashed within a matter of few minutes.

The remaining group now dispersed and ran across the river. eoraptors soon vanished into the woods. As Shyam flashed a smile full of thrill towards Mohan and Krishna, something came rushing back towards them, growling from the bushes. It was the same sceptic eoraptor. 'It's unbelievable!' shouted Mohan.

'This is not happening. Something has seriously gone amiss!' hollered Krishna. The eoraptor came forward, taking one step at a time.

'Krishna, I thought you had said we are in a simulation and no one can see us? Is that raptor coming for us?' Shyam asked worriedly.

'I do not know, Uncle! There will be a red dot on your left wrist just under your sleeve, press that. We need to get out of this simulation,' Krishna replied while looking into the eyes of the approaching raptor.

'There are no red dots on our wrists, son!' Shyam yelled in response as he and Mohan checked their wrists.

'He is fixated on me. You both just keep moving down the stream,' he said, while maintaining his composure.

The raptor leaped onto Krishna and before he could jump to safety, the creature was able to deliver deep cuts on Krishna's chest with his claws. He fell on the stream bed into the pebbles. Krishna was hurt and was lying just five feet away from the raptor, but it was still growling on the very spot. It was trying to smell and was looking around.

'We have been pushed on to their side. Now this hyper-intuitive predator is sensing me.' Krishna said while still lying in the water stream.

'You are hurt, let's get out of here.' Shyam was worried.

'It seems our bodies have gone into deep trance in the De-Accelerator. There should be a fall down the stream. I can hear it. We need to reach there,' Krishna was crawling away from the raptor.

He was right, there was a fall some 80 metres downstream. As the raptor again started making sense of his direction, Krishna leaped. His chest was aching and he found it hard to breathe, but he kept on leaping from one spot to another towards the fall. Meanwhile, the raptor was growing angry and in frenzy it too kept on leaping towards Krishna. It was clear that the raptor was not seeing but only sensing someone's presence.

The trio reached the edge of the stream. It was a very deep and straight fall. The transparent water, falling off the cliff was forming a mist cloud midway.

'We will have to jump off this cliff, only that would bring us out of our slumber,' Krishna said.

'Are you sure about that? Is there a faint possibility that we may hit the bottom?' Mohan asked.

'Shouldn't happen, we are in a simulation.'

'Tell this to that crazy dinosaur. Who knows? He might give the chase up!' Mohan replied.

'Something has gone wrong somewhere, but trust me, we need to do this to get out of this slumber.' The raptor still had not loosened the chase. It had gone berserk and was leaping forward towards Krishna, relentlessly.

'We have no other choice, we need to come out of this,' Shyam said. They held their breath and ran toward the end of the cliff and finally jumped. Few seconds into the fall; they saw the mist cloud hitting them into their face. They could now see nothing and were still falling heads down. And then they began to feel it; their body grew lighter and the flight slowed down. They could now see themselves falling from a distance; it was again an out-of-body experience.

•◆•

Krishna opened his eyes; he was still out of breath and was drenched in sweat. So were Shyam and Mohan. Still struggling to make sense of the visuals of the De-Accelerator chamber, Krishna reached to the red button on the right armrest of his chair. The straps were now gone. He could barely move as his chest was still aching and his body felt heavy. 'Are you okay, Uncle?'

'I am more worried about you. That raptor was a scary nut. Are your wounds still there? Do you need any medication?'

'I am fine. Those wounds were not for real. Nothing was, except for the crazy dino.'

'What was it? A system malfunction?' Mohan asked.

'We were pushed onto the server side of it. Our data was getting streamed back to Prithvi, and the crazy dino was sensing me.'

The fear was now evident in Shyam's eye. The Empowered

Group of the Council was banking on Krishna's project and the first rendezvous had not gone down too well. Shyam was now worried about the progress of the project. Gopal would not miss any chance to tear into him and Krishna if the project met any roadblocks.

Krishna could read the anxiety on Shyam's face. Before he could move to reassure him, he heard a chime. It was his wrist-device lying on the control panel.

'The Samganak has been attacked again,' Krishna said.

Mohan rose from his chair and went towards the lab hall, Krishna and Shyam followed. 'This malcode is now attacking our systems at will. It seems Samganak did defend itself, but after quite a struggle,' Mohan said.

Krishna read the log trail on the big screen and said, 'It was a deliberate attack, it went right up to the De-Accelerator.'

12

The Interactive Map

It was hot and humid. And, hundreds of feet below the surface, the conditions couldn't have been any better.

It was an old transition era bunker, designed to withstand any kind of warfare. It had a big central hall with numerous adjoining small chambers on the periphery. The whole bunker was carved out of big rocks.

Even before the commencement of Swarnim-Yuga, there was an imminent danger of the peace talks collapsing. The danger of a war breaking out was quite real and possible. The different factions mistrusted each other, neither side knew about the armaments still held by the other side and everyone on the talk-table had an agenda of his own. The foundation of a utopian society was being laid brick by brick. But the ground on which it was being laid was still shaky.

'This is a perfect place,' Mohan said.

'This place was right under our lab, and none of us ever knew about it,' Krishna said. 'I kept them under cover and made sure nobody knew about these bunkers. They were built before the declaration of Swarnim-Yuga but were never disclosed to anybody for security purposes. Samganak would be safe here. And now you folks, for the safety of the project, are not allowed to connect Samganak to any of the external data lines or network,' Shyam said.

All the apparatuses from Café Evolution were removed and

were shifted to the bunkers. The lab was not left vacant though. Dummy systems with some limited redundant functionality were installed in their places. Any malcode hacking into the system would still get system pings, but only proxy data would be left open.

'Uncle, we should raise this with the Security Committee,' Krishna said.

'Don't be naïve. I am not sure whom to trust and whom not to. I will use my network to check if something fishy is going around in the Council. And let's hope the dummy we have installed would gain access to the location of the attacking servers.'

'It's next to impossible. The attack overwhelms Samganak and leaves no trail.' Krishna replied.

'Tough situation to be in,' Shyam observed as he sat on a chair lying beside the big screen installed on the east-facing wall of the bunker. 'You said something about those raptors, didn't you? What was that?'

'Though the natural path of selections should not allow such massive and resource heavy creatures to continue to exist on a planet of the size of Prithvi, we still cannot rely on Nature alone.'

'I am not going in there for any kind of extermination mission,' Mohan said with a sense of anxiety and haste in his voice and that had Shyam laughing.

'No, you don't have to. I have set in motion some complex manoeuvres to take care of that,' Krishna replied.

'Of what nature?' Shyam asked.

'There is an asteroid belt circling the sun, quite near Prithvi. They move in a surprisingly very precise orbit and very rarely go astray. I have changed the Omechta coordinates of one of the big rock in the belt, to make it fall out of step with its orbit, gradually.'

'Omechta?'

'You would be lucky, Uncle Shyam, if he does tell you. Last

time I asked him, he did not.' Mohan said trying his best to only sound sarcastic and not jealous.

'We all know about space and time. The same space and time exists in all universes. Identical events can occur simultaneously in a space and time, and still be separated by the barrier of being in different universes. Here, Omechta comes into play. The variable which when changed can take you across universes. Mohan, you remember those carriers we launched into different universes? Those chambers manipulated their Omechta.' Krishna explained.

'You are basically smuggling objects in and out of different universes. Doesn't it disturb the balance of Nature?' Mohan asked.

'No, the objects thus transferred adopt the new Omechta quite nicely and the universe it has been transported to, doesn't object either, if done rightly. But it's a very taxing process. I chose a rock out of the asteroid belt with all the necessary features and then changed and changed back its Omechta in rapid succession. The result was…'

'It went out of synch with its compatriots and became unstable in its orbit,' Shyam filled in.

'You sneaked that meteor out of 1408?' exclaimed Mohan.

'And placed it back in a matter of a nano-second,' Krishna smiled.

'Are you on some special dose of Bhoomidium? Your capabilities are increasing by leaps and bounds.' Mohan said.

'I will take that as a compliment.'

'Are you sure when the rock will make an impact on Prithvi it will just wipe out the dinosaurs and not the other life forms? It won't melt the whole planet or will it?' Shyam asked.

'It will target only the territorial dinos. The smaller animals and the smaller dinosaurs with wings will survive. Everything is calculated and planned.' Krishna replied.

'But those winged dinos will shrink and become birds, won't they?' Mohan asked.

Krishna nodded in agreement. 'Here! This is that destined rock that I control. This meteor is made up of metals both heavy and light alike, measuring a kilometre in radius and on my one command it will decide the fate of the life on Prithvi.' He pointed towards the visuals of the meteor on the screen.

Shyam smiled and said, 'Now you are adding some melodrama to these celestial events that you control. Slow down, my boy.'

In all likelihood, Krishna was now coming across as arrogant to Shyam.

'I am just excited about how things are going in the right direction, despite all the odds. I have no reason to feel or act arrogant. As a matter of fact, it is not me who has been carrying out the project.' Krishna said.

'Son, now what would that mean?' said Shyam, who was now a little irked.

'The inhabitants of Madhavpur know me not only as Chief Scientific Advisor to the Council, but also as the only CD1++ on Bhoomi. When the best of the brains on Bhoomi cap at CD2++, did you ever not wonder, what made me go two notches over and above that?'

'We always thought you came in direct contact with nascent Bhoomidium and it had a profound effect on you. But more importantly, I am a little worried about the level of control and intervention you are exerting on 1408. We can still fix stuff on Bhoomi, but if the floodgates between these isolated worlds open up, we don't know what we might face. An alien invasion or a collapse of natural laws of physics.' Shyam said.

'There is something that I have concealed from you people all along,' Krishna spoke as he raised his sleeves almost shoulder high.

'What is that? You actually sustained bruises from that Jurassic incidence?' said Shyam seeing some sort of marks on Krishna's arms.

'These are marks of those dreams that drive Café Evolution and me. I have been carrying these around since my NYCAR days. In the middle of every other night, I wake up from these vivid dreams, drenched in sweat. Those voices in my dreams almost always solve my problems and tell me of future happenings. This element Bhoomidium, had it not been for those voices, wouldn't have materialized ever. I am not sure if this is my subconscious mind that speaks or they are some alien messages, but they are always right.'

As an amazed Shyam looked towards Mohan, the latter said, 'He told me about his dreams, but I didn't know what to make of them.'

'A subconscious mind can always engage you in a healthy conversation, but would never leave such marks,' Shyam spoke after a considerable pause.

'There is something else too,' Krishna then confessed.

Shyam gestured him to go ahead with it, but Krishna was still hesitant. After an uncomfortable bout of silence, he finally said, 'I will have to leave.'

Mohan and Shyam both gasped, almost in synch. Mohan found his voice first, 'Where? What happens to the project?'

'You will have to take care of it. I will hand over all my access codes and the encryption keys of Samganak to you.'

'In case you have already decided to leave, may I ask where will it be to?' Shyam asked.

'Uncle, do you remember the fables of an archaic hermit that used to do rounds when Madhavpur was being built?'

'People often talked about him based on lores. I am not sure if somebody actually saw him. Some accounts also said that he used to live outside city peripheries and guarded Madhavpur,' Shyam said.

'He still does,' Krishna said.

'And you believe it all has something to do with him? When was the last time you saw him?'

'I have seen him just once, that too from quite a distance. I was idling around on Govardhan and saw him standing beside his hut on Mount Meru.'

'There is no hut on Mount Meru or for that matter anywhere outside the city boundaries. But yes, I will believe your account. He moves around very quickly, you only get to hear fables about him and never get to track him.' Shyam said.

'These are times and events beyond our comprehension. We need an outsider's perspective and help, someone who is not bound by the laws of the city and the code. I need to find him, as soon as possible.' Krishna replied.

'Slow down, my boy. Let Mohan learn about the systems. I often get to hear from Mohan that you do not share encryption codes with him. Give him access and teach him how to programme Samganak while you are away.'

Krishna nodded.

•◆

After two days of fifteen-hour session each day, Mohan now knew the encryption keys and the roadmap of the project. Krishna made sure not to withhold any information. Mohan too was now underced the oath of secrecy.

Shyam said 'So, when do we expect you back, Krishna?'

'I checked the surveillance images, could not find any hut, neither permanent nor makeshift. So, basically I do not know where to search for the hermit,' Krishna replied.

'Take your sweet time. You should probably search the western front of the forests outside the city. I would do that if I were you. The eastern side of the Jambhu-Dweep culminates into the creek, the forbidden lands.' Shyam suggested.

'I know that, sir. The No-Go Area,' Krishna replied.

Shyam moved forward and after placing his arm across Krishna's shoulders said, 'I am sure you will find him, and I am sure you will get answers to all your questions. But I want you to know that you have already walked many extra miles for the Manava civilization. Just take it easy and don't be too hard on your own self, things will sort out for themselves.'

Krishna nodded.

'What were the last updates from Prithvi?' Shyam asked.

'The meteor struck as planned and a global winter ensued. The dust and soil particles engulfed the sky and temperatures on Prithvi dipped substantially. Thus wiping out most of the dinosaurian life there. Those, who survived, kept on shrinking in size and many grew wings. The biodiversity suffered too. Right now there are no dinosaurs and it will take a while before life flourishes in full force again on Prithvi. We expect the mammalian life form to dominate the planet now.' Krishna reported.

Shyam nodded and smiled. 'I have an interactive map for you, so you wouldn't have to waste much of your time in exploring unseen terrains.' He was right, strangely enough almost none of the Madhavpur dwellers would ever venture much out of the city limits. May be it was transition era's legacy when crossing the city limits could have been trouble.

'But, I cannot carry any location-seeking device with me, I don't want to blow my cover,' Krishna said.

Shyam looked into his wrist-phone, noticed the time and said, 'Your interactive map will arrive any time now.'

As Shyam completed his sentence the doorbell rang. Krishna closed his eyes, concentrated and unlocked the door.

'Hello, Shyam!' Vallabha said.

'And I was about to say that no one except for the three of us should know about this trip,' Krishna sighed.

'I never expected such a warm welcome, never thought I will be treated as an intruder to the league of the secret cabal!' Vallabha exclaimed.

'Whoa! Cool down, madam. No disrespect, but you do realize that we were in the middle of a conversation?' Krishna replied.

'Shyam, I think I should leave.' She said gently.

'Wait. This is my quest and for that I do not want to put anybody else in jeopardy,' Krishna said.

'Son, you don't have a say in this matter and Vallabha is the only one who has seen the whole of Jambhu-Dweep.'

'She has?'

'She has! I wrote her the consent which allowed her uninterrupted movement across the whole Jambhu-Dweep for her ecology-related studies.' Shyam explained.

'Ahaa! The interactive map doesn't seem that bad after all.' Krishna said, realizing the fact that he couldn't turn down Shyam's idea.

'Did you just call me a map? Huh! We are on a mission, and we are equal partners.' Vallabha retorted.

He looked at Shyam and said, 'Too interactive.'

Shyam could not help but laugh. He then clasped his hands together and said, 'Now listen, Krishna. Vallabha is an eminent ecologist and she is here on my request. So, when she says something you better listen. I am not letting you out in the wilderness alone.'

'Yes, I am one.' Vallabha said, confirming her eminent status.

'I understand,' Krishna said, and Vallabha smiled. She was

wearing a tightly draped orange-coloured saree. She was almost as tall as Krishna. But her slim stature made her look taller. Cream complexion, sharp nose, fish-shaped eyes, curvy eyebrows, thin long neck and facial contour of a warrior princess; she was a charming lady with a guileless attitude.

'Now Vallabha, I suggest you return,' Shyam said.

'But I have grown a certain degree of fondness for my map…' Krishna said playfully. Shyam then turned towards Vallabha, thus blatantly ignoring Krishna, and said, 'Take this map and be at the spot marked X at six tomorrow morning.' He then handed over a copy of the map to Krishna too.

'Tomorrow morning it is. Take care!' she said and left.

Krishna then turned towards Mohan and said, 'While I am gone, follow the manual, run required checks, and under no circumstances play around with Omechta parameters unnecessarily.'

Mohan nodded and hugged Krishna. With his head firmly placed over Krishna's right shoulder, a tear rolled down his cheek and settled on Krishna's collarbone.

'You have always been like a brother to me. Just got a little nostalgic thinking of all the olden times,' Mohan said.

'You too have always been like my younger brother,' Krishna replied.

Shyam then patted Krishna on his shoulder and said, 'May you find the answers you seek.' He then signalled Mohan and they both left for home.

•◆

The skies were still not properly illuminated by the patiently growing sunlight on the horizon. He was barely able to push himself out of the vent. The tunnels were deep, dark, and tiring. As he climbed up the vent and was dusting his robe, he heard some footsteps on his left.

'I collected some berries for you. You have a fondness for them, don't you?'

'I love them,' Krishna said. It was exact six and Vallabha was already there. It was a typical summer morning, filled with cool clement winds. She handed over a fistful of berries to him.

Krishna looked back from the mouth of the vent, and could see both Mount Govardhan and Mount Meru. It was the farthest from the city limit he had ever gone.

'You were lucky, that I came in here first. It was not an open vent, I had to push through all the soil and vegetation covering it.'

'Oh Vallabha! What would I do without you? Now will you tell me where to start looking?' he said. The sarcastically dry and thankless undertone irked Vallabha.

'You don't like me being here, do you?'

'You think this is an adventure trip, when it is not. And that's what I do not like.'

'The whole life is an adventure trip, come to think of it. Who would want to live that monotonous life anyway?'

'Directions, if you will.'

'We are going to the eastern front,' she curtly replied.

'To the creek?'

'You are seeking the hermit, you will get what you want.'

'Those are forbidden frontiers...' he said with a gleam in his eyes.

'That's what life is all about, seeking the forbidden.' Vallabha answered in a slow husky voice. Had it not been for a good dose of self-control, his facial expressions would have been that of bafflement.

'I will cover this vent up. This passage should remain a secret, as no one else knows about these transition era tunnels.' Krishna then turned and started covering the opening of the vent with soil and leaves. As he got up and turned back, he could see no one. Vallabha was nowhere to be seen.

'Now what?' he thought and then shouted out her name in a bid to find her. He could hear some giggling and sounds of dry leaves hustling from behind a tree surrounded with dark bushes.

'Here is the deal, Miss. You have precisely ten seconds before I move on.'

Krishna then waited for few moments and said, 'See you.'

As he was about to walk away, she replied from across the tree, 'Wait.'

'You actually have no patience, you are restless like a kid.' Vallabha said as she appeared from behind the thick vegetation.

'Are you insane? What is this?' Krishna exclaimed.

Vallabha tossed a small pouch towards Krishna and said, 'Keep this in your robe, will need it on our way back home.'

'You have no respect for anything. You know this is gross violation of the revered code. What do you want? A war?'

'Calm down! The code is only applicable within city limits. But then how would you know, you never ventured out.'

She had changed from her saree to dark beige-coloured half-trousers and a bright round-necked red t-shirt. She looked more athletic in her nicely fitting hiking outfit. Her skin was shining like a gold leaf in early morning sunshine.

Krishna was partly annoyed on the code issue, and partly pleasantly surprised. She had been Krishna's junior in both NYCAR and during his Madhavpur schooldays. She was more outgoing then Krishna and had a much bigger social circle. An occasional 'Hello' was all they had ever exchanged, that too had always been initiated by Vallabha. And now he couldn't help himself from staring and ogling at her. She was looking hot in her hiking outfit.

'Now if you are done running through the code in your mind,

that way please.' she said pointing towards her right.

'There is a foot trail here, quite strange.'

'We are a group of four friends, botany enthusiasts. This is our trail.'

'What do you study here?'

'We study various herbs and plants growing in and around Jambhu-Dweep.'

'Anything specific?'

'Bhoomidium.'

Now Vallabha had his attention. Before Krishna could ask anything she said, 'Yes, the levels are already low.'

'What role does it play in a plant's life?' he asked.

'It facilitates cell repair and longevity in normal plants. But, in case of carnivorous plants like the Venus Fly trap, well they have stopped trapping. They have started thriving only on photosynthesis. But of late many species are ageing and their numbers dwindling owing to the lack of Bhoomidium in the soil,' she said.

'Efforts are underway,' he replied with a smile.

During the next hour or so of hiking, neither of them spoke. As the day progressed it was becoming a little hot and humid. He raised his glance towards Vallabha, and noticed beads of sweat, glistening in bright daylight, rolling down her forehead and cheek.

'You look tired. Maybe we should halt for a while,' he said.

'Thanks for noticing, but the hill range that needs to be crossed is nearby. We ought to cross that before its dark.'

Krishna nodded and smiled while looking into her light brown eyes. Her eyes narrowed in response and she smiled in return. Even before Krishna could realize and extend his arm for support, she fumbled and fell to the ground. Her foot had landed in a shallow ditch. She let out a sharp cry of pain. Her ankle was hurt and her knees bruised.

'Are you okay?'

'Let's hope so,' was all she could say while biting her lower lip in pain.

'Let me help you get up, we will go and sit under that tree,' he then picked her up and helped her limp to the aragvadha tree some ten steps from that place.

'You should rest here for a while.'

She was still perspiring and the bruises were fresh. Krishna sat beside her and drew a pouch out his robe and said, 'Here wash the cut, it will also help cool your wounds.'

It was a high concentration of Bhoomidium mixed in distilled water. As she washed her knees with the solution, the bruises patched up and started looking better. The solution was now trickling down her legs from knee to the ankle. But it could only heal the superficial cuts and wounds. The twisted ankle could only be healed from inside and would have taken time.

'What motivates you, Krishna?'

'For what?' he asked.

'Come on! You are the most eligible bachelor in town, still you choose to remain single and spend all your productive years in that remotely placed lab of yours.'

'That's my work. That's who I am.'

Vallabha raised her right brow and said, 'And who decides that?'

'I made my own choices. I have some specific skillsets, which I could render for laying the foundation of the Manava society and its sustenance. That's what I am, that's what I was meant to be. My productive years are being spent well at my work.'

'So, the sustenance of the Manava society is what motivates you. I can say that, right?'

She expected a response from Krishna, but he gave none.

'What if I told you that there are people in Madhavpur who

are simply bored of this monotonous life?'

'Well, my suggestion to them would be to choose a preoccupation of interest and purpose.'

'Funny! It's funny that you think that life needs to be full of gravity and has to have a purpose,' she said. Krishna nodded with a casual shrug.

'What purpose are we solving here in Madhavpur, apart from our survival? Our purpose now it seems has become to ensure that we survive to work on a purpose. Working on a purpose has become a purpose for us.'

'So, what do you propose?' he asked.

'It's time we started leaving things to destiny. We run a treadmill in the name of life.'

Krishna was in no mood to get into that debate. He held a clear picture in his mind, the picture of sustenance of the society. 'My only suggestion is that you should loosen up a bit. I have had a degree of admiration for you from the schooldays itself. I am just saying what I felt like all this while,' Vallabha said.

These were the very words Krishna was apprehensive about from the beginning of the trip. It was not as if he never had any liking for her, but his heart was still filled with the reverberations of the fragrance of those fresh jasmine flowers. His heart was like an airtight box and no other fragrance, no matter how honey-laced it may be, it can never replace the stubborn wafts of those sweet smells.

Krishna stood up and bent towards Vallabha and firmly picked her up in his arms. With his right arm under her shoulder blades and left under her knee joints, she was now staring deep into his eyes. Krishna carried her across the mountainous trail. After an hour of walking across the hill range, they were now quite near the creek.

'These are the limits of Jambhu-Dweep, I will not go beyond

them,' Krishna said while placing Vallabha gently on a boulder under a tree. The sun was now descending and breeze had grown a little less hot.

'We won't have to,' Vallabha replied. She pointed towards some shrubs; he knew what it was. He went up to the shrubs and plucked a fresh green bulb. He then placed her right foot on his lap, and made a slit on the bulb. The milky white liquid then dripped on her ankle. After all the sap had dripped and the bulb went dry, he gently massaged the sap over her still hurting ankle. It took another five minutes before the pain relieved.

The poppy sap had kicked in and she was again on her feet, with her ever-jovial gait.

13

The Nefarious Plans

The room was dark and filled with smoke. It was hard to say as to what was darker, the room or the night sky outside. The only saving grace, that sky above had dense steel grey-coloured clouds, glowing in the moonlight. On the other hand, the only light or the hint of it that could be seen in that room was a pair of feeble red glowing objects. Any person sitting inside that room, from lack of any stimulus, would have turned insane in a matter of minutes. It was completely empty.

Suddenly, the automated door slid and a burst of light from the mildly lit alley entered the room. So, did a dark figure along with it. His face was not visible neither was his body, only his silhouette could have been estimated in the backlight of the pathway. The door closed, and nothing could be seen in the room except for those glowing indicator lights. But those were enough for the figure to make his way across the room.

He reached up to the glowing lights and pressed both the glowing indicators simultaneously. The upper surface of a table-like panel slid open. A panel on a transparent backlit glass now appeared. The wall behind the panel started glowing, gradually. It was a display, warming up slowly, so as to not to perturb the dark of the room. Even when it was fully lit, it was feeble and pale at best.

He punched in a series of code on the panel and then waited

for the commands to be processed by the system.

'Uplink Awaited'—read the screen.

He waited for a few more moments and then started walking up and down the length of the screen. He was growing impatient, and kept on turning his head toward the screen. It was stuck on that status.

'Paramganak! What is taking you so long?'

'Mercy, oh my master! The overcast has made it difficult to establish a secure connection. I am working on it.'

He growled in reply while walking the length of the room to and fro. Some images started showing on the screen, and a voice from across said, 'Command, oh my master! Ever merciful.'

Neither that heavy metallic reverberating voice nor that face belonged to any Manava. It was a face made out of dark alloy, with a protruding jaw and cylindrical black metallic teeth. The eyes were unlike anything else and glowed like red xenon. Ears were well rounded and the cheekbones were high and sharply contoured. He sported a rounded headgear with a pair of horns on it.

As the camera view on the screen adjusted, his body became visible. It was made out of the same dark alloy. At the end of his back was a tail made out of the dark alloy but with a sharp edge. He kept on waging his tail like a sword and wouldn't have restrained himself from whipping it on his enemies, if need be.

'Bhaydadh! Brief me on your preparation for war,' he said.

'My master! As you can see I have a full army of loyal mercenaries, who wouldn't think twice before rendering themselves to his highness's service,' replied that being.

The figure in dark broke into a fit of laughter, and as he zoomed out the view further, there was indeed an army of metallic beings working in what seemed like an abandoned factory. It was rather gloomy and dark. It was barely a structure with only metal beams intact, with no roof or walls. No wind was apparent nor was any illumination, neither natural nor artificial. It was dark, with a very feeble ambient light, which was apparent only after getting reflected from the fine silver-coloured dust beneath.

'Bhaydadh! My son, I have created you to fill fear into the heart of my enemies.'

And he was right. The very glimpse of that metallic creature was terrifying, even the name bestowed upon him—Bhaydadh—meant the one who instilled terror. 'Your blessing, my master,' the creature replied with his metallic tone dipped in servitude and filled with eternal gratitude.

'The Jarasandh Legion should be, on my command, kept prepared for the assault.'

The being kneeled on his left leg with his right leg placed forward, and placed his heavy metallic spiked mace head on the silver sand. He then placed his metallic squared chin on the tail end of the mace and said, 'Yes, my master.'

The figure in dark again broke into a fit of laughter, this time it was more deep and sombre and reeked of evil.

'We shall soon taste the sweet nectar of revenge, and will put an end to aeons of trickery and injustice. The fallen shall rise again and lay the empire of the righteous,' said the figure in dark before again breaking into laughter.

·❖·

In the outermost fetches of Jambhu-Dweep, after hours of walking around and many rounds of detours, Krishna and Vallabha finally arrived at the creek. It was already dark by now.

'It's dark and it seems it would rain tonight. I do not want to be around this creek for long,' Krishna said. It was not actually a creek but was called so. A natural boundary to the eastern front of Jambhu-Dweep, the water that ran through it was unimaginably brackish.

'I feel thirsty,' Vallabha said, who could now feel the pain coming back yet again.

'There is hardly any water left. And, the creek water is not palatable,' Krishna said.

'I know of a place where the creek water is sweet,' Vallabha replied. She then pointed north and they started walking upstream. By the time they reached there, it was already drizzling. It was the point of confluence of the Yamuna River into the creek, which explained the sweetness of the water there.

Krishna stood there in awe, as he saw the river after such a long period of time. After the shifting of the plates at the end of Kali-Yuga, all the major rivers either vanished or changed courses. The Yamuna started flowing toward further east into the creek, which in turn flowed into the Purva-Sagar. Its water was emerald green and was cool all year round.

'I haven't seen it for a while now, and now that I am standing by its shores, I feel a strange connection.' Krishna spoke in a voice laced with nostalgia.

'None of the Madhavpur inhabitants have seen its in some time. No one ventures out of city limits anymore. I often come and sit by her tranquil shores to listen to its music.'

Krishna helped her walk up to the river shore, she tried kneeling but couldn't. With all the walking around, her ankle pain was bouncing back. Krishna filled his flask and handed it over to her. He then pulled out another pouch and filled it with some more water.

'The rain is gaining momentum. We need to find some shelter, a tree maybe.

'I know of a cave at a hill's base nearby,' she said. Krishna nodded and then picked her up.

The cave was dark and humid, but still was their best refuge. Krishna drew some apparatuses out of his travel pouch and said, 'I hate to do this, but I will have to give you a shot.'

He then filled the prick-less injection with the diluted Bhoomidium solution. 'This might make you feel dizzy and nauseous for a while, but your pain needs to go.' Krishna said while applying the injection to her arm. The injection fragmented the solution into microscopic globules, which were then pushed across her skin using mild UV rays.

'It feels fine,' Vallabha said. Krishna then carefully removed her boots, and made her lean against the cave wall. She had started growing pale by now and the skin under her eyes looked darker. More than the pain, the fatigue of the day-long hike had clearly overwhelmed her. Krishna collected some dry shrubs growing inside the cave and laid them as a bed for her.

'You won't mind, if I lie on the inner side? I am not a big fan of thunderstorms, you see,' she said. Krishna nodded. 'And by your side?' she then said.

Krishna smiled and said, 'There isn't enough room in here anyway. But you need to sleep or the dose will make you feel quite uncomfortable.'

Only an iota of romantic feelings was all Vallabha expected but she got none. Krishna lay by her side, nearer to the mouth of the cave. She kept on turning and tossing, and would get up intermittently to look outward.

'I am not kidding, you actually need to take rest,' Krishna said.

'You never answered me. Why have you never settled?' Vallabha asked him.

'I am very happily settled with my work, and I thought we already settled the debate too.'

She gave up, and within a few minutes she was fast asleep. As

Krishna realized the halt of the barrage of questions and breathed relief, she in her sleep turned and placed her arm joyously across his chest. He smiled and slid a little away. It was still pouring heavily, the petrichor rising from the ground reminded him of that particular sweet face again.

•◆

He was not sure whether it was sharp chirping of the birds or the glaring sunlight entering the cave, which brought him out of his deep slumber. But as he woke up and turned, he couldn't find Vallabha around.

He leaped up and hurried out of the cave. The skies were clear and the grounds were still wet from last night's rain. He could not see her around. His best bet was to look around the Yamuna shores, which was some thousand-feet away from the cave. It was not uncommon for anybody, who has been administered with intravenous Bhoomidium, to feel acute thirst. He rushed toward the riverbank.

The wave fronts over the Yamuna were sparkling like emerald covered with molten gold, in the slant sunlight. The breeze flowing across Yamuna too had a tinge of sweet smell in it. He looked around but could not find any sign of her. He was completely baffled now.

As he was thinking of where next to search for her, a small circular wave front emerged some 10 feet from the river shore with that peculiar sound of the water separating. Her head appeared and then she slowly rose out of water, while walking towards the shore. Her red t-shirt and beige shorts were now completely drenched and were hugging her tight.

This girl never fails to amaze me. Krishna tried not to stare at her, as she came out of the river. Her hair had pearl-like beads of water, narrow streams were rolling down from her radiant forehead onto her sharp well-chiseled nose and her sleek toned legs were glowing with a thin layer of water over them. The cold water gave her quite apparent goosebumps all over her body. She knew that Krishna couldn't help but notice her.

Meanwhile, he was masking his amazement with a sense of curiosity on his face. 'What?' she asked, 'The first thing I felt after getting up this morning was this body heat. So, I went for a swim in the river.'

Krishna extended his hand with his fist closed.

'This is to pull me up or to join me in?' she asked with a mischievously sensuous smile on her face, while she stood a foot away from the shore.

He than unclenched his fist, thus revealing a small towel that he was holding.

'Neither. Take this and dry yourself. The picnic is over. We need to move on.'

'You need to move on, not we,' she said. Krishna gave her a puzzled look with a hint of impatience.

'You are still stuck in Kali-Yuga. Blinded by old memories and numbed by nostalgia, you can't even see my overtures. You, it seems, are still stuck in chapters of the past.'

Krishna tried collecting some words of speech to protest but couldn't. He was simply unprepared for a candid and forthright confrontation like this.

'Can't you see how much I want you?' Vallabha said bluntly.

'I can very well see that.'

'Then what are you afraid of?'

'Who told you I am interested in you? Stop assuming, lady!' Krishna retorted as he turned back and started moving.

'Very well then, I know my way back home,' she said.

Krishna turned, took a fast step forward and locked her in his embrace.

'You are hurting me.' Vallabha said in a shrill voice.

'Well, why? You don't want me anymore?' Krishna said with a devious grin on his face. 'I am here with some bigger issues on my hands. And I am not letting you ruin my mission for your petty gains,' he added, gradually loosening the embrace.

She was now a little intimidated, 'Okay! Okay!' she mumbled.

Krishna then completely loosened his grip. He was smiling and she was now frowning. She started following Krishna, 'Do you know your way around here? Where are we going?'

Krishna didn't reply. She stopped and yelled, 'You are being hurtful and rude!'

Krishna stopped, turned to reply, 'Good that you realized. Because that was what you were doing all along.'

She was still not moving. 'Now come on, I do not want to spend another night in some cave,' he said.

'Neither do I, but I must tell you, you are headed towards the wrong direction. Along the creek is our best bet,' replied a snubbed Vallabha.

'Now we are going to do it my way.'

She shrugged, 'Let's see.'

Krishna was now searching for some clues towards the creek-side foot of the hill range. The range base was full of flowering bushes. *If only I could find hints of recent settlement along the base,* Krishna wondered. Vallabha, meanwhile, was busy collecting specimens of shrubs and blossoming flowers along the way. She was busy hopping from one bush to another, when she noticed a bush with purplish-blue flowers. They looked quite unique and were unlike the whole other lot. A whole hill was covered with such bushes, colouring the hill purplish-blue.

'Neelakurinji!' exclaimed Vallabha. Krishna turned and gave her a long curious glance with a smile. He knew that she has found something of her interest.

'This flower blossoms only once in twelve years. It's quite rare and I am not giving up on an opportunity to collect it.'

She was busy choosing the right ones from the bushes, when Krishna heard something. *Some stone must have slid due to plucking the flowers.* But the noise was approaching them. Vallabha was still busy collecting her specimen, while Krishna could hear the sound growing. It took a moment before he became wary of the rustling sound. Bent over the bushes studying the flower, Vallabha was unaware of everything around her. Krishna started walking towards her. The noise started growing further, faster than the speed with which he was approaching Vallabha.

Finally, the creature making rustling sound leaped like a thunderbolt out of the bushes on the slope. Krishna leaped towards Vallabha and pushed her away out of its trajectory.

It was a fully-grown leopard that just leaped out of nowhere. The leopard clearly missed the intended prey in his first jump.

Vallabha dropped whatever she was carrying and screamed out of fear and disbelief. Krishna held her close to himself and asked her to stay quiet. The leopard was now back on it's feet and was going about in an arc around both of them. His eyes were now set on her, and he was growling in a threatening way. As the leopard moved a few feet forward, she got more scared. In her bid to step backwards towards the bushy slope, she fumbled and fell down. The leopard seeing her on the ground roared again and got into motion. She covered her eyes with her arm and yelled. The leopard sprung, aiming directly for Vallabha.

On seeing the leopard's unrelenting and belligerent behaviour, Krishna too rushed towards her. Midway, he reached out to his wrist-device and activated the Yocto-Suit. He slid his fingers down the front of his suit and it parted. As he reached near Vallabha, he drew her into his suit, and it got activated with a delay of a fraction of a second. Krishna then rolled over from the spot quickly to avoid being pounded by the leopard.

The leopard landed and skidded into the bushes behind. Bruised and perplexed, he was more furious than before. He kept on roaring in a mad frenzy for over half of a minute.

Before Vallabha could utter a word again, Krishna whispered to her, 'He cannot see us now, you are inside a stealth suit. Stay calm and quite.'

The leopard then began sniffing around and tried chasing fresh trails.

'He is not a dumb radar. He can still smell us out,' replied Vallabha.

'Sshhh...' he whispered back.

He stood up while tightly holding her and made sure that, they both were covered by the suit. And then began inching towards a tree nearby.

'Don't even think about that, leopards are tree dwellers.' Vallabha said in a hushed voice. Krishna with Vallabha in his Yocto-Suit went around the kadam tree twice and then moved towards the bush. The leopard followed the trails toward the tree and kept inspecting the tree trunk. This move had confused the big cat. Meanwhile, Krishna was slowly shifting towards his right, steering clear from the foothill bushes so as to not make any noise. With his eyes affixed over the movement of the leopard, he fumbled over a small rock and both he and Vallabha fell into the bushes. The fall made quite a loud thud sound and drew the big cat's attention. There was nothing that Krishna could have thought of now, and the feline attack upon them was inevitable. The leopard sprung into the air with no intention to display any clemency.

'Stop!' the loud words reverberated across the hill and the river basin. The leopard gave up the leap midway and using his tail turned in his flight. He landed and sat at the very spot of touchdown.

The main nerve centre of Krishna's suit located at the back was hurt and it gave up. Both were now visible, with no stealth. The big cat merely acknowledged the fact that he could now see them, but did not move.

Krishna turned towards the slopes above to see whose voice it was that had tamed the big cat. He could only hear the footsteps, but could see no one. He became cautious again.

'Relax, Vyaghraraj!' said a heavy voice emanating from the slopes just above them. 'They are neither intruders nor attackers. They are just wayfarers,' the voice continued.

As the voice grew closer, the person to whom it belonged to started appearing. As if he had passed through an invisible door mid-air, which made him visible again.

He had a flowing grey beard. His grey hair was matted into a knot above his head. His face showed no sign of wrinkles and his eyes were lively. He had a bare torso and wore a knee-length wrap made out of tiger skin around his loins. He seemed strong and held a wooden T-shaped stick in his right arm.

Krishna was taken aback, as he never knew that the person he was seeking possessed such supernatural powers, or that those powers existed at all for that matter.

'We are neither wayfarers nor adventurers.' Krishna said putting up an unmoved and nonchalant front.

'Then what business do you have here in these hinterlands. Oh resident of Madhavpur.'

'We have come here to seek answers,' he replied.

The hermit started laughing. He stood erect and raised his head high and laughed, 'This might not be the best place to be pensive, go to your city and look inwards for all your answers.'

'You know very well that we have been looking for you, you were here all along,' said Krishna.

'No, I didn't. I mind my own ways. I have these borders to protect, and you were on the verge of trespassing.'

'Is that the reason your leopard attacked us?' Krishna asked.

'Vyaghraraj is his name. He was on a vigil.'

'And who do you protect these borders from?' Krishna asked.

'From the storm, that is brewing.'

'Madhavpur is already under attack. They are after our last bastion.'

'And who are you to represent Madhavpur?'

Krishna then ran his hand under his robe and pulled out his Venu.

The hermit smiled. He then turned towards the big cat and signalled him to go back on his vigil. Vyaghraraj complied.

'The city is under severe threat, we believe that somebody from within is carrying out a sabotage,' Krishna said.

'I thought you were our Krishna.'

Though perplexed by the use of the word 'our', Krishna replied, 'Well, that is me.'

'No, I meant "the Krishna".'

Krishna kept quiet, waiting eagerly to know about the Krishna the hermit was referring to.

14

The Eternal Song

'I used to wander in Gokul, aimless and with no joy whatsoever. Me and in fact all of my friends use to miss him, so very much. We didn't even realize when our childhood zoomed past us, while either listening to his tales or on our lucky days playing with him on those beautiful Gokul evenings along the Yamuna. He was a natural charmer and always led the group that he chose to play with. He always used to dress in a yellow pristine dhoti and a nicely tied waistband. If his yellow attire resembled the vibrant energy of the universe, then the peacock feather nicely placed in his long matted hair resembled the eyes of the heavens above. Half of the village would give away anything just to see him smile, and the other half to hear him play his flute. As he grew, he started winning hearts of one and all...' narrated the hermit.

'But when he was gone, the very soul of Gokul subsided. As if he was our sole purpose of existence. I would milk the cows that belonged to our family, would sell the excess produce and would wander around the banks of the Yamuna for the rest of the day. Then one day word travelled from Mathura that Krishna was in need of new recruits for the Narayani Sena. I informed my family, delegated all my rights and duties to my younger brother, and left for Mathura. We were a bunch of thousand young men. We did get to hear our commander-in-chief, but I longed for those childhood games.'

Krishna was sitting beside him, with Vallabha on his side. It was not the first time he was hearing this story, but it was more of a passing memory. Something he heard once or maybe twice in his own childhood. He thought these were stories and traditions, and never realized that they could have been real narratives.

'The tensions between the Pandvas and the Kauravas started soaring high. And delegation after delegation started visiting Krishna in Dwarka. We all knew that a war was imminent and also knew with whom our commander would align—the Pandvas, the righteous inheritors to the throne of Hastinapur. We knew our Krishna would again fight for restoring the Dharma, and that is just what he did. We all were very excited that we would get to fight for our commander once again. But in a baffling turn of events, Krishna gifted us away. The Narayani Sena was loaned to the evil Kauravas. We were heartbroken. Not only we would be parted from our commander but would also have to fight against him. But orders were orders and for the love of Krishna we did march.'

Vallabha by now was smiling. Unlike Krishna, she remembered all the childhood tales of Lord Krishna and was pleased at getting to hear the first-hand account.

'A very fierce fight ensued. None in the whole Aryavrat could claim that he was not affected. Everyone had to choose his or her side, Dharma versus Adharma, righteousness versus treachery. We were a nerve-wrecked loaned-out group of soldiers, who had to fight against their own master. The whole set of parameters for dharma and adharma for us were different. We had to side with forces of evil, that was our dharma. The whole Sena was now growing paranoid and had second thoughts about what was our rightful duty,' his eyes were now heavier as he spoke. His heart still sank from the gravity of that past chain of events. He paused, rather his words came to a gradual halt.

'You basically then defected back to his side?' interjected Krishna.

Vallabha turned towards him with a jerk and said, 'Sshh! Let him speak. Don't be insensitive.'

'It was a bright and clear late autumn morning, with cold winds blowing from the east. We gathered our weapons and were dressed in our war suits and armours. We were not told much about the overall war plans, only the duties for the days were revealed to us. The thought of fighting against our own Krishna baffled us to no limits. We eventually would have defected but then we realized that we were not the ones alone in this dilemma.

'The great warrior, the most brilliant of all Pandvas, Prince Arjun too had similar conflicting thoughts going around in his mind. The one who wielded Gandiva, whose arrows could subjugate the Earth, heavens, and the underworlds alike, whose chariot in the Great War of Mahabharata was driven by Krishna himself—was finding it hard to raise his arms against the Kauravas—his brethren.

'He was tormented by the very thoughts of fighting his own grandfather, his gurus and cousins. He was shaky and perspiring even in the chilly autumn morning breeze.

'As we lined up in a formation with rest of the Kaurava legions led by great commanders, we saw a very unusual happening. Arjun asked Krishna to draw his chariot towards the middle of the battlefield. The conch-shells were yet to be blown; the Yudh was yet to begin.

'Even before the war drums could roll, Arjun was on his knees full of helplessness and remorse. He could visualize the annihilation of the Kauravas and the mere thought of destruction of his own family tree, sent cold shivers rolling down his spine. The Gandiva slipped from his hand.

'Krishna had held him by his shoulder and asked the reason

for his sorrow. Arjun said, "We are one Kuru family, they are my own blood. It was Pita-Maha who held me by my finger when I took my first step. It was Duryodhan and the Kauravas with whom we spent our childhood. Guru Dronacharya made the very hands, which wield the Gandiva today, steadfast. How do you expect me to inflict harm on them?"

'Krishna then revealed to him what generations since have come to know as the Bhagvad Gita. He gave lessons of dharma and duty to Arjun. The dark gloomy clouds of doubts finally started rising from Arjun's conscience. Krishna told him the essence of Karma and the importance of upholding one's dharma.

'We too then realized that it was now our duty to fight, on orders of our King, from the camp of Kauravas.

'A fierce battle for eighteen long days followed.

'Kauravas suffered a huge humiliating defeat at the hands of the Pandvas. There were collateral damages too, but dharma prevailed.'

'What did he say to Arjun that he had a change of heart?' asked Krishna.

The hermit smiled and said, 'He reiterated the wisdom which he at the beginning of life had taught to Surya.'

'The sun?'

The hermit nodded and said, 'The wisdom is eternal and has been passing on from one intelligent life form to another.'

'Now you got to narrate to me what wisdom are we talking about? What could have made killing your own bloodline a lesser sin?' Krishna said.

'Arjun did not just wake up one fine morning with a bloodthirsty throat. The very brothers, with whom he sympathized, ill-treated him and his family. The Kauravas cheated the Pandvas into exile and didn't even hesitate for a moment before insulting Draupadi in front of a full Kaurava court.'

'You are right, they did cross the line and sealed their own fate,' Vallabha added.

'I still remember that morning vividly; his folded hands were trembling. All he wanted was a last minute truce to save the kingdom and the family. That is when Krishna held him and made him see through the smoke screen into the eternal truth. He was heartbroken when he couldn't see Bhishma and the likes of Guru Dronacharya making it to the other end of the war. Krishna then told him how there has been no time when they have not been around. That those he saw, as relatives on battlefield were not people but rather manifestation of consciousness, which passed from one body to another. Arjun was not killing them. He was merely bringing an end to the temporary, transient, and ephemeral role that those consciousness were playing. "You forgot, but I remember," were his exact words. He then went on to explain to the Great Archer, how futile was it to worry about the end results when all he could control were his own actions. He taught Arjun the art of detachment from end results, and how to be dedicated to the duty alone and not to the end benefits that may follow. What Arjun feared the most was the fate of the family after the war, the scathes of the events would have left the family in tatters and completely directionless. This is when Krishna let him onto the most important secrets of all time…'

'And what was that?'

'Neither existing nor flourishing should be the sole goal of a conscious being. His ultimate goal has to be to devote his karma unto Krishna, and elevate himself to his abode.'

'What if you don't believe in Krishna or Godhead?' Krishna asked.

'You would still exist and chances are you could still flourish in your existence.'

Krishna couldn't connect the dots and remained silent, to which the hermit continued, 'But you remain stagnant in this transcendental journey of Jeev and Atman.'

Krishna was now even more curious. The hermit continued, 'Atman is the ever-flowing consciousness and Jeev is the form in which the Atman manifests. If you don't devote your karma unto Param-Atman or the Godhead, you never reach his abode and get entangled in cycles of beings and existences.'

'You mean survival of a civilization is a matter of trivial importance?' asked Krishna in a polite but firm manner.

'That's not the question. The question is survival for what?'

'To see another day, to be with your loved ones,' Krishna replied.

'Are you with your loved one, Krishna? Or your every other day is just another day?' the hermit asked him.

Up until this point he had been holding an eye contact with the hermit, but these utterances or the reminders that they were sort of, made him look into another direction. Those wide sparkling eyes were now being brutal to him.

'We at Madhavpur are rationalists and we do not rely on God. We have chiseled our own destination and it has worked well for us till of late,' Krishna replied.

'Then what brings you here?'

'I have been seeing these very powerful dreams and they tell me what to do and leave me with these dark blue marks,' he said while raising his sleeves and revealing the fresh marks.

The hermit smiled and said, 'And why did you choose to see me now?'

'I didn't, the turn of events did,' he replied.

The hermit held him by his arm and examined the marks closely. His eyes were now glittering with a thin film of moisture when he said, 'This is how Lord Krishna's complexion looked like when he took on the universal form. When, Arjun was having a hard time convincing himself to raise the Gandiva again that is when he gave him divine vision and then displayed his universal form. Krishna grew immeasurably; he now had thousands of neverending faces lined up one beside another. Few faces were smiling like freshly blossomed lotuses and few were gushing hellfire. His universal form was both awe-inspiring and fear-instilling. His skin grew dark like a young blue lotus. These are marks of Krishna, those dreams are the messages from his abode, which you now call the Core.'

'The Core?' Krishna repeated.

He nodded in affirmation and said, 'The Abode of Krishna.'

'This information was classified way back in a secret lab of NYCAR. How do you have access to it?' said Krishna, whose restlessness was now a little ostensible.

'I have heard it in my Lord's voice.'

'Whose jurisdiction do you follow? Theirs, right?' said Krishna.

'I only bow to his command,' replied the hermit smilingly.

Vallabha held Krishna by his arm and said to the hermit, 'How long have you been around and what's your purpose of being on Jambhu-Dweep?'

'I have been around for ages before you two even existed and my purpose has been the same since then—the protection of dharma,' he replied and placed his arm on the ground by his side to get up.

Vallabha seeing this folded her hands in a gesture of apology and said, 'Swami! We have come here to seek answers to our problems. Madhavpur is in great danger, our race and our civilization is in peril. We are just overwhelmed and astonished listening to the tales that you have narrated.'

'Those who relent the sacred thread of dharma, wither away into the darkness of anonymity. Your society works only on things that are necessary for a comfortable survival. Instead of dharma you chose to rely on what you call science. But then feeling insecure of your own advances, you placed a moratorium even on that. You people chose to abide by the Code but do so without understanding or indulging in it. Your society is living with no purpose apart from survival and with no meaning, whatsoever.'

'If we led such a meaningless existence, how come we earned enemies?' Krishna asked.

'Such societies have always been a ripe ground for genesis of evil. Meaningless living generates greed and greed begets evil.'

'Swami! We do not even know your name yet. How come you have lived through these ages, and is the rest of Narayani Sena still around?' Vallabha asked.

'They do not exist now, at least not on Bhoomi. I am the lone soldier of the Sena alive today. Gopaldas, that's my name.'

'You were blessed by Krishna himself, weren't you?' Vallabha said with a smile.

'We fought with all our vigour, drew enemy blood. But as the fate already had it, one after another the Kauravas fell. By the time the war ended, none from the Kauravas camp survived. On the day the war was decisively won, Krishna along with the Pandvas was touring the battlefield to take a note of the causalities from both the camps. Their first priority was to provide humanitarian aid to all the injured irrespective of the side they fought for. I was sitting alone and wrecked amidst my injured colleagues, when he in his pristine yellow dhoti and golden crown studded with rare gems and trademark peacock feather, went past me. I clung to his feet and said, "I am the divisional commander of your out-loaned Narayani Sena. Please forgive me for we fought against the righteous." He held me by my shoulders and pulled me up. "That was your duty, and you have lived up to your dharma."

'To which I replied, "Krishna don't you remember me, I am Gopal. Your Gokul awaits you; come along with us to your native place."

'He smiled and replied, "Someday I definitely will. For now I have many unfinished tasks. I have to prepare the world for the coming Yuga, which will be more challenging then this one." He then saw my fresh wounds and scars and smiled. He raised his hand and placed it over my head, and my wounds were gone. He then said, "I now relieve you from active services of the Sena."

'I grew baffled and out of fear of the fact that I might have annoyed Krishna, I trembled. But he said, "You will be on my special mission. Travel to all three corners of the Aryavrat and work for the people in need. Help the poor and the destitute. The state has been through a massive war unseen in ages, reach the extreme corners of the state and help rebuild it."

'Hearing this, tears of devotion had rolled down my cheeks, and I had embraced Krishna in joy. He said, "I bestow upon you the duty of guarding the mankind and helping the ones in need. As long as your heart will be filled with devotion to me, no harm will ever touch you."

'I have been venturing on Bhoomi ever since then, either helping the ones in need or meditating unto him.'

'Then why did you let Bhoomi turn into ruins before the split?' asked Vallabha.

'I might seem mystical and possessing supernatural powers but I have my limits and my own codes of conduct. All my capabilities are from boons and blessings of Krishna. I couldn't have jumped into battlefields with war cries and fought all evil by myself, as reinstatement of dharma is pure purview of Krishna alone. He clearly instructed Arjun—that whenever adharma would overwhelm dharma, he would take human form to protect the good-natured and to destroy the evil. My purpose was to serve the needy and I did. I travelled all corners of Jambhu-Dweep and served people under various guises. But as Kali-Yuga intensified and people started relenting dharma and generation after generation was born with no sense of right or wrong, I felt astonished. The things changed with such a pace that I decided to meditate unto him for assistance. For years or maybe centuries I sat in a reclusive cave in the depths of the Himalayas, contemplating upon him. And finally when I woke up, the world order had already changed. Jambhu-Dweep had shrunk and was now surrounded by sea from all four sides.'

'What did you do next, as none of the Madhavpur dwellers have ever seen you within city limits?' asked Vallabha.

'I travelled relentlessly, along the Mount Meru and Govardhan. I saw the city from its outskirts but couldn't figure out what it was all about. Much time had lapsed since I went away, and it took me a while to make sense of things. I kept on moving and finally reached the place which you refer to as the No-Go Area.' Gopaldas said while looking towards Krishna.

'I developed some good bonding with their chief and told him about myself. They requested me to guard Madhavpur, as the city dwellers in their view were naïve and needed care.'

'They actually said that?' Krishna asked incredulously.

Gopaldas smiled and said, 'Before I can help you any further, I need to know what lead to all this?'

'They didn't tell you anything?' asked Krishna.

'No. In fact they unanimously agreed to let bygones be bygones.'

'They never had much details anyway,' Krishna said.

'Tell me every fine detail of the turn of events which lead to the split.'

•◆

Krishna began narrating the tale that Gopaldas sought, 'It was early October of the year 2050. I woke up from my sleep sweating profusely. That was the very first time I had had one of those dreams. I saw something that is still etched on my memory like carvings on rocks. It was three in the morning and almost the whole university bore a deserted look, but that didn't stop me from rushing to my lab. My hands were still blue from the dreams and my best guess was some sleep time bruising, wrong posture perhaps. As I entered the lab and started checking out the newly installed equipment, I saw a pattern. There were blue markings on all the equipment, some too dark in shades and some fainter then others, but none two alike. Then I looked back at my hands and the colours on both my hands and equipment were same, just different shades.

'The compound I was working on, I started passing and processing it through the equipment with darker shade markings to the lighter ones. Up till here, I had been struggling to form the backbone carrier for my compound for a while now. As the night progressed into dawn, the process I was carrying out intuitionally started making sense to my conscious mind too. It must have been around seven or eight in the morning when the solution started turning to a brilliant saffron. That was it, I had thought. I had placed it under an analyser and the solution was indeed showing the property of healing damaged living cells. I kept to my lab that whole day and carried out tests after test, and each round of it just confirmed one thing, the ever-elusive elixir was now a reality. That evening a top-level meeting was called in NYCAR and the news was let out to the people who mattered, but with a caveat—to not let the word go out of the university.

'Professors, programme directors, and senior research faculties lined up to meet and congratulate me. Apart from my heightened level of anxiety they also noticed my glove-clad hands, though none asked about either.

'Shyam offered me a paid trip to Madhavpur. But how could I have accepted that when three elaborate rounds of safety testing for the compound were about to be done? In hindsight, I now think that my taking that trip could have meant a whole different turns of events in history. I kept to my lab. Senior researchers from related fields were drawn and a high-level team was formed. That whole autumn we kept on working relentlessly to establish safety and utility of the newly formed compound.

'It was Diwali evening. Mohan, Shyam, and I were all there at Times Square to celebrate and take a day off from our hectic schedules. The local Indian community in New York State organized a big fare on the Broadway just adjacent to the Times Square. The Square was glittering with display lights as usual.

'"What do you intend to call your new compound?" Uncle Shyam had asked me, as I had stood staring at the flickering light atop the buildings.

'"Bhoomidium," I had replied.

'Mohan had looked at me and smiled. It was derived from the name of his project—Bhoomi.

'"This is the best Diwali gift you could have ever given to me, Krishna," He'd said. And that was the last Diwali we had celebrated as humans.

'The following week there was another big event in New York, which I did not attend. The Friendly Chemical Company was launching a new product line called Xididium. They invited science grads from all over the United States and wanted them all to be informal brand ambassadors of the new product, so to speak. The Friendly Chemical Company—a chemical giant which otherwise used to deal in farm products like pesticide, herbicides, and synthetic fertilizers came up with what it called a 'Miracle of Science'. Cornered by declining sales of its main stream products, as a result of decline in human population and farm lands and increase in government regulations, it had come up with that radically different product. Ironically, it was meant to help save the already fast dwindling human population by increasing the shelf life of the essential farm produce. Once sprinkled on farm products before harvest, any foodstuff made from them was supposed to last longer at room temperatures. But fate had something else in store.

'By the beginning of the last month of the year, we were in the final rounds of testing Bhoomidium. The results were encouraging and implications were boundless.

'On one early winter morning, a noticeably different shipment from NYC arrived. It had "The Friendly Chemical Company" embossed all over it. The college on-campus security officers started unpacking it in my lab. The shipment had many gizmos and mementos nicely wrapped in golden foils, along with samples of Xididium. The security personnel then handed over to us a letter. I gave away all those freebies to the security personnels to be distributed among the campus support staff.

'The letter was on its company letterhead requesting NYCAR to conduct test for Safety Assurances of the soon-to-be launched Xididium. The letter had the handwritten concurrence of Shyam at the end of it.'

15

The Erstwhile Earth

It was somewhere between late afternoon and early evening. The sun had grown milder and winds cooler. The gusts of air sweeping from the creek side were combing through the neelakurinji bushes. The purplish-blue flowers were dancing to the tunes of the winds carrying smell of the brackish creek. It was a mesmerizing view of the rustic landscape, with the colourful flower bearing bushes across the foothills culminating into the green vegetation towards the summit of the hill range.

Krishna's narration was interrupted by the sudden increase in those very gusts, which now were ruffling everyone's hair. More so for Vallabha, her long silk-like tresses which were now glowing in the golden slant sunrays, came flowing down onto her beautiful and radiant face. She raised her hand, twirled her awry hair into a bunch and tucked them behind her ears.

Even before Krishna could continue, Gopaldas turned towards his right as he heard a mild purring. Vyaghraraj had returned from his patrol. He came and sat next to the hermit. Gopaldas then placed his hand over his head and closed his eyes for a while. He then said, 'Vyaghraraj, if you are not tired for the day, go and take note of the other side too.'

The big cat rose and walked for a hundred feet before dashing with full vigour into the bushes uphill.

'Anything significant?' Krishna asked.

'Yes, but not as significant as your story.' He smiled and requested Krishna to continue.

Krishna then continued, 'The compound we created was now clinically proven to help heal living cells and was ready to use. It was the last week of the year and almost all of America was in holiday fervour. We didn't take any break apart from roaming downtown on weekends and occasionally on some clear evenings too. Our team was now working on a safe mass delivery method for Bhoomidium. Alongside, a small team at my lab was also studying the company supplied Xididium. It was actually acting miraculously, as once it came in contact with any farm produce, any stuff made out of it did manage to stay longer in almost all food-adverse environments. Even moist breads would stay long, vegetable broths wouldn't ferment and fruits wouldn't overripe. This could have helped us to get much required food to the farthest possible areas of Bhoomi, wherever any impoverished people could be found. We were all excited on every front.

'Then one morning when I woke up to get ready for the lab, Mohan called me. He wanted me to switch on my TV. I tuned into the first news channel available and to my disbelief saw news of the release of Xididium for use in farmlands across the world. As a sub-note the news also said that few countries like India were not cooperating and have refused to use the purportedly under-studied chemical. They were blaming India's new strict and conservative regime for this, and said efforts were underway to persuade them. It was 31 December, the last day of the year 2050 and they were celebrating the release as a beginning of the New Year of Hope.

'I called Shyam and told him that this shouldn't have happened, as we were yet to evaluate the interactions between Bhoomidium and Xididium. He expressed his concerns, as he too was not consulted before the launch. He also showed his helplessness in this regard.

'"They are a big company with huge financial muscles. I can only recommend a moratorium to the US President's office," Shyam had said.

'But the ship had sailed from the shores and all we could do was to keep testing the samples. We shifted our focus back to the Bhoomidium project. We all reached a consensus that water would be the best way to introduce Bhoomidium into the environment and the food chain. It was to be introduced into all fresh water bodies nearby every human settlement, in Phase I. In Phase II, many underground water and fuel pipelines were to be laid to introduce Bhoomidium to the Bhoomi's core. The first process map for industrial level manufacturing of Bhoomidium was released and a grand production facility was to be built in Chicago, Illinois. It would have taken some three months for the facility to commission and the first batch was to be introduced into the Great Lakes.

'April of 2051 was the chosen month for the beginning of Operation Bhoomi, when a roadblock stuck. The Friendly Chemical Company raised a concern or a bogey as we at NYCAR called it, against systematic introduction of Bhoomidium. It claimed that Bhoomidium could destroy the effectiveness of Xididium if it reached farmlands through river water, which it eventually would have. Their initial research said so, they claimed. I summoned the manager of the team looking into the testing of the compound. They were partially right, Bhoomidium did tend to encircle the Xididium molecule and thus neutralized it. Only catch, it did so if Xididium tried entering any living cell. Bhoomidium was doing what it was supposed to do, to protect a living cell from all foreign particles. The manager did not report this scenario explicitly to me as Xididium was not supposed to invade human cell and Bhoomidium was functioning normally in encasing the invading astray molecules.

'I argued my case that Bhoomidium would not interfere with Xididium molecule unless it invaded living cells, which anyway it was not supposed to do. But my arguments were not appealing to the hearts already overwhelmed by pictures of starving humans. They required unhindered application of Xididium to control the famine and drought brought about by scarcity of food and logistics.

'As a final resort India was chosen, as it was already not participating in Xididium programme. A formal request was sent to the newly formed government in India at the time, and they asked for an elaborate report on the same. A copy of the research study was sent to them. Clearance from Indian authorities was received within a week of us providing the report.

'Bhoomidium was introduced into the Ganga and Yamuna, at their sources in the Himalayas. The initial results were encouraging, human health and soil quality started improving within a fortnight of the introduction.

'Then came a stream of news and updates from other parts of the world, which shifted all the focus away from Bhoomidium. Horrific news of massive die-offs of hordes of people started pouring in from already impoverished nations. Something went totally wrong in an effort to save people and a massive epidemic of sorts broke out. People affected by the unknown disease lost all their higher cognitive ability and before succumbing to the disease themselves, started attacking other healthy people.

'After initial self-absolving statements from the manufacturers of Xididium, authorities worldwide started seeing a pattern between usage of the chemical and the epidemic. We then were ordered to look for the possible causes of the outbreak, while immediate suspension of Xididium usage was brought into full force. We were supplied samples of farm produce and soil from cornfields of Iowa and Nebraska for examination. The samples were collected under a joint operation by the US Army and Air Force, as the epidemic took the Midwest in its grip.

'The corn samples were normal and no length of study found anything. But the soil was telling an altogether different tale. Xididium indeed was interacting with a particular soil bacterium to produce unforeseen chemicals. This particular strain of bacteria, which was quite common across all terrains and usually added to the health of cultivable soil, was using Xididium as a catalyst to produce some enzymes. These enzymes were detrimental to the cellular health of macroorganisms or the big animals. The enzymes, before destroying the cells of other vital organs in humans and animals, attacked the brain cell. In humans they attacked the brain cell in the pre-frontal cortex region, thus turning them into thoughtless and violent savages.

'I reported all my findings to Uncle Shyam and he agreed that this is what we call grim.

'We now had to work on a living infected animal to see if Bhoomidium could help. An infected mouse was brought from Nebraska. The enzyme increased his bite, rage, and restlessness tenfold. We just had a couple of days before the enzyme would have killed the specimen. It was tranquilized and administered straight shots of Bhoomidium concentrate.

'For the first few hours, all vital parameters of the specimen hovered around thin borderline, but then they started improving. Blood sample were drawn and it confirmed what we'd been hoping for. Bhoomidium was encircling and then disintegrating the harmful enzymes.

'The word was sent to the President's office in Washington, D.C. But the very next day news arrived that the Oval Office has been shifted to an undisclosed location in the state of New York.

The rumours had it that the airtight bunkers were being made operational in Poughkeepsie, a small town that was a couple of hours away from NYC. Nonetheless, we got back a message from the President's office that Bhoomidium can be released on a pilot basis into the Great Lake under great scientific supervision and with utmost care.

'The block of seven nations, which stood the survival battle of the twenty-first century now started succumbing to the Xididium induced epidemic outbreak. The only region untouched was the Gangetic plain of India. Wherever people faced an epidemic in the Indian subcontinent, they migrated to the plains. The new regime, which you would know, was based on Vedic values. They helped everyone on the subcontinent they could, and the Vedic values and culture started growing popular with one and all.

'Meanwhile, from rest of the blocks there were distress calls that were way too many in number to be dealt with one at a time. Within a week of injection, the areas surrounding the Great Lakes started showing some progress. The President's office ordered Bhoomidium from manufacturing facilities in batches. Delivery of Bhoomidium to all freshwater bodies around settlements was delegated to the US Air Force. They decided that launching ballistic missiles with Bhoomidium as warhead would be the best and quickest way to deliver it across the globe.

'The launches were successful and all major rivers now had substantial concentration of the elixir. But before it could settle itself in the local ecosystems, the casualty numbers had crossed beyond imagination. The loss of human life was immense and permanent. We were now a near-extinct race.

'The only way forward was to run extraction programmes from the seven nation blocks. Within a fortnight of the global operations, human search and reconnaissance missions in the nation blocks were deemed safe. Regular sorties ferried surviving people from the remotest corners of earth to the eastern coast of the US.

'Many were still sick and needed care, the amount of Bhoomidium that had gone into them could only subdue the enzyme. The first thing they needed the most was food, which every other country was in extreme shortage of. Warehouses were full with farm produces loaded with the lethal Xididium and nobody had cultivated anything afresh due to the outbreak. Many perished in the temporary camp due to debilitating health, cold weather, and lack of food.

'SOS signals were sent to the Indian authorities, honouring which they shipped food-aid to the US along with pamphlets and booklets stating importance of simple living. They threw open invitation to whosoever wanted to adopt the Vedic lifestyle, to come and live in India—guaranteeing plenty of food along with soothing natural and peaceful ways of living. But most of the recipients of the aid were in no condition to move.

'The soil quality of almost all affected nation blocks was damaged beyond imminent repair. It was a given fact that all the survivors would either have to migrate to the Gangetic plains or we will have to devise methods to bring uncultivated land near the Atlantic coast under cultivation. The latter seemed a more feasible option.

'My team got back to studying new soil for cultivation and for planning the Phase II of Operation Bhoomi. The pipelines were laid in parts of North America and the plains of India. They were interconnected and circulated Bhoomidium to and fro from Bhoomi's deep crust. The dredging and interconnection took well over six months.

'It was early October of 2051, when the supply for Phase II started. Many people, who could make it through, accepted India's offer and were taken to India aboard USAF military planes. The world population which was now concentrated in North America along the eastern coast and Northern plains of India (only Ganga and Yamuna were filled with Bhoomidium) had shrunk to baffling levels. Only around a million or so survived.

'The lines were opened up gradually as the concentration of Bhoomidium in crust was only to be brought up in small increments. Mohan's geo-sciences department had the onus of monitoring the situation. They constantly tracked the tectonic plates and fault lines, both on land and under the sea.

'It was a full month-long programme before Criticality could have been achieved. With Operation Bhoomi in its final phase of completion, all our focus shifted toward relief to the people suffering around. With large parts of advanced infrastructure sabotaged and damaged in epidemic affected area, resources were scarce. Even scarcer was manpower.

'Despite advance technological lead, the US was left with very little say in World Affairs. Dependent on Indian food-aid and manpower, it was now the Indian authorities, which had a psychological upper hand.

'A full month had passed since the valves were let open, and we were eagerly awaiting the Phase II to reach Criticality. It was a chilly November morning when the message from the geo-sciences department came in about Bhoomi's crust reaching the critical numbers. Everybody at NYCAR almost hugged each other; there was a wave of excitement and joy in the campus. The successful completion of the project was being touted as a belated Diwali gift. We all gathered that evening in the Grand Hall of the college to celebrate the feat with fine food, when Mohan's mobile phone rang and so did a dozen others—all belonging to the people working in the geo-sciences department.

'As he flipped open his phone and read the message, the cheerful expression on his face changed to one of sheer horror.

'"We need to evacuate the building. Quick! Form queues and move," Mohan had said. The alert was also copied to Shyam's phone and he too stood there frozen with horror, before Mohan jolted him and requested him to rush.

'As we all gathered in the open space outside at least 50 feet away from any building, and before I could turn towards Uncle Shyam and ask about the message, the ground shook. The tremors began as mild jolts and then within fraction of a second grew wildly turbulent. It seemed as if someone was pulling an invisible carpet from beneath our feet. I grabbed Uncle tightly, and made sure he stood firm.

'"The settlements!" he had exclaimed in disbelief.

'The earthquake lasted for around fifteen seconds. Almost all the buildings in the campus survived except for one, the Grand Hall. It came down like a house of cards. The sight of it terrified us to no end. Uncle was rightly worried about the people in temporary settlements; this would have proved a catastrophe for them.

'He called the President's hotline right away, the one maintained for direct contact with NYCAR. He requested the President to dispatch immediate help to the people in the settlements, and assured him that his team would study the long- and short-term effects of the quakes.

'Mohan's system, which studied geo-tectonic movement, predicted the quake by the lead of a minute. That was though not enough to secure everybody in America, but they definitely saved us from the collapsed Grand Hall.

'We sat in the reception of the geo-sciences department, while Mohan's entire team was analysing data to study the cause of the unusually widespread quakes. After a couple of hours, Mohan came running out of his lab and said, "The whole of America is sinking. All the continents have broken loose from their bases and are now sinking into the molten core. We do not have much time left here."

'Uncle had shaken his head in disbelief and had asked, "How much time, are we talking about?"

'Mohan had said, "A fortnight or so..."

'"Any fixes?"

'"Just one. All the continents while shifting are gravitating towards the new centre of the earth surface."

'"And that is?"

'"India. They would all eventually sink and attach to the base of Indian tectonic plate. Only Indian plains would be spared. We have nowhere else to go."

'Shyam pulled out his phone again and started making some important calls. We had just two days to confirm the results. The patterns were clear; Bhoomidium was interacting with the deep crust of Bhoomi and was making it unstable. Here, we were in a catch twenty-two. The very elixir we were banking upon to save our race was destroying the only planet we had. The supplies were cut-off and we were given a week's time to wind up NYCAR. Military transport aircrafts airlifted all the important equipment to the outskirts of the territory of India.

'The whole of NYCAR's various lab set-ups were docked in a remote, sealed room at the airport terminal. Indian authorities, after the quake incident were even more suspicious with anything to do with science and technology. And no one could openly criticize them either, for two reasons—they were our last hope for refuge and science had been biting us back, off late, way too often.

'The few hundred thousand people that were left were to be transported to India. The President's office was in constant talks with the Indian Government. Everything was to be either winded up or was to be abandoned. Whatever was necessary was neatly packed and shipped. Whatever couldn't be shipped was digitized and stored, for future reference.

'The Indian authorities had placed forward some tough conditions for providing asylum. They were probably still not fully aware of the gravity of the situation. A simple message was sent to the Indian High Command's Office reading—"The whole planet is sinking. If not us, then let the hapless refugees in."

'Within an hour, the Indian Government had agreed and the biggest exodus seen by mankind was initiated.

'Government officers, general public, VIPs, the army, and refugees from all other continents were divided into batches and on random basis were either sent by air or by the sea. The whole of the NYCAR staff and high-powered government officials were sent by air, though.

'On the day of our journey, we were still mid-air when news started coming in that at various places in North America there has been severe landslides and earthquakes. And the continent had already started sinking, with ocean water gushing into what was land a few hours ago. There were huge tsunamis and many ships which left almost a week before us, went down midway. It was like Nature's fury knew no end.

'It was our third day, waiting in a lounge on the same airport terminal where our shipments were being held up. The authorities said that they were working on an elaborate plan for our settlement. But none turned up to talk, except for the courteous stewards asking us for water and food every other hour.

'On my left was the sleeping area, a large floor laid with cushions to the point till a human eye could see. On my right was a big glass wall overlooking the runway. I walked up to the wall and placed both my hands firmly over it. I could see the airstrip in the dawn light. Behind the airstrip were vast beautiful meadows, and behind those meadows was River Sarayu. It was six in the morning and sun was rising on the horizon of Ayudhpur. The big illuminated sign at the end of the airstrip read in Sanskrit—"Welcome to the Birthplace of Lord Ram." At the end of the text was a bow and arrow symbol, glistening in the rising sun's maiden rays.

'"Mr Shyam, please proceed towards the main exit gate," an announcement was made in the waiting lounge.

'Uncle walked up to the President instead and said, "Sir, they have probably called out the wrong name."

'President along with his secret service took Uncle along to the exit door. Within fifteen minutes President and the group came back. The authorities wanted to talk to someone apolitical, so allowed only Uncle Shyam to stay back for discussion. The President had vested all his constitutional powers onto Uncle Shyam to negotiate with the authorities.

'Uncle did not turn up for the whole day, and we all were anxious to know as to what was going on. The bright and brilliant sky above River Sarayu soon turned dark and got covered with sparkling stars of the Milky Way, when Uncle appeared.

'Uncle Shyam returned along with a list of what they called the "code of conduct" to live in Ayudhpur. Not that there was anything wrong with the demands, but none of us were in a shape to adapt to them.

'"Is this the only choice we got?" said Mr President.

'"Pretty much yes, unless…" said Uncle.

'"Unless?"

'"We agree to settle in a completely different city, on land they would allocate us. The code would still be there but would be a little toned down." He then handed the document called "the Code" to the President.

The Code

The following document is binding on every Manava who wishes to reside in the territory of Madhavpur on Jambhu-Dweep.

1. All Manavas residing outside the territories of Ayudhpur shall respect the sovereignty and territorial integrity of Ayudhpur.
2. All Manavas residing outside the territories of Ayudhpur shall not trespass Ayudhpur.
3. All Manavas residing outside the territories of Ayudhpur shall not try imposing lifestyle foreign to the ways of Ayudhpur, on Ayudhpur.
4. All Manavas residing outside the territories of Ayudhpur shall not pass any legislation that may (knowingly or unknowingly) have an impact on Manavas residing in Ayudhpur.
5. All Manavas residing outside the territories of Ayudhpur shall refrain from raising any sort of armed force.
6. All Manavas residing outside the territories of Ayudhpur shall strive to emulate, when it comes to culture, the Manavas of Ayudhpur.
7. All Manavas residing outside the territories of Ayudhpur shall abstain from useless pursuit of frivolous technologies and place the least possible burden on the environment. They shall though pursue what is/will be necessary for the sustenance of the Manavas.
8. All Manavas residing outside the territories of Ayudhpur shall abstain from developing any advanced Artificial-Intelligent beings or devices.

9. All Manavas residing outside the territories of Ayudhpur shall be cooperative with each other and with all other Manavas in general.

10. All Manavas residing outside the territories of Ayudhpur shall acknowledge Lord Vishnu (or any Avatar they see him in) as the Supreme deity of the Manavas and the owner of all worlds.

'"We are free to follow our own will, but we will still have to follow the culture of the land, as instructed in the Code. They say they cannot let their values and ethos get diluted," said Uncle.

'The President nodded, knowing very well we had no other choice left and no other place to go. He patted on Uncle Shyam's shoulder and left. He was already very stressed out.

'We were then asked to prepare for a long journey towards the north-west.

'The city was to be called Madhavpur, and had to be built from scratch to fit our new lifestyle. All those ready to abide by dharma were free to take residency of Ayudhpur and those who wanted to live a modern life (but still be guided by the Code), had to move to Madhavpur.

'The land on which the city was to be built was leased to us. Leased to us in lieu of following the Code.'

16

Taming the Tides

'So, that's the reason for the perennial agony of all living beings?' Gopaldas asked, after Krishna further explained as to how Bhoomidium worked and why it was required in the first place.

'Yes! The cell or the smallest unit that constitutes life, evolved on Bhoomi under very harsh environment. It had to improve its own self through trial and error. Resources were scarce to let a single cell to live on and on. So, a cell would divide say up to 50 times and would then cease to exist, and also each of its offspring would adapt to the climate outside. Each new progeny was a better copy of its parent. It was a race for betterment, which never stopped. Even when Bhoomi became a better place to live, the cells would follow their archaic behaviour. Bhoomidium helped us fix this problem. It made the cell feel safe and secure and bolstered it,' Krishna said.

'Then what went wrong? With the elixir in place and a permanent homeland to settle, why did your population dwindle?' queried Gopaldas.

'The Phase II was disrupted after the catastrophe and a lot of study was required to attempt anything afresh of that sort. We had a whole society to build, so the Phase II was placed on hold till safety study was completed. Large amount of paperwork was exchanged for deciding jurisdiction on various world affairs. It seemed they just wanted clarity and were least interested in wielding any sort of authority outside their territory. We also shared the positive safety study for the laying of Bhoomidium pipes with them and they showed no objection. It was only by 2080 that Phase II went operational. And with the sunken continents supporting the Indian subcontinent plates, it was easy this time around. The current supply that was being drawn from one of our underground manufacturing facilities could only saturate the Bhoomi's crust by 2095. And it was the year 2100 when Criticality was reached. The journey was long and tiresome and many people, whose Bhoomidium levels had dropped, couldn't make it. Our numbers were reduced to an exact figure of 54,000,' Krishna explained.

'So, 108,000,' Gopaldas muttered under his breath.

Krishna raised his brow and asked, 'You mean to say exactly 54,000 people remained on the other side too?'

Gopaldas nodded and then stayed silent for a while. He then added, 'Now you say that you have run out of those fuels and your facilities are under attack by some unknown miscreant?' Krishna nodded in response.

'Interesting! Interesting that despite the attacks you chose to travel to the farthest point of Jambhu-Dweep, leaving the whole set-up to your friend?' Gopaldas asked.

'Those are less about attacks and more about provocations. The person behind could have easily perpetuated massive harm to our society but instead chose to throw challenges at us, the tricky ones. May be he is testing our mettle and our capabilities. And I knew for sure that answers to my question were here and not in Madhavpur.'

'Had I been you I would have rather turned inwards to look for the answers I seek,' the hermit said with a smile.

'Moreover, I wanted to smoke that rat out of his hole. With me going away, either he would stop altogether or would go all out with his plans. Either way this game of hide and seek has to end,' replied Krishna.

'The war is inevitable either way,' added Gopaldas.

'Vyaghraraj?'

'Indeed. He patrols not only the Jambhu-Dweep, but also frequents the borders of Purva-Dweep. They are preparing for war.'

'What prompted them to do so? We have not broken the Code, or have we?' Krishna sounded a little confused.

'It's not about the Code anymore, the Kamsa has risen,' replied Gopaldas.

Krishna looked at him puzzled.

'He who was born out of Desire or Kama and was subsequently slayed by Lord Krishna himself has risen again. He is the manifestation of Greed and Evil, and if left unchecked, would push the whole society into depths of darkness,' Gopaldas explained.

'You mean these attacks, all these are ancient and archaic evil forces surfacing again?' asked Krishna.

'Kama or desire is by no way an archaic force; it is very well ancient, but not archaic. Kama has plagued human kind since beginning. A noble person controls his desires and keeps such evil forces in check, while working for the betterment of his society. A greedy man filled with desire and fuelled by envy lets these forces control and drive him. And when they completely overtake a man full of greed, the Kamsa rises,' explained Gopaldas.

'So, before things spiral out of control, we will have to control them or else we could face an annexation?' asked Vallabha.

'Things already have spiraled out of control, from what I gather,' replied the hermit.

'How do we stop this?' asked Krishna.

'You can't, at least not alone. You will have to risk a visit to Ayudhpur and try brokering an agreement,' said Gopaldas.

'The two societies are beyond any kind of reconciliation. No talks can happen, we cannot interfere in their matters without breaking the Code,' said Krishna.

'I propose cooperation and not interference. They too know that peace cannot be achieved alone. Whom do you think Kamsa would turn to after he engulfs Madhavpur?' replied Gopaldas.

Krishna nodded. 'I will have to then drop Vallabha back home and ask the Council to choose a representative to visit Ayudhpur, if at all they allow that to happen.'

'You did approach the Council to get a resolution on those attacks. How well did it turn out? In this emergent hour bureaucracy is not the answer, diplomacy is,' said Gopaldas.

'Even then, she needs to be safely at home and an apt person needs to approach Ayudhpur as an ambassador of peace,' said Krishna.

'No one else can pull this off well, except for you Krishna. And she needs to be there with you to prove your intentions, that you actually seek peace.'

For Krishna, it seemed, there was no other choice.

'Do you still carry your flute around?' Gopaldas asked with a smile on his face and glitter in his eyes. Krishna pulled out his Venu in response.

'Your flute reminds me of my Lord, would you mind playing something for me?' he said as his eyes became moist with nostalgia.

As Krishna started playing, Gopaldas smiled more and pulled out from his right pocket what seemed like a peacock feather.

He placed the feather on his palm and as Krishna played higher notes, it started levitating. The feather hovered around his palm for a while and then flew. It swept towards Krishna and finally settled on his right arm. It then merged onto his upper arm skin and became a beautiful tattoo near his shoulder.

Krishna kept on playing his Venu incessantly, even upon seeing this. And finally when he stopped, he saw Gopaldas in tears of devotion with his hands folded in reverence.

'Arise! Oh Krishna! For you are the chosen one, chosen by the Lord himself,' Gopaldas exclaimed. Krishna did not move a muscle and waited for the hermit to complete. 'This Peacock feather was given to me by my Lord,' the hermit added.

Krishna nodded and then said, 'What all do I expect in Ayudhpur?'

'Familiar faces and surety of purpose among the tribe,' he replied.

'What kind of purpose?' said Krishna.

'Preservation of the Vedic Dharma.'

Krishna nodded, this was a ball game he was least prepared to play. He had no idea how he would deal with people so set in their ways.

'Why do you think they spared you these huge land tracts you now call Jambhu-Dweep. To fight and take it back from you, one fine day? They are the most unpretentious people I have ever come across. They are dedicated to their purpose and least interested in meddling in other people's affairs. But they do understand the utopian society of yours based on perceived constructs of science. They know well that it is the innate nature of your society to create a rulebook for every occurrence, even for things related to common sense and intuition. But above all they also understand that utopian worldviews don't always work. And evils like greed and desire can spring back from the dormant. Therefore, they keep their military preparations high to protect dharma and to protect the Manavas. No matter whether the ones in need are in Madhavpur or Ayudhpur.'

'They could see all this brewing?' asked Krishna.

'They always knew that it would happen. They were happy to

seek my services for the same. They wanted me to keep an eye on the vulnerable,' replied Gopaldas.

'Then you should come along and broker a peace pact, instead,' said Krishna.

'Firstly its your duty, your karma. And, secondly there is no conflict as far as I can see. It's all in your mind, in the collective consciousness of Madhavpur. They won't harm you or your society. They are preparing to act with brute force against what they think is enemy of the Manavas. I suggest that you present your case for cooperation, for the enemy is much stronger and it would require both wisdom and war to defeat him.'

Krishna got up from where he sat, so did Vallabha. 'Guide us with the way,' he said. The hermit pointed towards the creek and offered to come along till there.

They walked for almost three kilometres before reaching a particular point where Gopaldas halted. It was a coconut grove by the side of a golden sand beach. The creek water was much more emerald-like over there and the tides were low, revealing colourful coral reefs in the shallow waters. The shadows of the swinging coconut trees in the cool creek breeze were playing with the setting sunlight.

'This is the way forward. Beyond this, it's your journey. The currents of the creek are such that there is only one exact point along the length of it, from where you can sail and reach the shores of Purva-Dweep,' the hermit said.

'And how do you propose we cross this creek? Flying or swimming?' said Krishna sarcastically.

'Oh that! Well, let me lend you my preferred mode of transport.' He walked toward a patch of dense bush beside the row of coconut trees, and dragged a small boat out of it.

'Here, this will take you across. And yes you will have to row it, don't ask. Moreover you will have to row at an angle midway between your front and your right and at an initial speed enough to draw the boat thrice it's length within a count of ten,' Gopaldas said.

'That will take some serious effort, isn't that too fast. Are you sure you don't have a motor attachment for the boat lying somewhere in that undergrowth?' asked Krishna.

Gopaldas spoke with a smile, 'I said, don't ask. Row and propel. You need that kind of speed to beat the initial stream. The other shore is almost 30 kilometres apart, row fast until the shores become visible and then you can row at your own pace.'

'I can row too, I used to row for my high school team,' Vallabha said.

Krishna moved closer to the boat, and while inspecting it said, 'It has two oars, so there is no escaping from it for you.'

Vallabha shook her head in disbelief and shrugged, 'I would have happily rowed even if there had been only one.'

'Okay! You both will have ample of time to sort the rowing schedule out. Now listen, I know they owned this subcontinent and that you have had no conversation for a very long period. But fear not, and put forth your confident self. Speak from a point of vantage and on behalf of the residents of Madhavpur. And keep the trip short, Madhavpur might need you very soon,' he said with a hint of clairvoyance in his tone.

Krishna dragged the boat on the finely powdered sand, which was still warm enough to inspire a hasty hopping gait.

Seeing Krishna pulling the boat from the front while Vallabha pushed it from behind, the hermit smiled. He smiled looking at the teamwork of them both, for he could see that this team would soon develop fissures and will be put to test.

As Krishna looked back to bid farewell, he found no one around. The hermit was gone.

'Is it the same technology that your suit uses or is it some supernatural power conferred upon him?' asked Vallabha.

'Neither. He is blessed, no doubting that. But, the hermit has an almost limitless control over his mind. He understands the power of his conscious and subconscious mind and deploys them to his use. He is enlightened, so to speak. His control over his mind not only creates his reality but bend our realities too. The power he wields over his mind, makes ours to think that he has disappeared.'

'Almost hard to fathom,' she said.

'He was right in saying that neither did our society place full faith in science nor did we work on our spiritual growth.'

Vallabha nodded in agreement.

As they reached the water, they could feel the tides setting in. Pushing the boat well into the water, both hopped in. Krishna took both the oars and asked Vallabha to sit in the front and make sure they head in the right direction with the right speed.

The sun was setting behind them, leaving behind golden hues on the creek surface. As evening winds picked up, the restive water beneath the boat became livelier. The clear water illuminated with the golden-orange hues of the sunset, was patting the boat with small and light wavelets.

Vallabha saw something in the water beneath and extended her arm to touch the surface. It was a bale of turtles swimming very close to the boat. As she immersed her hand into the water, the group dispersed and dived deep into the sea. She looked behind and splashed a fist full of water on Krishna. He smiled and said, 'It's time for you to take to the oars, let's see how far you can row.'

As she stood up accepting the challenge, her right feet pressured the edge of the boat. She fumbled as the boat shook a bit and then lost her balance. With a great thud sound she pierced through the surface of the creek while going nose down. It took

Krishna a few moments to realize that this was not intentional and she was not pulling any prank on him.

He left the oars and stood on the edge of the boat. He could not see Vallabha around. He rolled up his sleeves and jumped into the sea. It was already dark enough and he couldn't see much in the water. He swam the length of the boat and then saw something dangling around. As he reached there, it was Vallabha.

As he closely examined, he saw her shorts' belt strap was entangled in an iron hook underneath the base of the boat. He had no other option but to pull open the belt and let it go. He then swam up to the surface with Vallabha and dragged her onto the boat.

She was unconscious and was not breathing at all. Krishna performed cardiopulmonary resuscitation on her for half a minute or so, until she finally breathed again and came back to consciousness. Her body was wet and cold.

Krishna made her lie on her back and said, 'You are fine. Don't worry.' She smiled and held his hand. 'It's only you who gets to rest, I need to row,' he said as he pulled back his hand gently and went back to the oars.

It was growing darker by the minute and now Krishna alone had to maintain the boat at the required speed and angle. He grabbed the oars with all the might of his grip, estimated the required angle and started rowing.

After rowing for an hour or so, he could now see some very feeble distant lights on what seemed like a shore. He slowed the boat down; his arms and shoulder were aching by then. Krishna then walked up to the front of the boat and sat beside Vallabha.

The slowing of the boat and the footsteps of Krishna brought her out of her slumber. She sat up by the corner of the boat and said, 'Are we out of the currents yet?'

'We are, and now you need to eat something while we halt here.'

Krishna pulled a slim can out of his robe and handed it over to her. He rested beside her, while she ate. The city lights doused few of his doubts about Ayudhpur; they, after all, had not given up completely on the modern ways of living.

This was a huge challenge for Krishna. He was landing on the forbidden lands without making an appointment and with no backing from his Council, whatsoever. All this while he had only been thinking that the people, who have forbidden any kind of reconnaissance, won't take this unscheduled visit very kindly.

The extent of segregation was such that the couple of satellites deployed in outer space by Madhavpur (for geo-monitoring purposes) were geo-synchronous and were not even allowed to cross over the Purva-Dweep's territory.

'We will have to wait here in these waters till dawn breaks,' said Krishna.

She nodded and reclined again. Krishna pulled out a package from his robe pocket and gave it to her. 'Here! Take this and keep yourself warm.'

'Tomorrow when we land in Ayudhpur, hope you remember your priorities.' Vallabha said with a slightly devious smile.

17

The Belligerent Love

The seagulls were now growing boldly boisterous with the pre-dawn daylights. They were hovering around the boat in circles. One of the smaller birds after circling about a couple of times perched on the edge of the boat. Krishna woke up, but tired from the last evening's vigorous rowing made no effort to chase away the seagull.

He got up and shook Vallabha, who was still sleeping beside him.

'Get up and prepare for landing,' Krishna said.

She now had to drape the saree, which she was using as a blanket for the night. 'I think that side of the shore is sparsely populated, we should land over there,' she said while pointing rightwards.

The morning breeze made the waves a little turbulent. The sound of oars cutting through the water along with the noise of the waves hitting against the boat made a medley of morning rhymes. The sun had just started rising across the shore, from behind the city of Ayudhpur.

After about half an hour of constant rowing, they reached the designated spot. Krishna then jumped into the shallow water near the shore and found a tree to anchor the boat.

'Here onwards I am not sure how to or whom to approach. We will have to tread very carefully,' whispered Krishna, as he helped

Vallabha get off the boat.

'We probably should find our way to the house of the chief of the city. We can then reason with him,' she suggested.

The city, it seemed, had still not woken up. Some 500 feet away from the shoreline there were many earthen-coloured huts in a row. Each hut-shaped structure was as big as a conch-shaped house, back home.

Seeing a mud-trail on the shore, they started moving along it southwards. The soft trail was covered with dense coconut trees on both sides. A shoulder-high wall separated the shoreline from the rest of the city. The boundary wall acted like a city border and also as a dyke against occasionally rising creek tides. The wall was decorated with intricate carvings of lotuses, peacocks, and elephants, resembling those on the roof of the Council Hall. Beyond the wall, there was an array of krishnachura trees. The bright red flowers added colours and hues to the incoming sunrays, filtering through the dense trees.

They kept on moving forward with nimble feet. But after walking about half a kilometre along the coastline, Vallabha said, 'How about turning on your stealth suit?'

'It won't cover us both,' hushed Krishna.

'Last time around it did, remember?' said Vallabha with a chuckle. Krishna narrowed his eyes and then he too smiled.

They could now hear voices at some distance that were rising and falling in a chorus. Krishna grew cautious and signalled Vallabha to slow down a bit further. The mud-trail was bending to its right some 10 feet from where they were located. They both approached the turn to gain sight of the source of the sound. The chorus was now clear—it was some kind of a war cry, which was apparent from the energy and enthusiasm of it.

Krishna stayed close to the wall and peeped. It was a group of young men and women practicing some sort of martial arts with arms. They wielded swords, long and broad. They were practicing moves in unison and with each move they let out the war cry which, had they been a notch louder, could have easily shaken the Bhoomi and the sky.

The men were dressed in brilliant saffron-coloured dhoti and women in saffron-coloured saris. Though the womenfolk in Madhavpur used to wear saris too, but he had never seen saris draped in such a glorious manner. Accompanied and complemented by heavy, yet, small nose rings.

As Vallabha stepped forward to look, they both heard a thumping sound from behind. Before Krishna could turn around completely and make any sense of where that sound came from, something came hurling toward him. He grabbed the object mid-air and shifted his focus to it. It was a sheathed sword with a peacock carved out of bronze on its handle. Underneath the crimson-coloured cover was the concealed blade of the sword. It was heavy and was propelled toward him by a masked warrior among a group of other five masked men. The masked warrior was probably head of the party.

The warrior signalled Krishna to lurch forward with his sword, while signalling his rest of the party to move backwards. The masked warrior intended a duel.

Krishna had no idea what to do with the sword. He had never handled anything like this in his life, neither in this Yuga nor in the previous one. He was not crafted out for such blood and gore. However, realizing that he was in an alien territory and had a compatriot to protect from any harm, Krishna pulled the sword out of the crimson cover. Its blade was shining in the morning light. As Krishna started swinging the sword, it started seeming lighter and swifter in movement. He started approaching the masked warrior.

The warrior sprang forward and attacked. The sword blows that Krishna was dealt with were not being placed with full vigour. It now seemed that the warrior wanted to give Krishna a fair chance, before capturing him. The sword fight was not intended to injure. Krishna sensed the intent and after dealing and defending a couple of sword swings, dropped his sword purposely.

The masked warrior, after making sure that the foe was defeated, signalled his party to blindfold the intruders.

They were driven in a wagon of some sort to the heart of the city. Still blindfolded, they were taken to a palace-like structure made out of limestone. Upon reaching the central hall of the palace, their folds were removed.

'Welcome, Krishna!' said a person in a baritone voice, while sitting on a grand chair in the centre of the hall.

The lights from the windows behind seemed too harsh to Krishna's eyes. As he readjusted his focus, he saw the expected. It was Shriram's voice, the chief of Ayudhpur.

Krishna did not utter a word, as Shriram continued, 'My apologies on behalf of Ayudhpur, for mistaking you for an intruder. Standard Operating Procedures, you see. A formal communication of arrival might have helped.'

'And I thought we had long severed all lines of communication to preserve the purity of His Highness's society,' replied Krishna.

'I am but an employee of the Kingdom of Lord Rama. And yes, we strive every hour of our existence to attain purity of thoughts and deeds,' replied Shriram.

'Then it seems that our means might be different but the end goal is the same,' Krishna said.

Shriram smiled and rose from his chair. 'Take them to our state guest house and help them undo the fatigue of the journey,' he instructed the masked warrior who had brought them here.

They were guided through the alleys, one after another, till they reached another big hall. The hall had high roofs with motifs similar to one on the boundary wall of the city. The ones in the hall were embedded with precious stones and embossed with gold leafs.

Across the hall there were chambers, one adjacent to another. The chambers had big beds along with all the furniture that a person would require for a comfortable stay. There were grand granite pillars, with colourful peacocks sitting atop giant lotuses carved on them—they were stunningly designed.

The masked warrior led them to the biggest chamber of all. As they both sat on the big sofa lying adjacent to the bed, Krishna said, 'We need separate personal spaces.'

The masked one nodded and with the voice muffled by the dark red scarf said, 'Vallabha, you follow me.'

Krishna now looked into the eyes of the masked person, trying to observe something. As the warrior turned to show Vallabha her chamber, Krishna asked, 'By what name should I address you?'

The person turned and gave him a long glare, to which Krishna said, 'Just in case if I need a partner to hone my sword skills.'

The warrior pulled away the mask and said, 'Radhika.'

As she walked out of the chamber, Vallabha followed her like a child with amazement in her eyes. Krishna placed his legs across the length of the sofa and lay with his eyes closed.

She knew it all the way and still fought with me and brought me to the palace tied and blindfolded. The face he used to long for, for just a glimpse of it, now seemed stranger than ever before. The more he realized that things have changed to such an extent, the more fondly he missed those Madhavpur evenings by the side of Radha-Kund.

His throat was dry, probably from the anguish of those distant memories. He reached out to the terracotta vessel placed next to the sofa. The vessel was nicely done in blue with small figures of boys and girls wielding bow and arrows drawn in orange, all over it. Each detail to the chamber was done very thoughtfully. The ceiling had intricate carvings depicting stories from the Puranas; the walls had beautiful paintings depicting various scenes from the epic, Ramayana. As Krishna drank the water, he found it to be very sweet.

He got up from the sofa and walked across the length of the room, toward the big window that was as high as Krishna and was set in a marble frame. The view outside was stunning. The lush green meadows had some ever-flowering bushes adorning the slopes.

At certain sections where the gradient of the meadows was not extreme, the holy River Sarayu could be seen. The meanders and hairpin bends in the course of the river brought the entire landscape to life, and made it look surreal.

While still looking into the mesmerizing views, he realized that he hadn't heard Radhika exiting the adjacent chamber yet. As he turned to take stock, he saw a familiar figure passing through the hall outside the chambers, disappearing into the corridors across the hall.

Vallabha entered the room and said, 'She is nice, not as daunting as she appears to be.'

'Yes, hospitality is what we came here for,' Krishna said drily.

'She carries a definite pain within her. No woman would ever have that much zeal, otherwise,' she said.

'We need a concrete plan to negotiate a treaty, and psychoanalysing the guards of the walled city won't help,' said Krishna.

'You do remember that she is the daughter of Shriram, the chief of Ayudhpur. You will have to put behind whatever ego issues you have, and will have to appeal to her emotions.'

'I hope there are better ways than that. Why use someone and risk bitterness spoiling the diplomatic relations later?' Krishna said.

'Whom are you lying to? You still have a soft corner in your heart for her. Any women can see it in your naïve eyes,' said Vallabha.

Krishna turned, with both his hands firmly clasped together behind his back, and said, 'I guess you are right.'

Vallabha then moved closer to Krishna and murmured something in his ears, and Krishna nodded in response to her.

•◆

It was now one in the afternoon, and a palace official came to Krishna's room to invite him for lunch.

Vallabha was already seated on the chair beside the giant oval dining table at the right wing of the hall. Radhika sat at the head of the table, with her back to Krishna's chamber. The first things Krishna noticed as he walked into the room was Radhika's silky, long hair and the golden glow of her skin. Her long neck was shining in the light. *She hasn't aged a bit, and looks as young as she did during her college days in Kali-Yuga. She should be grateful to me, my Bhoomidium has kept her young and jubilant.*

'I have been asked by the highest authorities of Ayudhpur, to give you company at lunch,' Radhika said in a firm and authoritative tone. Krishna nodded and sat beside her, facing Vallabha.

Vallabha was right about Radhika harbouring some sort of hurt, which baffled Krishna. It was his prerogative to feel hurt and betrayed, but he was being devoid of that luxury too.

'Well, why would a city guard with a blunt tongue be sent to host foreign diplomatic guests?' Krishna asked. Hearing his question, Vallabha could barely hold back her urge to gloat and chuckle. But she went unnoticed as Radhika's bright eyes were focused on Krishna alone.

'Because this blunt-tongued city guard also happens to be the Commander-in-Chief of Vaishnavi Sena, in charge of the internal security of Ayudhpur,' she replied curtly.

'I see. You have been assigned the task of keeping an eye on us,' Krishna said casually.

'I am here to host you as the official guest of Ayudhpur. Nothing more, nothing less.'

Krishna nodded and smiled. Food was served keeping in mind the culinary habits of the guests from Madhavpur. Both Vallabha and Krishna were pleasantly surprised by the hospitality being extended to them.

As they finished their food, coffee was served for him and sweetened lemon juice for Vallabha. He could smell the berry mix in the coffee, even before sipping it. He picked his cup and walked towards the huge window by the side of the table. Radhika followed.

Krishna, with his back to her, said, 'The waters of the River Sarayu never used to be this sweet.'

'It isn't just Sarayu anymore. The last massive quakes on Bhoomi diverted the flow of Ganga, and in a span of 200 years, River Ganga too converged into Sarayu,' replied Radhika.

'I see. A lot has changed here.'

'Indeed.'

'Come you both, let's go to my chamber for some post-lunch chatting,' Vallabha suggested, to which Radhika agreed.

As soon as they reached her chamber, she said, 'Just give me ten minutes for my post-lunch bath. Old habits, you see.'

Now it was only the two of them in the big room. For a few minutes an awkward silence prevailed, but finally Radhika spoke, 'She is cute and nice. Now, you not turning up does stand justified.'

Her words and the straight face with which they were spoken, took him aback. She looked pretty convinced and content with her conclusions.

'I did not come back, because we the people of Madhavpur were not supposed to. It was your kingdom which gave up on all contact.'

'I am not a big fan of alibis. She was your classmate in your college, wasn't she? You never cared to come back and see me,' she said facing away from him.

'She was never there in the picture. As a matter of fact, she is a friend of Meera's,' said Krishna.

'Meera?' the very mention of the name left her stunned.

'Yes, Meera! Your sister, whom you never even enquired about,' said Krishna.

'She left the family against our parents' wish! If she can make her own choices, she can take care of her own self too. Anyway, the point remains that you are not trustworthy. You promised, but never turned up,' she said with a tinge of bitterness and hurt in her voice.

'Why do you care anyway? You are happily settled with Raghav, aren't you?' shot back Krishna.

'Raghav? He is just a colleague of mine.'

'Are you sure about that? Because, that's not what I have heard,' he said whatever Vallabha told him to.

'You betrayed, I didn't. You lied and trashed all the promises we made to each other,' she replied.

'Me? I spent three days stranded on that airport of yours. You knew we had come there, barely escaping a catastrophe. Did you ever turn up to see if we were okay?'

'I had committed myself to the cause of dharma. Things could have been different, if you had ever turned up even once during your NYCAR years,' she said.

As he walked closer to her, he saw a tear roll down her cheek.

He came within her arm's distance and could hear her sobbing.

'I was committed to my cause. My work was critical to the survival of my race, rather our race. I had definite plans for us, but things didn't turn up the way they should have. I couldn't have left my people helpless there [in NYCAR],' he said while holding Radhika by her arms.

'My father had to consolidate our society and bring everyone onto the right path of dharma. Even here in places outside Purva-Dweep, where your Bhoomidium didn't reach by rivers, we faced massive epidemics and outbreaks. When I got nothing but excuses for your next visit, I gave up on you. I had to be with my father—that was my dharma,' she said.

As Krishna consoled her and made her sit on the nearby sofa, Vallabha came in.

'Things can change,' he said to Radhika. They both understood what he meant.

·◆·

It was early evening when he was done browsing through the copy of the Ramayana, placed by his bedside. He got up from his bed to take a glimpse of the famed evenings of Ayudhpur, from his window. Someone knocked on the door and asked, 'Sir, what time would you prefer your dinner? Our Chief would like to enjoy his dinner in your company.'

'I don't wish to keep him waiting for long. After sunset, would be fine.'

The officer nodded and left.

This was a signal that Ayudhpur was finally ready to listen to what Krishna had to offer. He instructed Vallabha accordingly.

Krishna and Vallabha were already seated at the grand table of the central dining hall of the palace, even before Shriram arrived.

Krishna was still looking around to see the intricate details that had gone down in ornamenting the hall, and then Shriram arrived, dressed in a saffron-coloured robe along with the sacred thread tied diagonally across his waist and shoulder.

He took his chair, sat down gently like a royal person does and said, 'Speak to me with no qualms, as a son would with his father.'

18

The New-Found Love

This part of the palace was located fairly close to the River Sarayu, and the sound of the waves of the water flowing down the river was audible through the open window glasses. It was a beautiful evening, and the early autumn nip of the cold was already being felt in the evening breeze. The branches of krishnachura trees planted just outside that section of the palace, were swinging to the autumn breeze. The swaying branches were cutting through the path of the city lights across the river, giving an illusion of them being some distant twinkling stars.

Shriram had finished eating his dinner, and after making sure that Krishna and Vallabha were sitting comfortably, he himself was pacing up and down the length of the table. The overall mood was quite sombre in the room.

'The entire thing cannot be true…' said Shriram.

Krishna kept his silence, he wanted Shriram to reconcile, to absorb all that he had heard.

'Things have grown too complex, haven't they?' said Shriram and Krishna nodded. 'That's the reason we never let our guard down,' he continued.

'And we don't even have that much of deterrence. The Code prohibited us from having any as such,' replied Krishna.

Shriram nodded in agreement, 'We, from the Kali-Yuga days,

have always been peaceful and contemplative beings. But the world always saw it as our weakness and tried attacking and enslaving us, as far as history goes back. Our monuments were destroyed during the Kali-Yuga, our religious canons offered to flames. We were invaded, tortured, hounded around and insulted. When we finally broke away from all shackles and established a dharma-based society for ourselves, we vowed never to let that happen again. And you, the Madhavpur people, are a society of mixed ethnicity and beliefs. We had no other choice but to impose moratorium on you, and barred you from having any sort of an army. Nonetheless, we have always valued your society for what it is and have been grateful to it for mixing water bodies on Bhoomi with Amrit-tatva. And we will always be there to help you in any of your fights, if the need be. It was an unsaid promise, right from the inception of the Swarnim-Yuga.'

On hearing these comforting words, Krishna stood up from his chair and said, 'Sir, we will require your assistance and cooperation to fend off any obstacles during the completion of Café Evolution.'

'As per the negotiated deal, Madhavpur has full right to work in the best interest of Manavas when it comes to the preservation of Bhoomi, using any tested modern means available,' said Shriram.

'We have always employed our acumen for betterment of both the societies. But this time around it's difficult. We are being overwhelmed. The warning signs bode of an enemy who is not only prepared but also not afraid of provoking us. I am of the opinion that it is not something that Madhavpur is prepared to deal with,' said Krishna.

'I will have to consult my group of ministers. Meanwhile, I hereby invite you for the morning prayers, tomorrow at the city centre,' Shriram said.

Krishna accepted his invitation and then Shriram left the hall with his entourage of guards. He knew what the morning prayers will have in store.

By ten o'clock almost all of Ayudhpur was covered underneath the sheath of sleep, barring one. Krishna was still wide awake and didn't feel like resting. The autumn night's moon was looking magnificent from his window. The view of the moon was covering at least quarter of the window. The bypassing clouds would cover the moon every now and then, but its bright silver moonlight was not concealable.

As Krishna was going through memory maps of his plans for the following day, he heard a knock on the big wooden door of his chamber. He sat upright and said, 'Come on in.' It was Vallabha. She walked up to Krishna's bed and sat on the settee beside.

'I am a little worried about you,' she said.

Krishna knew what she meant, but that was not his focus right now. 'Even if we develop a substantial understanding here with Shriram, you will have to do a lot of persuasion back home. Some of them might be completely unwilling to reconcile with changed ground situations,' she said.

'People back home do get quite rigid at times. My first priority is to establish a tacit understanding with Ayudhpur,' he replied.

She got up to leave but then said, 'You should ask her, at least before we leave.'

Krishna took a while to respond, 'I don't want to complicate it anymore for her.' He said so because he had seen Meera miss her family to no avail. And somewhere down the lane he blamed himself for Meera getting ostracized from her own family. A year before Phase II began, Mohan had visited home. And Mohan, on Krishna's behalf, hand-delivered a gift to Radhika at her place. It was then that Mohan met Meera and both developed a liking for each other. When everybody started moving from the Ayudhpur airport after the apocalypse, Meera left her parent's home and joined Mohan midway towards Madhavpur. They were the first couple to get married in the newly found city. Shriram never brought up the topic during the negotiations on the Code, which lasted six months, but he was hurt. He was neither rude nor mean, but wanted both his daughters to live life in accordance with dharma.

During his last meeting with Shriram, Shyam had assured him that he would take care of Meera as his own daughter. Then the Code came into force and all contacts between the two neighbours had ceased.

•◆

It was 5.30 in the morning and Krishna was already up. He took his bath and was dressed in a fresh and crisp saffron-coloured dhoti.

'Shall we move?' Vallabha asked as she entered his chamber. She froze and stood at the gate, as she got a glimpse of Krishna. He was well-chiseled, even more than what she expected. The water droplets from his matted hair dribbled down his well-defined shoulders to his well-crafted abdomen. The peacock feather tattoo was wet and glistening on the juncture of his well-carved biceps and shoulders.

Krishna looked up and saw Vallabha. She was draped in a beautiful saree.

'Almost time,' replied Krishna.

The rituals began with invocation of hymns from the oldest texts—the Rig Veda. Shriram stood at the centre of the assembly, and the city priests stood beside him. They were facing a large statue of Lord Rama.

Carved out of the most beautiful piece of granite, it stood 150-feet tall. With his right foot placed forward, his left hand held the bow and his right hand extended to bless. The statue was designed with utmost details and the mild smile on Lord Rama's face was mesmerizing.

The Chief of Ayudhpur, Shriram, was the first to offer flowers of devotion at the Lord's feet, followed by ceremonial sounds of conch-shells. The whole ensemble of people then sang Sanskrit hymns in praise of Lord Rama. The very realization of the fact that the place where the statue stood was revered as the birthplace of Lord Rama filled Krishna with a sense of spiritual ecstasy.

As the ceremony completed, Shriram said, 'Let me show you around our town. It is not as intricately designed as yours, but we like it simple.'

'The interiors are very beautiful and very thoughtfully designed. Ours looks good from the outside, but yours looks good from inside, no matter how much of a simple facade it carries,' said Krishna.

Shriram smiled.

Vallabha, meanwhile, went with Radhika, to visit the command centre of Vaishnavi Sena. And Shriram took Krishna to the forest cover behind the city limits. It was a sort of jogging track that passed right through the middle of one of the densest forest Krishna had ever seen.

'We call it Tapo-Vann. Beautiful, isn't it?' Shriram pointed towards his right. The view to his right was magnificent, with golden sunrays filtering through the dark dense forest. He could see a herd of different kind of deer there, of which few were resting and few were grazing.

'It is! Beyond words! But this might not last,' replied Krishna.

'But I will have to consult the elders and the sages. I cannot commit to any migration,' replied Shriram.

'Whether to migrate or not is not the question. The question is of survival. If you want your civilization with all your values to continue, there is only one-way out,' said Krishna.

'What kind of a migration are we talking about here?'

'I cannot comment on the distance of our possible next destination, but it won't be on this planet definitely.'

'Do you have means for such a mass migration that too across heavenly bodies?'

Krishna nodded and said, 'We are working on it in full swing.'

⋅◆

'What is your day like in Madhavpur?' Radhika asked Vallabha.

Vallabha was lost in thoughts of her own. The old-fashioned looks of the building around and the weapon-wielding battalion of girls, it made her envious to no end. Pulling herself out of her thoughts she said, 'I am an ecologist. I study plants and it's species in and around Jambhu-Dweep.'

'Travel and exploration, something I find interesting too,' said Radhika.

'It is 10 per cent exploration and 90 per cent a regular desk job. A lot of briefing to the Council goes through my office,' replied Vallabha. Radhika smiled in response.

'I like what you get to do over here,' Vallabha said.

'I vowed my allegiance to the cause. I vowed to never let our guard down,' she replied.

'Ever thought of living in Madhavpur?' Vallabha asked.

Radhika smiled and said, 'That isn't going to happen anytime soon.'

Meanwhile, Shriram was done with his morning walk with Krishna. They both exited toward the other end of the city. The cantonment was a couple of hundred feet from that point. He knew his daughter would be there, looking after the daily affairs.

They both reached there and on spotting Radhika, Shriram

turned toward Krishna and said, 'So we have an agreement over here.'

Krishna extended his hand and said, 'Yes, but I am speaking in my personal capacity. I will do my best to convince my Council. This is something that they take very seriously.'

'Krishna, I would urge you to enjoy your stay here. As and when you want to leave for Madhavpur, just let me know. I will have arrangements made,' Shriram said.

'We will have to make an urgent move and will require the directions to the shore,' replied Krishna.

To which Shriram laughed and said, 'Oh, of course you would! I made my army seize your boat, and they handed it over to the engineering department. They have fitted the boat with a solar-powered engine. You won't have to row home.'

'Gopaldas won't be very excited about the tweaks in his boat,' replied Krishna and along with Vallabha returned to their chambers to gather whatever stuff they had. Krishna also refilled his stock of food, water, and other essentials for the journey.

Post-breakfast, which was served in a more informal setting of the lawn outside the chamber for them, they informed Shriram of their departure. Within a moment's notice an officer turned up to escort them.

'I am Raghav, a Commander in the Narayani Sena,' he spoke in a formal tone. He was over six-and-half-feet tall and had a build of a war tank.

A wagon with a tilted conch-shell embossed over it, pulled over outside the palace. As Vallabha was boarding the wagon, she ran her fingers over the embossed symbol. 'This is the official seal of the Narayani Sena, we call it Panchjanya,' Raghav explained to her.

Seated firmly inside the wagon, Krishna examined the ceiling of the vehicle. It was a composite solar panel. 'So you are not totally technology-averse, are you?' he asked sarcastically.

'We are not averse to anything, except for overreach. We believe excess of anything is what brings about evil,' replied Raghav. His voice was so deep that it seemed like it was reverberating inside the wagon coach. Vallabha grew even more envious. She was envious of the level of freedom the residents of Ayudhpur had. No rushing to office, no sitting around in enclosed buildings, and they had such exciting work to fill their days.

'Is there any particular point on shore, we should start off from?' Vallabha asked.

'There is one, I will guide you till there.'

As the wagon halted near the shoreline, Raghav made sure to embark first. He then crossed the road and went beyond the array of coconut trees. He dragged the boat out and with the help of the wagon driver placed it over the roof of the wagon. 'The jetty is nearby, I will explain the new controls of the boat to you there,' he said.

'Is it the same place where we arrived?' asked Vallabha.

'It's almost two kilometres upstream from there.'

After understanding their way back through the creek, they started off from Ayudhpur. The sun was now past it's day's vigour and was on a gradual descent. The winds were much cooler and balmier then what they were two days ago.

Vallabha was sitting right across Krishna, and noticed how he was looking more content than before. She turned and faced the front of the boat. The boat's onboard engine controls were programmed to manoeuvre the creek on autopilot. With no rowing or steering to do, she chose to bask in the mild sunshine and the pleasant breeze.

As the boat progressed, the shore shrunk on the horizon.

The two worlds are in fact quite worlds apart, Krishna couldn't help but think.

19

Hope Besieged

Amidst the lightly saturated dawn lights spread across the eastern horizon, the upper crest of the sun had just started appearing. A faint moon could still be seen over the western horizon, with each passing second losing its sheen to the growing brilliance of the sun. The chilly uphill wafts of winds were growing stronger by the minute.

'The winters are near, it seems,' said Vallabha as they were climbing down the hill range towards the city.

'It's already cold around here,' he said. The Indian subcontinent plate had gradually shifted northwards in the past million years. The territorial features blocking the polar winds had also vanished due to the sinking of the continents. These two factors combined to bring sub-zero temperatures and heavy snowfall during winters across both Jambhu-Dweep and Purva-Dweep. Something the erstwhile Gangetic plains had never witnessed in its long history.

The easternmost rows of houses on the city's end had started glowing in the emerging sunlight. The city was quiet and the MagVahn was yet to ply. 'It seems we will have to walk our way back to home, though they usually start MagVahn by this time,' said Vallabha.

'They do but it also depends on the traffic, and somehow the city is sporting an uncanny deserted look.' Krishna spoke with an undertone of concern in his voice.

'Do you want to stop by Mohan's?' Vallabha asked.

'No. As soon as we enter city limit, we split. Do not mention our trip or divulge any details to anyone,' he ordered.

Vallabha then headed straight to her home, she had to reach her office and submit the report of the study (which she had used as pretext for her absence). Krishna headed for his lab.

As he entered the lab and placed his stuff on the side table, he noticed his belongings had been shifted—his desk was now not facing the window. He called Mohan and said, 'How soon can you turn up, Mohan? Were there any guests in the lab? I do not like my things being moved around.'

'I will be there in an hour or so,' said Mohan.

He went upstairs to take his bath and change. By the time he had his breakfast and coffee, Mohan was already there.

'Good to see you after so many days,' said Mohan.

'My work desk?' he said with his right eyebrow raised.

'Come on, Krishna, is that so? Can't I even enjoy the view from the window for a couple of days and that too when you are out of town?' Mohan asked earnestly.

'How is it going in Madhavpur?' Krishna asked.

'It is going great,' he replied in a jubilant tone.

'Is everything good? No nasty cyberattacks, no Bhoomidium facilities going down?'

'None. And, now you need to hurry up,' said Mohan.

'For?'

'The lunch! You need to be there, everyone important needs to be there.'

'What lunch?'

'Vasu's lunch,' Mohan explained.

'What if I have other preoccupations to deal with?'

'He is a Councillor, an Empowered Councillor. We should not be disrespectful.'

'You carry on, I have some work to do,' Krishna said and turned towards his work desk.

'Your call, but I must tell you, my friend, you will miss out on a lot,' said Mohan.

'And what would that be?' Krishna was curious.

'It was meant to be a surprise, but now let me give you some hint. He wants to felicitate us for our work.'

'Why would he do that?'

'I invited him over and showed him our work,' Mohan said proudly. But even before he could have added in any more details, Krishna almost yelled at him.

'Are you nuts!'

'No, I am not. He is an honourable Councillor and is concerned about Madhavpur. He just wanted to make sure we are setting our sails in the right direction. What's wrong in that?'

Krishna inhaled a long breath and closed his eyes for a moment. 'Was he all alone or other Councillors were there too?'

'No, just him.'

'Not even Uncle Shyam?'

'Nobody.'

'What details have you let him onto?' Krishna asked.

'General procedures, our philosophy, and where our project have reached.'

'What about encryption codes? Don't tell me he knows that too!'

'He doesn't. In fact he himself refused to know the technical details,' replied Mohan.

'What time is the lunch?' Krishna asked anxiously.

'One o'clock,' replied Mohan.

'Go home, I will see you there,' said Krishna.

After some reluctance, Mohan did leave. Krishna found his behaviour quite unreasonable and now he was curious about the lunch. *What could be the reason behind the newly found camaraderie between Mohan and his ex-boss?*

May be he was over-analysing after all, as Vasu was always the kind of guy who would walk an extra mile to make sure everyone was attended to. And, Mohan was as guileless as ever. He did not even care to dress his best. He picked up the invitation meant for him from his desk and left the lab. He required no invitation but still wanted to read it once to check for any finer details. There was nothing in it that Krishna needed to be sceptical about.

•→

There were queues outside the Council hall. The midday heat was sweltering, and Krishna chose to wait for his turn in the queue. He was almost the fortieth person in the queue when Gopal appeared and said, 'There is a separate passage for the VIPs.'

'I am fine here. I do not want to skip the line,' he replied.

'Come along, I will show you the arrangements,' said Gopal.

On second thoughts, it was a chance for Krishna to know beforehand what the function was all about. He left the queue and walked along with Gopal.

'It was not about skipping the line, per se, my boy. That queue was for the audience, you may have to be on the dais,' he informed Krishna.

It was the fifth time that Krishna had tried calling Uncle Shyam, but he was still unreachable. Krishna then dropped him a message saying, 'Do not go into the Council building and meet me in the lab, late afternoon.'

He got no reply to the text either. He then couldn't control his curiosity and asked, 'Gopal, do you have any clue where Uncle Shyam could be?'

'Have not seen him around, must be busy somewhere.' he replied.

As they entered the assembly hall of the building, he saw Mohan there busy with getting things done before the programme could begin. The sight was perplexing, how could chemistries change in just a couple of days of his absence? Things were not adding up. Krishna paced up and approached Mohan, he then took him by his arm to a corner and said, 'Have you checked upon Uncle? His phone is not working.'

'I haven't seen him too for a couple of days. He must be busy,' he replied.

This was not the kind of reply expected from Mohan. Such callousness took Krishna aback. A person who had brought up Mohan like his own son deserved better in return. He left the already preoccupied Mohan and walked back.

'There, the first two rows are reserved for us,' Gopal said. He then walked along with him to the sitting area.

Suddenly crowds started pouring in and within a matter of a minute or so all the seats in the hall got filled. As soon as everyone was seated, the lights were gradually dimmed.

This whole new way of conducting Council business was perplexing Krishna. This Council hall had never witnessed anything so pompous in it's entire history.

A spotlight turned on and after traversing the whole breath of the hall, got fixed onto the rightmost corner of the stage. It was Vasudevan, standing there with his arms wide open. He was grinning and brimming with grandeur.

He then walked toward the centre stage and started speaking, 'Good day, ladies and gentlemen. Today we have gathered here for a very special reason. Mark my words, a very special reason indeed. This goes back to a couple of days. I was busy working in my office when my phone rang. It was not an ordinary phone call, my dear friends. Mark my words, not an ordinary phone call. We have always fought for our right to survive and our freedom. Haven't we?'

To which the gathering cheered, 'Yes.'

'We have dedicated our every living moment for the one goal: Sustenance of our race. Haven't we?' This time the cheer was not only louder but also reverberated through the hall.

'I was busy working for the greater good of our society, when that call came. A self-determined and hard-working boy spoke from the other end of the receiver. He was perturbed. He knew something, which we didn't. He knew that our citadel Madhavpur is at risk, we are at risk. He was worried for us.' Vasudevan said and then took a pause, heightening anxiety among his spellbound audience. There was now an uncanny silence in the hall.

'He was at the centre of it all; he had faced it first-hand. He is none other than our Mohan. He sought my help, as his lab facilities were under attack. There was a lurking enemy. Can we ever choose inaction and silence, when somebody cast an evil eye on our city? Can we?' said Vasudevan.

The gathering shouted with a fervour unheard of in Madhavpur—'No! Never!'

Krishna understood what Vasudevan was up to. He was trying to charm the gathering and bring them into a state of collective trance.

'I had no choice either. For the greater good of the Manavas, I left the work desk then and there. I went around the length and breadth of Madhavpur, until I found what I sought. In a secret dungeon just outside the city limit, there was someone hiding. He was unlike us. Big, powerful, and covered with strange metals and alloys; he was sitting there carrying out his devious plans. I was a little hesitant as I knew nothing about that being, but I did not retreat. That was not an option. I stared into his eyes. They were big and were glowing red with rage and anger. My glance held him in a stupor, and despite being all-powerful he did not move. My eyes burning with determination and dedication towards my homeland, held him captive. My dear friends, then I saw the impossible—a tear rolled down his metallic eye. He knew with whom he was dealing with. He sat down on his knees and was begging for mercy. But I showed none. None, my dear friends, none.'

The only thing crazier than his account was the self-confidence with which he was narrating it. Krishna was still finding it difficult to comprehend and assimilate the changed realities. Vasudevan had never been known for melodrama and crazy public narrations.

'He was an alien and upon confrontation was feeling guilty of his misdeeds. He confessed to have attacked our scientific facilities and even our elixir supplies.' The mention of Bhoomidium alerted Krishna. This meant Mohan has divulged information far from required to him. He thought of sneaking out of the hall to find Shyam, to make sense of all that was happening, when Vasudevan resumed, 'May I now present to you—Bhaydadh, our henceforth loyal soldier.'

A transparent glass capsule, some seven-feet tall, started descending from the roof of the hall, over the stage. The case was levitating over the stage now. As the audience gasped in awe and fear, Vasudevan calmly said, 'There is no need to panic. He is that alien, which I had taken captive. He has surrendered and has defected his evil side. He has now pledged his allegiance to us and would help us guard Madhavpur.'

Krishna too was shocked. What Vasudevan was speaking and

suggesting was sheer madness, outright violation of the Code. This was a coup... How come the people were not questioning it? Krishna then held Gopal by his arm and said, 'This is crazy. How can he unilaterally take such decisions? He is violating the Code. You need to veto him, right now!'

'He is right in what he is doing. He is our last hope against this invasion. He has captured that evil alien and persuaded him to fight for us. When you cannot annihilate your enemy, its better to lure him on your side.' Gopal stated matter-of-factly.

Krishna could do or say nothing and stared blankly at him. Even if this alien was the perpetrator, why was Vasudevan using him to project himself as a saviour? Wasn't it his duty to turn the matter over to the Council, and what was the whole pomp and show all about?

Things were not summing up well. If the alien had the technology enough to hack and attack the Samganak, why would he so easily submit to Vasudevan? What was the felicitation that Mohan was talking about? Krishna's head was buzzing with all sorts of questions.

'Now, I request Mohan to come up on stage and explain to us what kind of a being this creature is,' announced Vasudevan. Mohan raced his way to the stage. *This was after all a felicitation ceremony for Mohan and not us. And to make me feel jealous, Mohan made sure I attended.* The one thing that Krishna could not understand was whether this switch in loyalty was sudden or was this in the making for long. Whatever it was, he was caught completely off guard.

'Thanks, Vasu! My dear friends, welcome to this great gala. For we have successfully not only intercepted but also devised the strategy to avert this catastrophe. For when, we have not even partially forgotten how we barely made it through the last one, another catastrophe came knocking at our doors. This foe-turned-friend comes from a civilization much advanced than ours. For they are bad, and have no shame in pursuing technological advances for bullying others. Unlike us, they lack restraint. And mind you I say so only when this creature is asleep. Before he comes back to consciousness we would like you people to know, what potential dangers and perils he could cast.'

Mohan walked across the stage, on its left there was a small round table placed, which was hard to see in the dim lights of the hall. Harder was to figure out what was lying on that small table. Mohan walked up to it and picked up from the table what seemed like a weapon of a sort.

'This is what he was in possession of when Vasu found him,' Mohan said while brandishing that weapon in air for display and for full public view.

'This is some sort of high-cosmic energy gun. There is a small video clip that we would like you to see, to help you understand the threat.' He then started a holographic video projection with help of a remote lying on the same table.

It was a short two-minute clip of that creature handling and shooting from the weapon onto the trees and rocks, somewhere around the forest surrounding Madhavpur. The weapon emitted a neon-blue beam and evapourated any material it struck. The clip was intense enough to instil chilling fear into the hearts of all those who were present in the hall.

'We have persuaded him to submit his weapons to us, but we cannot say with surety that the other beings of his race would be willing to do the same without any concessions from our end. They are swift, nimble, powerful, and smart. Let me show you some more clippings we found in his possession.'

Mohan then started the projection of another video. The hall lights were dimmed further for this one. The video showed a detailed insight into the colonies of the aliens. It showed everything from, their big footsteps on the dark grey-coloured ultra fine sand-like soil to them fighting each other with spiked maces as a war drill. No Manava in Swarnim-Yug after the establishment of Madhavpur had ever witnessed such violence, not even in videos and simulation.

Vasudevan appeared back on the stage and said, 'Such is the level of barbarism they can inflict upon us, if we let it be.'

'We shouldn't let it be!' shouted a bunch of boys from the back of the hall in unison.

'Vasu is playing with people's psyche. They are perpetuating fear psychosis. There is something phony about these aliens,' Krishna whispered into Gopal's ear.

'You might be right but truth of the moment is that I am scared, I do not know how else to react.'

'Where are Vitthal and Narayan?' Krishna enquired.

'They have been assigned work for improvement in internal security of Madhavpur. They must be busy somewhere,' Gopal said.

'So they all know about the latest developments, where is Uncle then?' Krishna asked.

'All the Empowered Councillors attended a short brief by Vasu, except for Shyam. We were all very busy assimilating the facts and somehow overlooked his absence in the panicky state,' Gopal said.

'Just don't panic, Gopal. That would be the last thing any Manava ought to do at this moment,' Krishna said.

'No, we are perfectly fine now. Vasu and Mohan have stepped up to the challenge and have the situation under their control.'

Krishna couldn't sense any urgency to trace Uncle Shyam, in Gopal's voice. And this lack of concern, that too for the Head of the State, was baffling him. Moreover, he was concerned about Shyam's safety. If he had to slip away from the gathering, to look for Uncle, now was the time.

Krishna half-rose from his seat and with a posture crooked enough to not block anybody's view, started crouching sidewards. The hall was dimly lit and he wanted a quiet exit without anybody noticing. But as soon as he moved a few feet away from his seat, the lights grew brighter. A spotlight swept through the length of the stage and pinpointed on Krishna. He froze in the spot.

'Krishna it seems has run out of patience for our problems,' said Vasudevan in a pitched voice, 'nonetheless, the next part of this session is about you, willy-nilly.' Krishna turned and looked at Vasudevan, there was something unbecoming about the smile that he saw on his face.

'We have administered this alien a tranquilizer, on the pretext that it would help him acclimatize to our planet. He would wake up any minute now, we don't have much time at hand. So without wasting any time further, let me ask you this: Are we ready for some sacrifices to avert this oncoming storm? Raise your hand if you are!' Vasudevan prompted.

Almost everybody raised their hands, barring Krishna, who stood there like a deer caught in headlights.

'Good. Now here are the conditions, which these aliens have demanded. Firstly, they want me as their single point of contact and also want me in command. As I am the only one they say they can trust.'

Almost all the hands went up, and everybody nodded in agreement.

'Secondly...now, here is the interesting as well as the tricky part,' he said while smiling gleefully, 'they want two people confined. Are we ready for this?'

He again got an overwhelming response with everybody agreeing without even knowing the names. 'Krishna! Come up on the stage. Sorry my child, I love you more than anyone, but I will have to do this. If it comes down to my brethren, my race—I will have to play a tough father,' he added.

Krishna kept his calm. The people in the hall, especially the young lot at the back, started raising slogans. They wanted Krishna to voluntarily turn himself in.

'Come on, my child. We cannot wait for this unreasonable alien to wake up from his slumber.'

20

The Deluded Wisdom

It was hot and humid, with the sun shining bright right over his head. Apart from the unusual noon heat, Krishna couldn't find a single possible fault with the day. The meadows running in front of him were spectacular, with green grass covering each hill around him. The colour of the grass looked extra saturated, to the limit where the colour itself could hurt the eye, if stared at uninterrupted for too long. The sky above too was a glazing dark blue, dark to the limit where it appeared to be surreal.

His eyes would stray from one visual to another like a child in a candy store. The visuals were so very pleasing that Krishna wondered why he never knew of such a place ever before.

He then thought he saw something or somebody across the small valley. He was curious and all charged up. He wanted to know who that person could have been. The figure was sporting something like a full body wrap around; implying it was a girl. He ran downhill towards the valley. His sole focus was now to know the identity of that girl standing there; the bright colours all around him were now not enticing him anymore.

As he approached the figure, he stopped and stood some 10 feet away in amazement. It was a woman clad in a bright-coloured sari with her back towards him. She was walking around in a manner, which could have easily been called an enticing dance. It was almost as surreal as a pleasant, vivid, and desire-evoking dream.

'Who is she?' The part grace and elegance in her gait suggests that she is Radhika and the part intoxication in it suggests that she can be Vallabha as well.

His heart was pounding with anticipation; he had to know who she was. He raced towards her and stopped only at an arm's length. He placed his hand gently over her shoulder and wished that the lady would turn.

It took the figure a while to set her body in a turning motion, but eventually she turned.

To his horror, the full body wrap-around was not concealing either Radhika or Vallabha, it was Bhaydadh the demon alien in disguise. He grabbed Krishna by both his shoulders and his red glowing eyes pierced through him. Krishna by no means was prepared for such a treachery; his bones were almost crushing under those metallic claw-like hands. His ribcage was almost collapsing, leaving him grasping for air. He tried speaking, but couldn't. Meanwhile the grip was growing stronger and the feeling of suffocation was now turning to being excruciating. The alien being didn't stop at this. He started opening his jaw and started displaying his rounded cylindrical metal teeth to intimidate Krishna. The creature then started emanating a very high bass sound, and along came a storm of slime from his mouth. The slime was too watery and landed on Krishna's face.

As Krishna looked around the whole background, which just few minutes ago was full of vibrant colours, had now gone black and white. He could see ash-coloured hills and a pale sky, but could not see or feel any colours around him. *This is a dream. This is actually a dream I am trapped in. I have to snap myself out of it.*

As he reminded himself about it being a dream, a second roar emanated from that metallic throat along with more slime. He woke up. His head was heavy from some kind of impact and his eyes could barely stay open. His limbs were aching terribly.

As he regained consciousness, he could see a faint figure of something black and metallic. It was not a senseless dream after all; the alien was actually around. He could still feel something on his face. It was water that had been splashed on him to wake him up.

As Bhaydadh stood there with another tumbler full of water, Vasudevan said, 'Nothing to be worried about Krishna, we had just tranquilized you.'

He tried moving his arms but couldn't. His legs and arms were tightly chained against a metallic board fixed to the wall. Finally, he could look around and start making sense of his surroundings. It was the same bunker, which up until now was doubling up as his lab. His entire set-up including the Samganak was there in front of him, fully operational. Vasu having access to the facility was not a good sign to begin with, but then neither was he being in chains. His only hope was now the encryption codes.

'Who was that second person to be confined too, you were talking about?' Krishna asked. Vasu smiled and with his newly gained access to the thought command control, opened a chamber carved inside the bunker wall. Inside it was Shyam, also chained to the chamber wall, battered and unconscious.

'Vasu!' shouted Krishna in anger.

But the man raised his right hand and said, 'Nah! Vasudevan is gone. Call me Kamsa. I am an incarnation of the legendary hero, King Kamsa.'

'Let Uncle go, Vasu. Talk to me, for whatever your demands are.'

'Look my son, none of your questions will be answered if not addressed with proper salutation,' Vasudevan replied.

'King Kamsa, or whatever fancy honorary title you have bestowed upon your own self; just let him go,' Krishna said.

Vasudevan now burst into a laughing frenzy, he laughed till he had to grab the corner of the nearby table, to balance himself. 'Now don't tell me that you don't recognize me, Krishna. I was your worst nemesis, until you used all kind of trickeries to defeat me. I was righteous and my goals justified, but you played all kind of tricks to further your own selfish motives,' he said.

'I am not sure what delirium you are in, my only concern is safety of my Uncle. Let him go and we will talk,' replied Krishna.

'We sure will talk, with or without your Uncle,' he replied, sneeringly.

'That is not going to happen. You won't get any cooperation from me, until you release Uncle,' said Krishna.

To which Vasudevan again burst into that deep dark laughter of his. 'Kid, you will talk if you want your Uncle to see another day.'

He knew that Vasudevan was in no mood to relent, and probably he had no choice but to keep him engaged in talks till he found a way out. 'You cannot coerce us, neither me nor Uncle,' said Krishna.

'Your Uncle needs no coercion; he has been sleeping like a baby for many hours now. I have been injecting him with tranquilizers. But your non-cooperation would mean that I might have to replace that with a beam into his sleeping head,' he said picking the cosmic energy gun from the table.

'You can kill us both anytime, but it won't solve your purpose. Let Uncle go,' said Krishna.

'I can, for that matter, not only kill you both but also can run over entire Madhavpur before marching onwards to Ayudhpur. Your foolhardiness is making you underestimate my capabilities,' he said.

'With what, this tin can of yours?' Krishna said with a chuckle. It was a calculated risk of poking Vasudevan that he was taking.

'You are right. My mistake, it is. I cannot just jump into action, without narrating the prologue. It seems you remember nothing from the day's presentation with the Council,' he said smilingly. He then switched on the display meant for the Samganak. It was loading commands and operations files, which did not belong to Samganak.

'And why only a prologue, let me show you a detailed trailer for what I have in store for you Bhoomi inhabitants,' he further stated.

The giant screen was now populated with imageries of huge manufacturing plants and war drills of those aliens on a silvery dusty rocky terrain. 'What would be your guess, what is this place?' he then asked with a sense of pride.

'Some makeshift movie studio somewhere in the jungles of Madhavpur, or better still some cheap animation?' said Krishna mockingly.

'Kid, you have practically spent last two million years in that stinking lab of yours. Must say not venturing out does makes a man myopic and stupid,' he replied, while looking for any change of expression on Krishna's face. 'This is the moon. The dark side of the moon.'

'The moon cannot harbour life,' replied Krishna.

'Who told you that they are living? They are sophisticated robots, designed to serve me,' he replied.

'So, you made them? And placed them on moon too?' said Krishna.

'No. I did not make them, at least not all of them. While Madhavpur inhabitants thought that all enterprises in the city belonged to the state, one man was busy building his own empire. Albeit, on a faraway rock,' he said.

'The Moon Inspection Mission, wasn't it? We should never have trusted you,' said Krishna.

'Yes, the mission I volunteered for. I volunteered because I knew that the asteroid that had struck the moon had all kind of rare elements, required for my dreams,' he said.

After the moon had stabilized in its lower orbit, a spacecraft was sent to the moon to see if the only satellite of Bhoomi was doing well. Vasudevan was the only Manava aboard that flight. He had to stay there for a month for carrying out various studies, but the project got extended to three months.

Now everything started making sense to Krishna. Vasudevan had mislead everybody and misused the state sponsored trip to somehow set up a robot-manufacturing plant on the moon, and being on the darker side everything went unnoticed.

'All along you thought you were doing something remarkable in your lab, and to an extent you actually did. But I used the whole universe to my advantage and used the hidden side of the moon as my laboratory. I carried along maps of cosmic cells and smart bots with me and within a tight span of three months I single-handedly constructed Bhaydadh, my most trusted associate. I also secured alternate cryptic code for our then defunct satellite monitoring the dark side, for myself. I then operationalized it to communicate with Bhaydadh. He then, on my command, built plants to mass manufacture cosmic cells and a whole Jarasandh legion of warrior bots,' he said.

Krishna was assimilating each bit of information that Vasu was letting out voluntarily. He was not unaware of the concept of the Cosmic Cell, a highly controversial source of energy proposed towards the end of the twenty-first century. The cell was supposed to draw or borrow pure cosmic energy from any random location in the whole universe, and after putting that energy to use would replace the deficit thus created by borrowing energy from another coordinate in space-time. This random shuffling of energy from one place of universe to another made everyone sceptical. Thus an idea that could have provided Bhoomi with never depleting energy source was shelved.

'What do you want now?' said Krishna.

'Justice,' he replied.

'What justice? When you are the one breaking every rule possible in the rulebook,' Krishna replied.

'I intend to bring over an end to the prevailing hypocrisy and deliver justice. Justice to the name of people who have been persecuted all along the history for expressing honest desires. I would bring an end to the hypocrisy of setting up of rules and norms, which makes an ambitious yet honest person feel guilty and ashamed of expressing his desires,' he said.

'You do understand that whatever justifications you are conjuring up for your act of treason, are not making any sense at all,' replied Krishna.

'Look at me Krishna, I am the same Kamsa you tricked and fooled aeons ago. But, you will not fool me now,' he said, as his facial muscles got stiff and expressions became full of vengeance.

'I did not trick anybody in setting up my kingdom, neither were my plans of expansions unjustified. Still you killed me citing dharma. You have always been a master at propaganda; you wronged me and then led world into believing that I was evil. When it should have been you who should have been scrutinized,' he further said.

'I remember nothing, nor was I present in the times, that you cite. Even if that person resembled me, why avenge now?' Krishna asked.

'You are too smart to forget anything. But you overlooked something. You thought that you could kill manifestation of desire, which in actuality you can't. And unlike you I don't condone anything. I rose from the ashes and waited for the right time to strike. I wouldn't let residents of Madhavpur suffer injustice at your hands,' he said.

Krishna couldn't believe his ears, either he didn't hear it right or he was listening to the most conceited man ever. The odds favoured the latter.

'You thought your trickeries and deceit would go unnoticed this time around too? You were outright dishonest from the beginning, you lied even when under oath. You lead us into believing that you were searching for an inhabitable planet, while you had other plans. Even when you confessed after being overwhelmed by my attacks, you didn't disclose the whole truth. You deceived everybody. Old habit. The thing you never realized was that I had a close eye on you,' he further stated.

Vasudevan was busy narrating his grudges when Krishna interrupted and said, 'So says a person, who not only broke all laws of the land but also raised an undercover army? You are talking of deception? You even deceived your boss who supported you through thick and thin.'

Vasudevan grew restless and started seething with anger. 'My time is precious you see, I do not have all the day for all your crap,' he then signalled Bhaydadh, who moved ahead and with his metallic fist delivered a blow to Krishna's neck.

As he felt the same excruciating pain radiating out of his neck toward his head and chest, he started losing focus of his vision. Things were blacking out, but in a fraction of second before that he saw something.

Mohan was standing by the bunker door next to the Samganak screen, with his arm folded and with composure in his body language.

21

Betrayal: Best Served Cold

Mohan was programming the Samganak with astute adroitness and without any remorse. It was now beyond doubt that Vasudevan wanted an unlimited access to the Samganak systems and Mohan was by his aide.

'He is coming back to consciousness; do you want me to smack him again?' Bhaydadh asked in his dry metallic voice.

'No! Does he look like a punching bag to you?' interjected Mohan.

Vasudevan looked towards Mohan with his brows raised and announced, 'Do not. You might break his neck for good. Will use serum to tranquilize him if required.'

But doubt still lurked in Vasudevan's sceptical eyes, sensing which Mohan said, 'Don't give me that look, Vasu! We are a team. Let us fully understand this toy of his, before we actually exterminate him.'

Krishna chose to keep his eyes half-shut, but he could listen to what Mohan was saying. Handing over the manual and encryption codes to Mohan was a big mistake, he realized. But now much can't be done about it anyway. They chose to remain demilitarized unlike Ayudhpur and no one ever envisioned this implosion. 'Water,' he murmured. Vasu signalled Bhaydadh and he made him sip water from a bottle.

Shyam was also up by now, but was quite silent. He stood there clamped to the metallic board. Krishna seeing everybody busy in setting up Samganak, looked at his uncle asking for his wellness with a signal of his eyes. Shyam nodded and made sure Krishna understood that he was feeling much better.

He was feeling guilty of placing his uncle in such a perilous condition, but then he had no other option when he left in search of Gopaldas.

Krishna then noticed Mohan struggling at an encrypted screen; he seized the opportunity and promptly said, 'If you are finding it hard to grasp feel free to ask me, you CD2++ dumb head!'

Mohan turned and smiled, 'I love your arrogance. I just love it. Because your arrogance has brought you to this pathetic condition of yours, and the funny part is your arrogance didn't even let you see this coming.'

'I am happy for myself, no matter what. I served my people. What did you get out of this treachery?' Krishna said.

'First and foremost, I am just about to get rid of the most irritating, arrogant, and callous man. Second, we are a team and we will rule the New World,' said Mohan while looking towards Vasudevan.

'Rule the New World? You crappy buffoons don't even understand the project or how to execute a transition,' Krishna retorted. His tone was acrimonious and was now aggravating Vasudevan.

'Speak with all your force and foolhardiness, for you and your Uncle won't see the other end of the tunnel. You won't survive to see the righteous kingdom of King Kamsa,' Vasudevan said as he broke into laughter.

'The way your ex-student is fumbling with coding the procedures, I have my fair share of doubts,' he smiled. It was his desperate bid at securing his Uncle a release, by making Vasudevan or Mohan seek help.

Vasudevan then walked up to him and said, 'You think you are the smartest chap around, and everybody else is a clueless moron? Right? Mohan tell him what we are up to.'

'Your Majesty! Any moment now, the solar flares will have subsided and the link will be almost back,' Mohan said while punching in commands incessantly.

'You think those videos were bluff? I have a full legion ready on moon. My one command would transport them here,' said Vasudevan.

Mohan was now almost ready with his set-up, 'Your Majesty! This is done. We can start the teleportation.'

'I have already mastered the technique of playing around with space coordinates of the time-space matrix. I can mobilize my army across the universe, without any physical transportation. And you are going to be a lucky spectator of first such operation on a grand scale,' said Vasudevan and he then signalled Mohan to start the procedure.

The Samganak screen was now showing live visuals from the dark side of the moon. On the same screen in an inset, the Council building of Madhavpur was also visible. A whole legion of robotic army was standing in a formation in front of a rectangular arch made of a glowing substance. They started marching in formation into that arch. As soon as the hordes of robots came under glowing light of the arch, they disappeared. The teleported bots were getting beamed on to the lush green lawns besides the Council building, from a wide ray emanating from a cloud-like formation some 50 feet up in the otherwise clear sky.

Rows after rows of robots were now gathering on the lawns. Krishna now grew nervous, and even the expression on Uncle's otherwise calm face grew tense. In a matter of minutes, the teleportation of the bots was complete. Around two thousand alien bots were now standing in a formation. Vasudevan grabbed the left lapel of his robe and said, 'Legion, take your position.'

The Jarasandh legion now occupied each and every street and avenue of Madhavpur. They (armed with barbed maces and cosmic gun tucked in their belts) stood guard to resist movement of any sort in the city.

Vasudevan then walked towards the Samganak panel and started speaking onto a speaker embedded in the control panel:

> 'Dear residents of Madhavpur, this is your King Kamsa speaking. We have successfully negotiated with the alien race, and they have agreed to render their military services to the city. Prosperity of our city has always been a matter of envy to everyone else; but it has now started attracting aliens from even far-fetched galaxies. This reasonable race has forged with us an alliance and has vowed to protect us from other plausible alien invaders. They mean no harm to us, but what I would like to suggest is that, try and stay indoors until our newly found friends get accustomed to the city. I take pride in now declaring that the righteous Kamsa-Rajya has been established, and now we don't have to live under any repressive code. Stay healthy, stay safe.'

He then turned towards Krishna and said, 'I really liked whatever you have done on Prithvi, now from here on, I myself will take full care of our new abode.'

•◆

As Vasudevan's or the new (self-anointed) King Kamsa's voice reverberated through each empty lane and avenue of Madhavpur, voices of dissent started surfacing.

Gopal was pacing up and down his living room. Madhvi, Gopal's wife, had never seen him so tense and overwhelmed. 'What is the matter?' she asked.

'Something doesn't seem right, Madhvi! Everyone is now under house arrest, and the city is under a curfew. These visuals do not bode well. Something much troublesome and nefarious is on its way,' he replied.

'Vasu is probably looking out for our best interests. Moreover, he already discussed everything in detail with you all,' she said.

'This is not what we agreed upon. He was to broker peace with these strange beings, but he has now become their commander. He promised that Madhavpur will remain sovereign and the Council too shall remain relevant. But this takeover of the city and he elevating himself to be a king—this was never put across to the Council. This is nothing less than a coup and he is using those strange metallic beings to his cause. He has destroyed the very fabric of the Madhavpur society and is dragging us towards some kind of tyrannical rule.'

'Have you shared your concerns with Shyam?' she asked.

'He has been untraceable for many days now. I was befooled like everyone else. We have not witnessed anything like this for aeons. And when this sudden drama cropped up, it made us blind to the obvious. I even let go of the fact that Shyam has been missing for so many days. Krishna was right, he warned me about this farce. I was hooked onto that sham, I did not listen to him. He was our last hope and we turned him over to this megalomaniac Vasu. What have we done? Moreover, how did we allow him to arm-twist us all into this.'

'Have you tried calling Vasu? Any chance we can talk some sense into him?'

'I did try to reach him out, but to no avail. Heck, we don't even know from where is he operating all this nonsense of his. I should have checked him at the beginning. I failed my people and let them slide into this darkness,' he said dejectedly.

'It isn't too late; reach out to all other Empowered Councillors and build consensus. This siege of our city has to end,' she replied.

He nodded and called Vitthal and Narayan. He then instructed them to meet him at his house. They were his next-door neighbours. Infact all Empowered Councillors were, except for Vasudevan. Vasudevan used to live near his enterprise Vasu Corp's office. Generally, residential housing was not allowed in commercial avenues. But, his was an exception. He had special permission just for the same. Now it all made sense. He lived in a reclusive commercial avenue to escape public scrutiny while working on his nefarious plans.

The robot soldiers were marching up and down the streets. They were not in a column, but rather in a line formation. They were heavily armed and their stature itself was intimidating to any regular Manava. As Vitthal and Narayan stepped out of their houses, the marching line came to a halt. Two marching soldiers, just outside their houses, looked at each other. One of them in its heavy metallic voice informed someone over a communication channel (through a device on his right arm), about the breach of the orders.

'Gently ask them to step back,' said another metallic voice from the other end.

The soldiers then moved a step forward breaking the formation and said, 'Sir! We ask you to move inside. It's not safe for you here.'

The very voice sent shivers down their spine, but the two of them still mustered some courage to hold their ground. It was then that Gopal came rushing out of his house. Seeing the increasing number of people out of their houses, the soldiers on patrol started walking forward.

Gopal then shouted, 'Stop! We are Vasudevan's friends. Let us just go and talk to him.'

The two soldiers who had stepped ahead earlier, looked at each other again. One of them called Vasudevan and said, 'My Majesty, there are three men who call themselves your friend, they want to come and see you.'

'There are no friends and foes in the empire of Kamsa. All are equal. Deny them access and send them packing,' he replied. The communication channel was still on, when the soldier iterated, 'Sir! Move indoors. It's an order.'

To which Gopal said, 'I am one of the highly placed Councillors of this city. Don't you dare threaten me. You step aside and let me go talk to Vasudevan.'

'Majesty! He is not relenting,' the soldier reported back to Vasudevan.

'Use force if necessary, I want no Manavas on the streets,' Vasudevan replied curtly. The soldier now stepped forward and rushed towards Gopal. Seeing which, Gopal clenched his fist and as soon as that being was in his arm's length, he punched him in his face.

Gopal's hand was now bruised and bleeding from the impact on the robot's metallic face. The metal-faced was now smiling. He then punched Gopal on his flanks and grabbed him by his neck. Seeing this, Madhvi came rushing from her courtyard and intervened. The robot then let go of Gopal and clenched her by her jaw. She was now bleeding profusely from her mouth.

Gopal while still lying on the ground in his own pool of blood, yelled, 'Let her go. You have no right to hurt her or anybody around here.'

The robot switched his glance towards Gopal and smiled deviously.

Meanwhile, in the lab, Mohan was able to hear these voices blaring from Vasudevan's communication channel. 'Ask that soldier to back down, Majesty! Now!' he said.

'I will not! And don't you interfere in administrative matters,' Vasudevan yelled back.

'From the sound of it, it's Gopal and Madhvi. Let them go, please.' Mohan pleaded again. Vasudevan was now staring at him, when he further said, 'Those are influential people. You kill them and you lose trust of each and every Manava. How will you rule subjects that don't trust you any longer? Let them go.'

Vasudevan nodded in agreement and yelled into the communication channel, 'Leave them.'

The robot loosened his grip and then let her go. Madhvi then dropped to the ground. Gopal got up and helped her up.

'Ask them to stay indoors or else no one in Madhavpur lives,' Vasudevan said over the line.

Even after listening to Vasudevan's voice blaring through the channel, Gopal was standing steadfast. Narayan then yelled, 'Gopal! This will not solve anything. There is no reasoning with these metal heads or Vasudevan. Let's stay inside. Any move and we place every Manava in jeopardy.'

Gopal sighed and nodded. They all went inside Gopal's home. They crossed through the courtyard and stood in the living room, which looked directly over the street.

Vasudevan then spoke into his communication device again, this time to his entire legion. He said, 'Legion! Quit the Patrol mode and activate the Sentry mode.'

The Jarasandh legion had three pre-programmed wartime modes. First, was Patrol mode, when they would patrol a designated area in a formation for show of strength. Second, was Sentry mode, for which they were taught to stand their ground and keep a lookout in all directions. Third, was Annihilate mode, where they were free to use any brute force on the designated enemy.

⋅◆⋅

With the Gopal-led rebellion curbed, Vasudevan now wanted to take control of Prithvi. Now, this would have been a real test of how much Mohan actually understood the encryption keys. Krishna had himself designed the system to make unsolicited access to the control of Omechta difficult. The Omechta code needed a level of understanding of the system and a level of intelligence to decipher it.

'In case you think we haven't yet cracked the Omechta code, let me remind you the ease with which I disintegrated the Bhoomidium molecule. If I can make people Bhoomidium-deficient, then I can also systematically administer Bhoomidium to people and notch their intellect up from a CD2++ to CD1++,' Vasudevan said. Mohan was now smiling, looking at Krishna with his arms folded.

'You handed over the manual to me cause you thought that even in case of espionage, no one would understand the final codes, right?' Mohan said sarcastically.

'No, I handed over the manual because I trusted you as much as I would have trusted my younger brother,' said Krishna.

'Those who constantly and remorselessly use deception as their weapon of choice, should not expect honesty in return,' Vasudevan then turned towards Mohan swiftly and said, 'Mohan! Prepare for the transition.'

Mohan without even giving a moment's thought got back to the programming panel and started working through the final phase of access. Line after line, Samganak was prompting for entry of the encrypted codes. And to Krishna's disbelief Mohan was punching in proper commands, as if he had been practicing it all along. Not an iota of doubt was left in his mind that Mohan would eventually be able to gain access to the Omechta keys.

After almost five minutes of coding, the system displayed the most-coveted symbol—the Omechta Key. The symbol was a golden-coloured key with two parallel horizontal lines running through the Key's head. Shyam looked at Krishna, they both now knew that things were beyond any control.

Mohan was now invoking the Transfer module of the Omechta control. But it was too early to sneak anything into Prithvi, or so thought Krishna.

'Unlike you, I am not a lab rat. I will visit my soon-to-be kingdom and see to it that it is being nurtured properly,' said Vasudevan.

Krishna was puzzled as to what he meant by visiting. The look on his face prompted Vasudevan to say, 'We have mastered the technique of transferring to and forth substantial amount of matter by manipulating Omechta parameters in your system. Hold your breath, and see our technological prowess.'

Vasudevan then broke into fits of laughter again. The cacophonic bouts of laughter were now growing more dark and sombre. It reverberated with a bitter dose of lunacy and an overreach of confidence.

Mohan, meanwhile, was busy ensuring each parameter was punched in correctly. Vasudevan was now standing just behind Mohan watching him work on the panel. 'The systems are now ready. The conversion factor is still one to billion; tell me how long do you want to stay on Prithvi?' Mohan asked.

'Make it a full Prithvi day. I will carry out my own assessment as to by when we can start the migration.' Vasudevan replied.

'Your Majesty! The area, which is currently inhabitable, is quite large. You would require much more time than that. Let's me make it ten Prithvi days? A matter of fractions of seconds here,' Mohan

'No, make it two days. No more, no less. I want to be back as soon as possible and then I will start wrapping up things on Bhoomi,' he said.

'Are you sure, you want to do this?' Shyam now gathered his battered voice and spoke. Vasudevan turned and while looking at Shyam said, 'Oh! You bet. I so want to take Bhoomi and then Prithvi by storm. What surprises me is that you asked, because as far as my functional memory goes, I never asked you such questions. I always only rendered my unconditional support. I want to do this? Hell, yes. I didn't utter a word when you used your contacts in the President's office to become the director. I never challenged you when you skipped the line and went ahead alone for negotiations with Ayudhpur authorities and then went on to become the City Head for life. Did I ever question you? Never. Now, you have no moral right to question me when finally it's my turn to grasp the glittering glorious trophy that I have been eyeing for ages. You got all your glory by just being good and jovial, while I have worked for it. I have sacrificed, I have waited, and I have ambushed. All in all I have earned it, and now I am going to cherish it,' Vasudevan said and laughed again.

Shyam sneaked a look at Krishna, but Krishna was blank. He had no last-minute tricks to pull.

Vasudevan then called Bhaydadh, and he stepped forward and kneeled on his right leg. He offered his barbed mace to Vasu, who signalled Mohan to take it. Mohan grabbed the mace and placed it next to the Samganak.

Mohan punched in a few commands into the panel and the wall on the right side of the panel retracted vertically. A six-foot tall glass chamber came out of the vent.

'Mohan, test the device with this mace first. And, what do you call the process?' said Vasudevan.

'Brahmportation.'

Mohan placed the mace inside the chamber and dashed back to the panel. He then promptly punched in commands into the Samganak. 'Your Majesty! It would be back in fraction of a second,' and then he pushed the final button. The mace was gone even before Mohan could bat another eyelid, leaving behind agitated air molecules fighting each other to occupy the vacant space in the chamber. And even before the gleam in Vasudevan's eyes could grow to its pinnacle, the mace returned. He again broke into a bout of laughter, just that this time the undertone was not that of madness. It sounded more like a laugh of a sprinter who in his last five metres of the race knew, that he was yards ahead of everyone else.

Mohan too was smiling. His was full of contentment, the contentment of a child who could now walk without holding anyone's finger. He had yearned full access over the Samganak for long, and now he had it.

'Now, programme the computer to transport me. I would need that mace too, just in case. I don't yet want to use cosmic gun over there, lest I tweak mass-energy balance in that nascent world,' he said.

Mohan nodded and started preparing the Samganak again. Vasudevan was now strolling up and down the bunker hall. Done with his programming, Mohan turned towards Vasudevan and nodded. Vasudevan walked up to the chamber and placed himself in it. He had to squeeze himself to fit along with the mace. The chamber then closed. He then signalled thumbs up from inside the chamber and Mohan nodded in reply.

He turned and looked at Krishna, before actually pressing the button. He wanted to see his reaction, but got nothing. He then went ahead and pressed it. The chamber was now empty and with the speed of a thunderbolt, Mohan punched in commands to get visuals from Prithvi.

He then pointed toward the screen and said, 'Bhaydadh, see our master has now travelled beyond this universe onto Prithvi.'

Bhaydadh nodded. 'Master will be back any moment now, till then keep a close eye on him,' Mohan said pointing towards Krishna.

Bhaydadh nodded again and turned, facing Krishna.

The very next moment, a loud sound emanated from the chamber. The mace was back, while Vasudevan was not. Mohan leaped towards the chamber, slid open its door and grabbed the mace.

Even before Krishna could make sense of the events, Mohan charged with the mace in his hand. Some two feet away from Bhaydadh's back, he jumped vertically off the ground and struck him at the back of his neck. The shining blue crystal on the joint of his upper back and neck shattered into pieces, and he collapsed. Even before he could perceive the medley of sounds and noises behind his back and turn, Mohan had struck the cosmic cell of Bhaydadh. 'We at Mohan's Brahmportation Services provide end to end services,' said Mohan with an emphasis on the word 'end'.

Shyam smiled and sighed with relief. 'Set us free, then you can deliver your rehearsed dialogues all day long,' said Krishna. Mohan then freed Krishna, whose hands were aching, and he was supporting his left wrist with his right hand. He walked towards Shyam and asked, 'Are you okay or should I call some medical assistance in?'

'I am okay, and the trouble is not over yet,' he replied pointing toward the city visuals on screen. The city streets were full with the bots. They were all in Sentinel mode.

Krishna reached for the back of his collar and pressing the

fabric there said, 'They will soon be taken care of.'

'I had not programmed his return. And because of his voluntarily lowered Epi-cortical functions, he had no way of knowing, that I hadn't,' Mohan explained.

'Lowered?' asked Shyam.

'Yes, he injected himself with the antagonist of Bhoomidium to lower his rationality. He said he wanted primordial desires of his to take over. He wanted sheer sense of revenge, with no barriers of morality or rationality. Crazy,' said Mohan.

'And this is not how you teleport a living being across the universe. I am pretty sure those were fabricated visuals of Vasudevan on Prithvi,' said Krishna. Mohan grinned and nodded.

Krishna was now checking the Samganak for its integrity. The health of Café Evolution was now his major concern. He started progress-checking procedures on it.

'What was the deal with the crazy guy anyway?' Shyam asked.

'He was always the jealous sort, reading the wrong kind of mythology. The notion of being a victim had housed in his mind and he sympathized with every evil force in history ever defeated. He, as he confessed too, always envied you. He wanted a kingdom of his own, where everybody would submit to his will. He always knew about our progress and wanted to take over well before the migration could take place,' said Mohan.

'So, you joined him to sabotage his plan from within?' Shyam prompted.

'I knew his plans since long. There was some technical briefing to the Council going on when he noticed me frowning at Krishna overriding something that I had said. He took it for a fault line between us and approached me in a very subtle manner. I played it down. A few months ago though, he pushed a video clip to my wrist-phone, which was quite strange, as all lines to the device were highly secured and encrypted. It was the show of strength of his computer system—Paramganak, which he designed before lowering his own CD levels. The video was basically what you people saw the other day, bots all around preparing for war. He offered me a deal either to cooperate or be a part of those who get annihilated. He also used to track Meera and slyly even threatened me once regarding her. I was worried about Meera, and figured that joining him for the time being would be in everyone's best interest. We were no match for his robot army. I planned for this day all along, when I could safely get rid of this mad man.' Mohan concluded.

22

No Holds Barred

The sound of the chrome-plated base cutting through the thin layer of trapped air was mingling well with the sound of parting waves, underneath. The force that the air column faced was being transferred to the wave crests below, forcing them to split. The mid-morning sunrays were first bouncing off the highly reflective surface of the chrome, and then were illuminating the parting crests.

'How far are we from the shore?' Shriram asked.

'We should already have been there, sir! It's taking longer than usual. The shore is still some 10 kilometres ahead, as per the readings,' said Raghav.

The navigation systems couldn't have been wrong, still the fact that the route appeared to be longer worried Shriram. 'Boat speed?' he asked.

'Everything is fine onboard, sir.'

It was a solar-powered LevNauk, capable of hovering over water by charging its surface. It could carry around hundred men at a time, and the whole fleet being commanded by Shriram himself had ten LevNauk in a geese like V-formation.

'As soon as we approach the shore, signal everybody to throttle down the engines and make no noise,' said Shriram.

Shriram was busy taking briefings from his Council of ministers, the night before when the device made out of that special fabric sounded alarm. Krishna before leaving used the fabric of his Yocto-Suit to make a signal receiver. He had re-programmed the particles to receive a very specialized frequency, only to be emitted by the Yocto-Particle at the back of the collar of his robe.

As soon as alarm sounded, he knew that they would have to leave for Madhavpur, first thing in the morning. The troops and their equipment were ready in anticipation. The administration of Ayudhpur was handed over to the Vaishnavi Sena, commanded by Radhika.

Raghav checked the control panel and then raised his sight; with his right hand acting as a visor above his eyes he could now see the shore. He took the mouthpiece of the phone and announced, 'Throttle down your engine, and keep moving toward the shore with absolute calm.'

Within the next fifteen minutes all the boats were lined up on the shore, and the troops started assembling.

Shriram reached the head of the troop formation and said, 'Young men, history is testimony to the fact that Ayudhpur has never even thought of annexing or capturing any foreign land. Our preparedness and our capabilities are for our own defence, so that amidst peace our civilization could prosper. But today for greater good of the whole Manava race, we have taken upon our own self to render our services to our only neighbour, Madhavpur. This operation is not meant to annex any territory on Jambhu-Dweep or to showcase our superior strength. We are here to defend the residents of Madhavpur from, what I have understood, is an alien invasion. The enemy is unknown and its strength is unknown too. The gap and distance between the two cities makes it quite difficult to gather any information through telepathy or any other form of brainwave communication. Whatever information we have, has been rallied by Gopaldas, our trusted ally and friend of the entire Manava race. From my fair understanding the enemy is a mechanized being and carries both conventional and energy altering weapons. We need to march forward in the most meticulous manner, while gathering information about the strength and position of enemy garrisons. Keeping in mind the fragile diplomatic relations between the two cities, it's an order from your Chief Commander that under no circumstances should any resident be hurt. Your entire stock of arrows is as usual geared with self-destruction mode. In case any of the weapons miss their intended target, activate the mode using your brainwaves. We will not stop till we completely neutralize the enemy. For Manavas!'

'For Manavas!' shouted the troop.

Raghav then pulled out some maps and started explaining the course ahead to his sub-divisional commanders. It was almost midday and the troop had to march towards the city limits. As Shriram was walking past the troop formation (for final inspection of preparedness) a cool gust of wind column, ruffled his hair. He could smell a very familiar whiff in the air. Shriram promptly turned and said, 'Welcome Gopaldas, the Commander Emeritus of Bhoomi's most valiant troop ever.'

Gopaldas had always been a commander, on the special request of Shriram's, of Ayudhpur's Narayani Sena since its inception, but some hundred thousand years back he had voluntarily retired, as uncertainty prevailed over the fate of Madhavpur. In case of any confrontation between the two cities, he never wanted to provide any one side with an upper hand.

'I am not here to render my services again. I can at very best just show you the right path,' Gopaldas said with a smile.

'We were never after your services Gopaldas, we always sought your guidance. And that's all we need,' said Shriram.

'The bots have been teleported from the dark side of the

moon; they are in thousands all over the city. The adversary is technologically superior,' said Gopaldas.

'What about Krishna and Shyam? Where are they?' said Shriram.

'Couldn't trace them, my brainwaves won't reach them. But if Krishna has signalled you, they must be on Jambhu-Dweep,' said Gopaldas.

'He could be in his bunker, he was telling me about. But then again we can't be sure till we reach there,' said Shriram.

'But before that we need to secure the city. We need to first reach the western borders of the city, from there we need to wait and watch,' Gopaldas said.

Shriram nodded and Raghav signalled the Sena to prepare for the march. Gopaldas picked the shortest and fastest possible route across the dense jungles of Jambhu-Dweep. By the time the clock struck four, they were already trekking across the foot of the hill range.

'That's Mount Meru, the highest peak around. We will get a good sight of the enemy formation from there.' Gopaldas was pointing towards the hill.

Shriram's Sena was now occupying not only Mount Meru but also two more hills, alongside. Gopaldas chose a tree and sat in a lotus position underneath its shadow. With his eyes close he channelled all his energy focusing on locating Krishna across the city. His eyeballs could now be seen moving rapidly underneath his closed eyelids. He sat there for some good ten minutes and then opened his eyes and said, 'He is there in his lab, and is responding.'

'Ask him to relax his mind—both conscious and subconscious, and retrieve whatever information you can,' said Shriram.

'He has eliminated the commander of the invading enemy. He says, the troop which still doesn't know about the fate of their commander, needs to be neutralized,' replied Gopaldas.

'Who was he?' he asked.

'Vasudevan!'

With the mere mention of that name, visuals from a distant memory popped up in Shriram's mind. Vasudevan was one person who never appealed to him right from the beginning. And had it not been for him, Vasudevan actually might have succeeded in leading the negotiations and could have very well claimed stake to the post of Head Council.

'The robotic army is connected with each another via a special communication channel. They can act in tandem with each other just like a school of fish and we cannot take them down while that communication channel is still up,' said Gopaldas.

'And how do we disable that?' Shriram asked.

'Krishna will. He will try and hack into the system and jam it. We can then strike and take them out, one by one,' Gopaldas replied.

'Do we wait for dusk and strike under the cover of night?' Shriram asked again.

'No, they are mechanized and would have better night vision capability than us,' Gopaldas replied. He closed his eyes again, for, there was some communication from Krishna. 'He would be able to lock down the system in another thirty minutes. We need to start encircling the city from the west-end.'

'He is learning quite rapidly. I never thought any resident of Madhavpur would be so apt at using brainwaves,' Shriram remarked.

'He is no ordinary Manava. You will get to know more about him soon enough,' he said and smiled.

Within fifteen minutes the Narayani Sena was sitting tight, ambushing behind the rocks just a few hundred feet from the westernmost street of Madhavpur.

'Even before we bring the network down, tell me how loud would the impact of that metal clunk on the asphalt surface be?' Krishna asked.

Mohan while punching data on his computing device said, 'Given the strength of the surface and composition of the bots, 120 decibels!'

'How do we manage that?'

Mohan turned his handheld device, which was now accessing Paramganak, towards Krishna and said, 'Look here, they are programmed to ignore any ambient noise up to 110 decibels. If they are taken down street after street, the sound will grow feebler anyway.'

'If you can see the core of the codes, just turn them off or put them on self-destruction mode,' Krishna said.

'Nah! I don't have access codes for that, that megalomaniac never trusted me with those,' he replied.

'Then hack it,' Krishna ordered.

'I can and that too probably in fifteen minutes, but any kind of bypassing through the security check will initiate self-destruction module on Paramganak, first.'

'Give me the camera feed from the 1st Street, and look for any movement or heat signature,' Krishna said.

Mohan drew the camera feed from atop the museum building, and started scanning the hill range for any motion or heat signature. No motion or movement could be detected, but the heat signatures were present all across the range. 'They are already there,' he declared.

Krishna closed his eyes, placed his forefingers on both side of his temples and stayed in that position for a while. 'They will strike in another five minutes, taking down all bots one street after another. We need to hurry up and jam the module,' he said as he rushed toward the Samganak.

All preparations were done; he just had to enable the Interference field to bring the bot's communication channels down.

'It's up!' said Krishna.

'Do we need to signal them?' Mohan asked.

'They must be on their way,' said Krishna. Mohan turned and started more camera feeds from the 1st Street.

Meanwhile, Shriram said to Gopal Das, 'I will order my troops to initiate stealth mode.' He was referring to the tactical use of brainwaves, by which they used to trick their opponents into not seeing them. But the tactical manoeuvre was to be used with great care, as it was a big energy consuming exercise, prolonged use of which could leave soldiers tired and fatigued in battlefield.

'They are metal heads and have no organic brains. You would just end up tiring your soldiers and bot's circuitry would still respond to our visuals,' replied Gopaldas.

The idea was dropped, and a plain vanilla signal of mounting an attack was displayed. Shriram extended his right arm with the palm open and then very ostensibly pulled in his fingers, clenching his fist.

The robot guards were rotating in sync, keeping a vigil on all four directions. As soon as they turned east, a massive shower of arrows sprang forward from behind the rocks and bushes. Each arrow with precision down to thousandth part of a millimetre, travelled parallel to each other with the same speed, same direction, and same time of release. And to top it all none missed its target. As soon as the arrows pierced through the blue-coloured crystal, the cell shattered and its pieces fell to the ground. And with a delay of couple of seconds, the whole array of bots fell with a thud.

'Hundred and one decibels—as noted on the 2nd Street,' said Mohan.

'We were lucky, that a belligerent person like Vasudevan was never in power. Any war with Ayudhpurians would have been a catastrophe. They are fighting machines,' said Krishna. Mohan smiled and nodded in agreement.

The Narayani Sena operated with the precision of clockwork, and in the next 30 minutes had crossed onto the last street on the eastern side of the city. As the Sena men reached the last street in a bid to totally liberate Madhavpur, Shriram signalled to halt. 'Something is not right. Raghav, do you notice any movement behind us?'

Raghav replied in a negative, after thoroughly checking the city streets behind. It was something else, of which Shriram by now was only conscious and not aware.

'We can go back and check, later. This is the last array of the alien bots remaining, let's finish them off,' suggested Raghav.

Shriram nodded and Raghav signalled for attack. Now, everyone was holding their breath waiting for the bots to turn. As Shriram remained a bit apprehensive, tension in the group grew to a nerve-wrecking high.

The sentinels then turned and were now facing west. They were to stay in that position for no more than 30 seconds. After a while, as bots turned and as the raised metallic boots of the bots came down thumping (signalling full rotation) the clinched forefingers and thumbs relaxed and let go of the arrows.

The massive shower of arrows flew past the street in complete sync piercing the obstructing winds and smashed their target with precision. As Shriram refocused his vision from his archers towards the bots, he saw blue crystals of the cells shattering and falling on ground. But something was still not right. It was an arrow, launched from the exact middle of the formation. The robot it was meant for was still standing tall, facing the Sena. It hadn't quite reached its target. Rather the robot had caught it mid-air.

Raghav too now noticed the anomaly, and in an instant prepared his own bow to shoot at the target himself. Shriram held his hand, as the surviving bot's neck-studded cell crystal was now not facing them. There was no other way to take these bots down, without energy-modifying weaponry. The armour was simply too strong.

The robot was as tall as the others, but still there was something more to him. His eyes were not simply red, but were rather fiery red. His metallic shoulder blades were more prominent, his jawline much deeper and gait much bolder. On his upper right arm, near his shoulder, was embossed 'Jarasandh' with two crossing thunderbolts running across it.

'He is Jarasandh, the Field Commander of the whole Jarasandh Legion. The only advanced AI-enabled robot left behind on moon by Vasu. He even commanded Bhaydadh, and took orders only from Vasu.' Mohan said while looking at the camera feed.

'We should have factored that in earlier!' said Krishna.

'I didn't know he would be here, just recognized him seeing the coat of arms embossed on his shoulder. Him being here means Vasu was quite serious about his threats,' he replied.

Meanwhile, Jarasandh was looking around. The very sight of his bots lying all around agitated him to no end. His eyes grew brighter with rage and his fists clenched in angst.

Raghav signalled everybody to move back and said to Shriram, 'My Lord! Let me handle this.'

Both were now taking firm steps towards each other. The giant bot's footsteps were leaving behind a trail of cracked asphalt. Shriram knew that this was not an equal fight and was constantly pushing a message into Raghav's mind to use his service sword as soon as he gets a clear shot on the bot's cell.

As both halted at a distance of a mere foot from each other, Raghav gave Jarasandh a stare down. Jarasandh, almost sneeringly smiled for a fraction of a second and then his face expression again turned into that of rage and angst. He grabbed him by his neck, and started contracting his metallic grip. Raghav was suffocating within a matter of a few seconds. His eyes were now bulging and the jugular vein above the metallic grip grew prominent (swollen with constricted blood supply). He struggled for almost half a minute and then with all his determination raised his hand, and reached for the blue crystal at the back of the bot's head. Sensing the imminent, Jarasandh loosened his grip (freeing his throat) and rushed to hold him by his wrists. Now Raghav was struggling to free both his hands. By no measure was Raghav a being of frail stature; still the organic body was no match to the cleverly designed alloy metal of the bot. He kept on struggling to twist his wrist in a manner to gain some grip on Jarsandh's forearm. Seeing these hitherto futile trials to fight back, Jarasandh smiled and raised him above the ground by his wrists. He then threw Raghav like a weightless pillow across the street. The flight was only to be broken by an impact on the compound wall of a house. He was battered and bleeding, but still refused to back down. As he struggled to get up on his feet, Jarasandh had already rushed there. He kicked him on his shoulder and then picked him up by his arms. He then again held his neck in a final bid to strangulate him. Jarasandh was smiling with delight.

Meanwhile, a soldier from the Sena tried sneaking onto the opposite side of the street to get a clear shot of the bot. Jarasandh pulled his cosmic gun and shot at his feet. The soldier retreated. Raghav was helpless and was getting suffocated more with each passing second. His skin was now almost blue due to lack of oxygen. In a final try, he again raised his arm and reached for the most vulnerable spot of the bot. As Jarasandh saw his arm swing towards his neck, he flipped in hurry. Jarasandh's back was now facing towards the wall of the house.

Raghav could barely raise his head or arm now. His vision was turning blurry and his senses were becoming lull with the passage of each moment. He was not sure whether it was his fading vision or the sky above had turned dark. Even before he could render a thought to the same, Jarasandh leaned in to knock him on his head with his own.

The very next movement a liquid started oozing from Jarasandha's neck and was landing on Raghav's arms. It was the blue crystal, which now had turned into a fluid. Jarasandha's grip loosened and eventually with a delay of a fraction of a second, he fell on the ground.

It took a gasping Raghav a couple of seconds before he could collect a cohesive thought. As he looked up, it was Vallabha, standing behind the fallen bot. She had been watching the whole fight from behind the compound wall of her house, and as soon as Jarasandh's back was up against her wall, she struck him on the neck with the heaviest hammer she could find around.

'You are welcome,' said Vallabha.

Everybody rushed in and Shriram held Raghav by his arm. 'He needs immediate medical care. Young lady, where do you have hospitals around here?' he said.

'Two streets eastward,' she replied.

Meanwhile in the lab, Krishna was pacing up and down. He said, 'Check if any of those robots are still remaining.'

'None,' replied Mohan, as he was done scanning each camera feed of the city.

23

The Kakudmi Manoeuvre

'Yes! As we speak,' Krishna was saying as he explained to Shriram about Mohan's new find. Bhoomi's core was now fast running out of Bhoomidium. Because of which the continental plates had grown unstable again; a factor that everyone missed out on due to the turmoil.

'How do we slow it down?' enquired Shriram.

'As per the briefing I received from Mohan, we cannot,' said Shyam. The expression on Shriram's face grew sombre.

'I need numbers. How much time, at what rate and all that,' he said.

'Okay, let me put it this way. Purva-Dweep will drift away and sink anytime and it is happening at a fairly variable but good speed,' said Mohan.

'I think, we too have noticed the shift. It took us longer than usual to cross the creek,' Raghav reminded Shriram.

Shriram was the only person in the room who was reluctant to believe that they might have to make a move for good. He stood up and took a long breath, regaining his composure. 'There is a whole civilization on that mass of land, where do I take them?'

'We need to bring them here. We need your go-ahead to prepare, it's going to take time and we cannot afford that luxury,' said Shyam.

'Where do I settle my people? Whose constitution would be applicable?' Shriram asked.

'There isn't any time for negotiations; furthermore this won't be the final migration. We will have to leave Madhavpur too. With double the population, the already low-levels of Bhoomidium would deplete in half the time,' said Krishna.

'And the half-time being?' Shriram enquired.

'Six months,' replied Krishna.

'And believe you me, you won't like walking to the edge. That's the upper limit,' added Shyam.

Shriram nodded and said, 'Gather the means and form the teams.'

It was not an easy task, to reverse engineer a heavy-lift helicopter in a day. But the dedicated team at Vasu Corps did manage to pull the feat, and also modified the production line for mass-producing hundreds of such copters. After getting rid of Vasudevan and his robotic army, Shyam quickly moved in to call the Council meet. And with a voice vote, unanimous decision of nationalizing Vasu Corps was taken. He knew that the enormous production facility owned by Vasudevan could not be allowed to rot as an aftermath of the conflict.

The helicopter had gone out of production since the early Swarnim-age, when the sea-locked Madhavpur decided to put up the last of the specimen in the museum.

•◆

Next day, Krishna took Shriram out for an evening coffee to Café Moksha, where the latter expressed his desire to visit Govardhan. Krishna smiled on hearing the request and Shriram asked him what was so amusing about it.

'You have already been there, you launched the first wave of attack from its foothill,' replied Krishna.

'Then I need to go and visit again.'

Krishna gulped his coffee in a single go and said, 'Let's go then.'

They walked all their way to the hill, it was barely five in the evening and winds were already cold as ice. Strolling all their way up to the foothill, Krishna said, 'This is the fabled mountain. The sunsets are awesome from the peak.'

'Will it be fine, to climb up the mountain?' Shriram asked.

'I do it all the time, I love spending my evenings here.'

Shriram was still looking stuck in the dichotomy, seeing which Krishna said, 'Isn't the ground we walk upon all his creation?' Shriram smiled and nodded. The sun was now almost beneath the horizon, only a fair amount of its crest could be seen by the time they both reached the pinnacle. The colour streaks left behind by the setting sun were now dominating the evening skies of Madhavpur.

'Aren't we almost there? Isn't it time to just fade into antiquity?' said Shriram, looking at the glory of colours across the horizon.

'Depends,' replied Krishna.

'I am not sure if migration to another planet is what my people would vote for,' he said.

'Then you must have some other options in considering,' replied Krishna.

'As per my fair understanding, as soon as the Bhoomidium levels would go down, will the natural processes of reproduction begin again?' Shriram enquired. After reaching Criticality, the immortal race of the Manavas had not seen even a single addition to its population. The life consciousness at cellular-level sensed no danger and had no reason to make its safe copies by way of reproduction.

'It will, but that won't help the cause. I am sure you must have thought it through,' said Krishna. Shriram shook his head in negation.

'Then now is the time. Because our understanding points towards just one possibility—anarchy,' replied Krishna.

The last traces of self-generated optimism vanished from Shriram's face, just like the fading evening colour streaks on the horizon.

'The first capability to completely shut with lowered Bhoomidium would be the Epi-Cortex and next would be the Pre-Frontal Cortex. The Manavas would become human again, and that too ailing humans. They would not hesitate from fighting or inflicting harm upon one another at the slightest provocation. The dwindling resources on Bhoomi would add fuel to the fire,' Krishna elaborated.

'What actual options do we have then?'

'When we faced a similar situation at the end of the Kali-Yuga, we migrated. I fear, the same story is about to repeat.'

'What if I ask my people before airlifting them and they decide not to leave Ayudhpur?' Shriram asked.

'Then they go down with the island. But why do you even think along those lines? Do Ayudhpurians not look forward to life?'

'The dilemma is that we are staunch believers of Lord Rama and Karma-Yoga. We find it hard to justify an existence without purpose. If mere existence becomes the purpose of existence, then the whole meaning of life vanishes in thin air,' said Shriram.

'And how do you stop that? By giving up on living?' Krishna said. A long silence ensued. 'When life becomes a mere struggle for existence, you concentrate on finding a purpose. Your people need to see another day to find one. Assimilation of both civilization and moving to a better place for a better tomorrow, should be our first priority,' Krishna added.

'Tell me more about this planet.'

'It is more or less like our own. Has rivers, oceans, forests and by the time we reach there, it will also have humans.'

'Do we have enough spaceships to reach there, or we plan sorties?' asked Shriram.

'Spaceships won't do,' he smiled.

'Where is this planet?'

'Universe-1408. The planet, or Prithvi, as we call it is in a parallel universe. We will need something beyond spaceships for that.'

'A universe beyond our own?' said a visibly surprised Shriram.

'There are plenty, this one was of the right age to populate with life.'

'You mean whatever life you were talking about on that planet was…'

'Started by me. And no, in no way this is in contradiction to the work of God. He leaves traces and signs all across for us to pick up, and then allows us to solve our own problems,' said Krishna.

'Gopaldas was right; you are not an ordinary person. Now let's get moving, I need to know when can the rescue mission begin.' Krishna nodded and smiled. As they began to descend, the autumn moon could be seen on the eastern horizon. It was appearing bigger and brighter than ever before.

•→

'The helicopters have started rolling out of the production line, incidentally they are identical to those that I used to operate,' said Raghav as they both reached the new command centre of joint operations (headquarters of the erstwhile Vasu Corps).

Raghav had been a squadron leader in the Indian Air Force (during the Kali-Yuga), before global population shrunk and every surviving person had to move to Ayudhpur, for better management of remaining resources.

'Good! Also identify other pilots, so that we can begin extraction operations at the earliest. How many sorties will we require?' Shriram asked.

'Around ten, with an average of 50–55 person aboard each chopper,' Raghav replied.

'Around hundred machines, that would be. By when will the production be over? When can we start?' Shriram then asked.

'By tomorrow evening,' he replied.

He nodded and then looked towards Mohan, who was standing to his left. 'Even with the increasing width of the creek, each sortie shouldn't take more than two to three hours. If we start tomorrow we will have a couple of weeks before Purva-Dweep drifts far away and eventually sinks,' said Mohan.

'Day after tomorrow's morning, it would be then,' Shriram concluded.

•◆•

The night had grown darker and the temperatures outside were hovering around zero degree. The night sky was hazy with light mist and trees were swinging with intermittent gusts of winds. Just two hours short of midnight, the streets of Madhavpur sported a deserted look. The only commercial building around with its lights still on was Vasu Corps.

The cold alley leading up to the main entrance of the building was drenched in complete silence, when sound from distinct footsteps broke the monotony. Draped in a shoulder to toe saffron-coloured wrap-around, the sleek and tall figure easily manoeuvred her way around the building complex. Heading straight for the administrative office at the top right of the building.

Raghav was comfortably seated in his chair while Mohan was sitting over the contour of the big office desk in the middle of the room going through the finer details of the flying machines, when they both heard the sudden unexpected clunking of the office door.

'Food for both of you,' said Vallabha.

'I cannot imagine you being so cordial just for me,' said Mohan with a smile.

'You guessed it right, Mohan. We owe them a lot, they took good care of us,' she replied as she placed the brown bags on the table and then pointed at Raghav.

'Much appreciated, Vallabha,' Raghav said as both his and Vallabha's eyes locked on each other's for longer than usual. She smiled and slowly made her way back.

'I think she has developed a fondness for you,' Mohan said, once she was out of earshot.

'Same here, I have a lot of respect for her. The valour with which she fought that robot commander is commendable,' he replied.

'Come on, you know what I mean,' Mohan persisted.

'Yes, I do. But me reciprocating the fondness would be gross violation of the Code,' he replied firmly.

'That would indeed be, but we can take care of that while getting the new one drafted.'

•◆•

Shyam, meanwhile, was feeling restless at his own place and decided to go to the lab where Shriram was putting up with Krishna. 'Hope you have briefed Shri about the project Café Evolution,' he said as he entered the hall of the lab.

'Yes sir, I have. But, not sure how impressed the gentleman is with my work…' Krishna replied.

'A lot,' said Shriram.

'You still have your doubts? Right. That's natural, it is going to be a leap of faith.' Shyam said.

'Somewhat! It is all new to me. Parallel worlds, life seeding and then movement across universes,' said Shriram.

'This is nothing new we are trying, or are we?' Shyam said in response.

'What are you referring to?'

'King Kakudmi, remember?'

'From the great tradition of Bhagavata Purana?' he said with the lines of puzzlement slowly melting away from his face.

'He did travel across the universes to pay visit to Lord Brahma,' said Shyam.

'And the time swept by at an accelerated pace...' added Shriram.

'Exactly. We are trying the same, just that we are going to a younger universe. And we do not have to fear a time-lapse as we do not have to return to Bhoomi,' said Shyam.

'What if we do not get adapted to the new place?' Shriram asked.

Shyam looked towards Krishna for a response. 'Since the inception of life on Prithvi we have been monitoring a very vast range of parameters. On top of that we have automated programmes scanning these parameters round the clock for even minute changes, lest we miss out on something. So, we run a pretty good chance on surviving on our new abode,' Krishna assured Shriram.

'And given the life on the new planet, who all could be our neighbours?' Shriram asked.

'Ah! You mean the substantial co-dwellers, besides the variety of flora and fauna?' said Krishna.

He nodded. 'Humans, plain vanilla humans,' said Krishna.

Shriram rolled his eyes in disappointment and said, 'Then why don't we stay over here, let the Bhoomidium dry up and we become humans again—plain vanilla mortal humans?' replied Shriram.

'We are well past that bridge, as a matter of fact, that bridge is burnt and has gone up in thin air. We did not start Bhoomidium interception at a healthy stage or out of choice. We were sick back then, and were vanishing by millions. With the load of toxins in our bodies, we were no longer the perfect humans to begin with,' Krishna replied.

'Moreover, we would have stayed nonetheless, had these continental plates have not been shifting and sinking randomly,' added Shyam.

Shriram nodded and said, 'We will have to decide upon the structure of the society even before making the move.'

'The project has not yet reached those milestones, where we get to decide structures,' Krishna replied.

'Let the kids focus on the rescue plan, Shri, we will definitely sit down and decide every details once we make some substantial progress,' added Shyam.

24

The Much-Awaited Reunion

The last possible colour streaks on the western horizons of Madhavpur had merged and faded into the growing dark of the night. The moon was bright as usual. The upper reaches of the hill range had just received some snowfall, bouncing on which the moonlight was making the hills glow like silver on that cloudy night.

The winds from north sweeping across the hills were generating snowy mist across the range. And from behind that misty screen came out the machine made out of shiny black metal. Its rotors were cutting through the thick winter air and its engine's noise reverberating through the silent streets of the city.

An array of makeshift helipads was created just along the foothill of the range. The first sortie consisting of fifty machines had now begun under the command of Raghav. The remaining fifty under the command of Mohan were supposed to start once Team-One had been lifted off from Ayudhpur.

'Start beaming the coordinates' trail and time to destination,' Raghav spoke into his mouthpiece across to Mohan sitting in the Control Room.

'Here you go, connected the stream to the ground systems. It will take you across,' he replied. The fleet then flew across the horizon toward the creek, in a V-formation.

It was ten in the night when the fleet started touching ground, one after another on the outskirts of the city. Raghav had clear instructions from his Chief to reach straight for the Commander on duty of the Vaishnavi Sena. But the ever-vigilant Sena head saved him some trouble, as the noises from the fleet had alerted and drawn her to the landing site.

'Here! These are the orders from Shriram. I need access to the Public Announcement System right away,' he said to the Sena Head, handing her a copy of the same. Raghav then dashed to the security office besides the palace and went straight for the microphone.

'Good evening, everyone. I am Raghav, and I need you to quietly and in a very orderly manner assemble near the statue of Lord Rama,' he said, realizing well what he had just said. The on-duty deployed Vaishnavi Sena members sprang into action to make sure the assembly occurred smoothly without any panic.

Raghav then picked a folded piece of paper from his right pocket and scanned through it again. He then tucked the paper into his pocket and started walking toward the assembly venue.

In a matter of forty-five to fifty minutes almost all feet were on ground. Raghav grew tense, as now he had to carry out the task he was delegated with, with clockwork's precision. He stepped forward, folded his hand and bowed to the Lord's statue and stated in a calm but firm voice, 'Shriram wanted to be here among us but for some reason he cannot join for now. We have secured Madhavpur from the alien attack, and everybody down to the last person is safe. People are happy in the twin-city, so should we be. Any harm to the Madhavpur-dwellers would have been harm to the race of Manavas. For, they are us and we are them. We being their elders have helped them in their hour of need. But we still have some work chalked out for us, for our struggle has just begun,'

He paused to take in people's reactions, what he saw were faces as calm as the winter moon. Probably the extent of the exercise had given them a fair idea of something coming. 'We have been ordered to move by our Chief. Still the last word, he has left open to us to decide democratically.'

A Padh-Adheesh stepped forward and said, 'While leaving, no such matter was discussed with any of us. What has changed in the matter of time?'

'Nothing has changed during this particular time frame, sir. It has been happening all the while. The tectonic plates below Ayudhpur have been volatile for long, and now they are drifting apart.'

'At what pace? What's the severity of the situation?' asked another elderly man.

'We will sink, in a matter of weeks may be. The only temporary solution is to move to Madhavpur,' he replied.

'Temporary?' the Padh-Adheesh said.

'Yes. We might have to migrate further, the details of which rest with Shriram and the Madhavpur Head—Shyam,' he replied.

'Give us some time,' said the Padh-Adheesh.

All the twelve Padh-Adheesh(s) stepped forward, and formed distinct groups with their area inhabitants. And after at least half an hour of discussion, one of them approached Raghav and said, 'Is there any rescuing of our town possible?'

'I wish there was, but the whole island is going down. We will have to start evacuating in the next few hours,' he replied. The Padh-Adheesh then went ahead and gathered all remaining chieftains for discussion.

The eldest one spoke after another round of talks, 'We shall move. We cannot gather our belongings in a few hours, but just wish that the Sena Chief would take care of them and get them shipped afterwards.'

Raghav nodded and handed over the copies of evacuation plans to the twelve chieftains. The chieftains in turn instructed the local populace. The elderly and the womenfolk were to form the first batches of the sortie.

It took another hour before the shortlisted people were finally in their place on the helicopters. Raghav contacted and signalled the control command back at Madhavpur. Mohan left the command centre to Vallabha and accompanied the lead helicopter of the fleet of Team-Two.

For two long days the sorties continued on a war footing, day and night. The fully automated construction machines were building accommodation for the incoming Ayudhpurians. All but last evacuation lift-off was remaining, when Vallabha called Krishna in his lab and said, 'This is definitely a problem. I will put you through.'

She then connected him to Mohan, who was stuck in Ayudhpur.

'There is a situation here. A whole bunch of people, aren't ready to be evacuated!' said Mohan in a tone laced with anxiety.

'Calm down! Who are they and what do they want?' said Krishna.

'A whole bunch of them are there, among whom the most vocal is Radhika. They want us to take boats and leave the helicopters behind, so that they can stay back till the island is afloat.'

'Let me arrange a talk between them and Shriram,' Krishna replied.

'Please do. I cannot risk my crew by taking the creek route,' said Mohan.

Even Shriram struggled convincing Radhika and the whole lot of officers from Narayani and Vaishnavi Sena. 'We will have to leave for Ayudhpur now,' said Shriram after an hour-long talk over the phone.

Krishna nodded. It took Raghav fifteen minutes to prepare

his machine, and within a matter of an hour they were in the city.

'Sir, it's comforting to see you in person. We all hope that there is no pressure from the governing bodies of Madhavpur on you,' said an officer from the debating lot.

'Oh! Stop being a fear-monger. I had to stay back to make sure that inbound people had access to all basic needs and accommodation,' Shriram replied.

'Father! Are you sure?' said Radhika.

'Yes! Everything is fine between us. We have released Madhavpur from the evil clutches of Kamsa. We never had any differences; we just had different parallel philosophies to protect,' said Shriram.

'Father, can few of us stay here till this theory of shifting plates is verified by our own scholars?' she then said.

'Come on, there is no end to mistrust and scepticism. What do you all want? You want to witness the whole island sinking? Is that what will make you believe?' he said while facing the group of gathered people. He then turned towards Radhika and said, 'What do you want? Until you see a dozen men going down, you won't believe? Will you? If I lose any of these brilliant men from our security forces, who would protect the people in our voyage ahead?'

Radhika grabbed her father by his arm and drew him to a corner and said, 'What makes those Madhavpurians so trustworthy before you? Remember the last apocalypse? It was a result of their actions.'

Shriram instantly moved his arm, forcing her to release her grip. 'There will be no one-on-one chitchats or discreet group talks. The matter concerns all,' he said facing the whole group, 'we have no other option; there is no future on this island. As a matter of fact we might even have to abandon this planet too in the very near future. We should be thankful to them and their advanced monitoring systems, that we got ample time well-ahead of the sinking.'

'Father! Do you actually want us to abandon the very land where our Lord was once born?' Radhika cried out loud.

'Tell me of a time when he was or is or will not be around,' replied Shriram.

'But how could we let his birthplace sink? We need to do something at least?'

'Tell me of an inch of space on Bhoomi or for that matter in this whole universe that does not belong to him?'

'But it was our duty to protect his land!' she said with tears in her eyes.

'Even a grass-blade wouldn't move, if it is not on his action plan. He made us with thinking brains and evolving minds. We are his beloved children and he wants us to work for our own betterment,' he said. He then moved forward and embraced Radhika and said, 'He has something much better for us in store, my girl. He will always be with us.'

Radhika while still clinging onto his father and with tears rolling down her cheeks, nodded in agreement. 'An hour and we will be moving,' Shriram declared and then started moving towards Krishna, saying, 'Hurry up! Before I have to waste some more vocal chord tissues, convincing these knuckleheads.'

'These are trying times for all, she needs your love and affection,' replied Krishna.

'She was well past eighteen some two million years ago. She is a grown-up and should act like one,' said Shriram.

'You should not be harsh with her,' he replied.

'I should not have made her harsh. I should have let her choose her path along with Meera,' said Shriram.

The days and night were merging into a seamless interplay of light and darkness for Krishna. He and the people around him were working hard to make all arrangements look picture-perfect. Madhavpur was now hosting people twice its capacity. The electricity supply, the water supply, the heating supply and the Bhoomidium supply—everything was to be doubled up in capacity.

Mohan had a dedicated server for monitoring the situation at the isolated and abandoned city of Ayudhpur. But after a week of vacating the island, Shriram ordered closure of the monitoring. He couldn't bare to witness the island going down into the sea.

But there were few other very odd readings appearing on the surveillance screen.

◆

It was a nice sunny morning with the temperature many degrees below the freezing point outside. Shyam and Shriram had gathered in the lab to take stock of the progress.

Krishna then signalled Mohan to keep his presentation ready as they were all expecting the remaining Empowered Councillors any moment.

'Is leaping across the Omechta realm finally possible?' Shyam asked.

'Yes and guess who left us some clues on how to make it possible?' said Krishna.

'Of course, the Demon King did,' Shyam said.

The lab bell rang and Krishna unlocked the door with thought command. It was the trio—Vitthal, Gopal, and Narayan.

'In the cold northern regions of Prithvi...' began Mohan, even before everyone could grab a chair and settle down. '...we have observed early primates running on two feet while carrying essential food supplies with their forelimbs. Or, what now seems to be their functional hands. They are doing so to presumably reduce their contact with cold grounds beneath as well as to multi-task while they are out in snow. These were last updates, after which it became a bit difficult to trace the species as they started spreading across the frozen landmasses. Our systems are quite efficient but energy and computational power required for searching such thinly distributed populace of a particular species is not actually worth it,' said Mohan.

'Where do we stand now?' Gopal asked.

'Turns out, we shall find out together.' said Mohan with a smile, while turning towards Samganak and re-establishing the connections. There were not many visuals available on the screen; rather Samganak was generating readable crunched data.

'The primate species have branched into many other sub-species, but one of them, as we expected, has gained prominence and has been able to migrate and find warm sea-coasts,' said Mohan.

'Are they Homo sapiens yet?' Vitthal enquired.

'Not exactly, majorly because we don't have yardstick enough to reach those sort of conclusions,' Krishna explained.

Gopal gave him another of his trademark hypercritical glares and said, 'I mean, is it just a scientific definition we are looking for? The exact carbon copy of the people who we don't want to be?'

'Even before humans dominated the globe, there were many cousins of his, few of them surviving in isolation and few other working in small groups. What made Homo sapiens undisputed leaders were their superior social skills,' replied Krishna.

'So the species we have traced on Prithvi, are they capable of those refined social skills?' Vitthal asked.

'All the human cousins had almost similar brains, the different wiring of which made all the difference. The subtle change brought about by incidental inculcation of certain habits along the evolution path,' said Krishna.

'So, we can only observe and not predict,' said Gopal.

'I couldn't have put it any better myself,' said Krishna.

'The fittest would survive, their population would grow,' said Mohan.

'How much more time are we looking at? Mind you, I am in no hurry, but is their some exact timelines where we will have to make a compulsory move?' Narayan asked.

'Yes, decisive choices are hardly ever made in lack of compulsion. The Empowered Group will have to consult with all the councillors from both the cities to come to a fair understanding, as to when to go and populate Prithvi,' replied Krishna.

'Aren't those scientific decisions? Calculations? Where does consensus fit in there?' Gopal asked.

'What I meant was, at what stage of human evolution should we go and join the Prithvi inhabitants is something for the Empowered Council to decide,' Krishna stated

'I think we all would prefer living with a rational and intelligent race. Equals at the very least,' said Shyam.

Everybody nodded in agreement, some quite ostensibly and some in a fairly subtle way.

'When do we place Bhoomidium on Prithvi?' Vitthal asked.

'We cannot do that now, without altering foolproof natural ways of evolution. It's too early,' Krishna replied.

'Seems fair, let the right species grow and reach a critical level of cortical development,' added Shyam.

'Good going, make sure the right species prosper well,' Gopal insisted too.

'They will, either by cooperation or by competition,' Krishna said.

25

Beyond the Realm

'It sounds just straight out of a love story.'

'You can say so.'

Radhika blushed and said, 'I always had a soft corner for love stories. Especially when people separated by situations, waited for one another.'

'I never waited. Not in the literal sense,' Krishna answered.

The very words and the lack of any affection or emotion they were said with displeased Radhika. 'Why?' she asked.

'Because I knew you would do that for me,' he replied, smiling ear to ear.

She narrowed her eyes with her mouth wide open and then with a wait of a couple of seconds, punched him on his right arm. Just beneath his shoulder. 'Okay, lady! That hurt,' he said.

'Did it?' she was smiling. Then she reached for the right cuff of his robe, and lifted his sleeves up to his shoulder. She was amazed at what she saw, 'No way that light punch could have given you such a bruise.'

But before Krishna could say any further, he realized that Radhika was having a closer look at what she thought was a blue-coloured bruise.

'Is this a tattoo? No, wait. This is deep in your skin. What are these patterns?' she said.

He further raised the sleeve and said, 'Look closely.'

As she saw the mark in its full glory, the muscles around her eyes relaxed and her facial expression mellowed. 'What is it?' she asked.

'A cosmic eye,' he replied.

'Whose?' she said.

'His. He who knows all, sees all, and pervades all.'

'Where did you get it from?'

'A feather in Gopaldas's possession left this mark.'

'What does it mean?'

'An indication that I need to take charge and lead, is what he said.'

'Do you believe him?'

'Do I believe him blindly on everything? No. Do I trust his intellect? Yes.'

'That doesn't answer my question, sweetheart,' she replied, understanding very well that Krishna was trapping her in wordplay.

'I wouldn't know for sure. Your world seems full of mysticism, spirituality, and meaning,' said Krishna.

'For the record, Gopaldas belongs to both worlds, yours and mine,' she said.

'But he never came in contact with us,' said Krishna.

'You know the reason. To understand him you need mysticism, spirituality, and meaning,' she said smilingly.

'Then I stand corrected, I understood neither him nor what he said,' he replied.

'He couldn't have said it in any simpler words,' she replied.

'It's not happening, not now, and not any time sooner,' said Krishna.

'Scared of the responsibility it would bring along?'

'Not in the slightest! Even today, all the responsibility of my actions and fruits of action inspired by me, lay with me. I respect hierarchy. And, just because I am the one who does all the calculations around here, doesn't mean I am the wisest one to command everyone around,' replied Krishna.

Radhika was about to respond, when at the very last moment she pulled back her words. It was obvious to her that Krishna was a bit upset now.

'Coming back to our story, rather our love story. Won't it be the first one to stretch across two different universes? A love story beyond the realms of reality...' she said and then blushed again.

'Our love story? I am not sure you actually formally professed your love for me,' he said with a playful sparkle in his eyes.

She again narrowed her eyes and again punched on his right arm playfully. As soon as her tightly clinched soft fist landed on his arm, he felt a wobbling.

No way that this shaking is from her punch. But the vibration grew and became wilder, along with a rising sound of rumbling. Before he could change his perspective, Radhika said, 'The ground below is trembling. It's a quake.'

He held her arm and rushed towards the emergency exit door. The migration facility was built in hurry and was only meant to serve as a temporary accommodation. He feared whether the structure would be able to take full impact of a quake of this magnitude.

By the time the major shocks and following minor tremors subsided, everyone in that building was out in the open. Krishna, though, could see some major cracks and fault-lines developing on the walls of the facility.

'Come along, I need to reach my lab. I cannot leave you here,' said Krishna. He then raised his left arm and called Mohan.

'It's Purva-Dweep. The two plates are smashing into each other frantically,' said Mohan. Krishna disconnected the call, sensing another minor tremor. The MagVahn services were shut by now, he had to walk all the way through.

As Krishna reached the lab and made Radhika sit on a chair besides his work desk, Mohan said, 'The Purva-Dweep plate won't relent. It will keep hitting our continent for a day or two more.'

'Anybody hurt?' asked Krishna.

'Nobody, but our energy-generation facilities beneath the city have been hit hard with displaced rocks and soil,' he replied.

'What about solar?' said Krishna.

'The solar farm took some beating too. Apparently, a lot of trees fell over them,' he replied.

'What's the deficit level?'

'We are running at only 35 per cent of the capacity. We will be able to bring that up a bit in few weeks,' said Mohan. Krishna shook his head vehemently and said, 'Run the resource check, down to the last rare metals we have with us.' He then pulled up his cuff and called Shyam.

It took Shyam, Shriram, and everybody else important about fifteen minutes to reach the place.

'Mohan, run a parallel batch for both, the seismic activity underneath and the progress check on Prithvi's data stream,' Krishna said. Everybody had a fair idea that things were not going down as expected and the quake could have changed certain factors in the whole equation.

'Do we have any way to stop the sinking plate from impacting our island?' said Shyam.

'I guess it would stop eventually even without any intervention from our side, but then we have a bigger problem on our hands right now,' replied Krishna.

'Is it about power? I could see a whole section of the grid giving up,' said Shriram.

'The generation facilities underneath have taken a hit. We are running quite low, at a third of our capacity and requirement,' said Krishna.

'I had my engineers visit the basement, they say it could be brought back in a week,' said Gopal.

Meanwhile, the colours on the Samganak display changed. The seismic simulation report was now up. 'The impact has started a chain of sequence which would pull down the whole of the Jambhu-Dweep in a matter of months. The jolts were just the tip of the iceberg,' said Mohan, as his face went pale.

'This is exactly what I feared,' murmured Krishna.

'But fixing power has to be our first priority, winter is at peak,' said Gopal sensing some plausible change of game plan.

'I fear, we will have to manage,' said Krishna.

Shyam stood up and said, 'We have thousands of people, who have taken shelter here. We cannot leave them out in the cold.'

'We can make alternate arrangement and each Madhavpurian can accommodate guests at his/her place,' Krishna suggested.

'Do you need the generation floor below to set up some kind of equipment?' Vitthal asked.

'That's not the idea. I do not need the space, but the components. We have so much of rare metals with us and if we spend that on fixing power generation, we would be stuck in a warm and cosy but sinking island forever,' he replied.

'You are suggesting, we expedite the migration process?' said Shriram.

'On a war footing, our last bastion is going down too. I would rather spend every waking hour of mine building the Brahmportation mechanism for the great migration,' replied Krishna.

'Where are we on the evolution scale on Prithvi?' Gopal asked.

'Gopal, I now have very concrete evidences which suggest

that the Time-Space-Omechta framework is not linear. It has curves. The time conversion scales between our world and 1408 are changing cyclically. They are in a slow phase for now, but if we do not move in time it might change. We might have to live in a post-human world,' replied Krishna.

'The conversion scale could accelerate? Have we understood the pattern?' said Shyam.

'No! It is too complex to calculate,' Mohan interjected.

'Why are we playing with something that we have not understood fully?' said Gopal.

'We do not intend to stay in inter-universe space. That's the realm of Omechta, we don't need to decode it to the last bit for passing through it,' replied Krishna.

'When do we move, and what kind of people do we expect to see on this new planet?' Shriram asked what was on everyone's mind.

'How sophisticated they are, what level of cortical development will they be at when we reach?' added Shyam.

'They are arranging themselves in cooperating societies and are fairly intelligent. Moreover, I will time the operation as to reach somewhere around what was our twenty-first century,' he replied.

'And that would be?' asked Shyam.

'In a fortnight's time.'

There was not much left to discuss, so everyone left the lab. Everyone's duty was cut out clearly, and there was very little if any time left for any further consensus-building.

'I will be at Meera's. I should leave you to your work,' said Radhika to Krishna. She smiled and left the lab.

As she was walking out, Krishna couldn't help but notice her silhouette getting outlined in the light pouring in from the open lab's door. The glistening streak of her tightly tied golden-brownish hair, pulled a string or two in his heart. He was being pulled between the poles of two different ideas. Was it her beauty that has kept him spellbound for aeons or was it an idea named 'Radhika' that had captured his imagination all this while.

As Radhika stepped out and the door closed, those thoughts faded in the background. He could now hear Mohan say something that had sneaked quietly under the bridge of his attention.

'I think I missed what you just said,' Krishna said.

'I said I will need a comprehensive list of rare elements required and the blueprint of the set-up,' Mohan repeated.

Krishna nodded in response.

◆

Within a matter of weeks the extreme cold started to subside. The winter was now past it's peak. The big arch-like structure for mass transporting was also taking shape.

It was erected on the foot of Mount Govardhan, so that there could be some sort of shielding from the different fluxes emanating out of the Bhoomi's plate movement.

The Space-Time-Omechta surrounding the different universes was also rising and ebbing following the hyper complex patterns, which was difficult to calculate using present computational power. The field thus generated by the arch to create suitable Omechta warp for Brahmportation, had to read, guess (by extrapolation) and mimic the variations. The constant calculations was placing extraordinary burden on the generators.

On the tenth day from the last quake, the arch was up and running.

'Looks great!' said Mohan with his hand busy punching test codes and commands on the portable Samganak panel, which he had established besides the arch.

'That's the problem...' said Krishna, compelling Mohan to raise his brow and narrow his eyes in suspicion.

'It should work great, looks won't matter,' said Krishna.

Mohan laughed, 'Yes, it will.'

It took twenty round trips of various inanimate articles across the realms of Omechta (into 1408) before Krishna found the systems to be reliable, repeatable, and satisfactory. Mohan then volunteered to Brahmport himself and that worked too.

The generators, which utilized a very specialized and limited fuel, were already running hot. 'The field calculations are putting the generators in jeopardy,' said Mohan.

'Cannot help, as and when the Omechta realm would fluctuate so would the power required for the calculations,' said Krishna.

'What's causing these tremendous fluctuations? They were not there when we started studying them, were they?' said Mohan.

'One plausible reason could be that we are moving across it. What happens in one universe depends upon what are the occurrences in older universes, remember?' he replied.

'That means we have to do a fanatic amount of calculations for the changing Omechta realm, because the realm is also fanatically calculating our moves,' said Mohan.

'It is a possibility,' he said.

Many more tests with different permutation were carried out, till Krishna was satisfied with the system. And till, no further fuel could be spared for testing.

On the thirteenth night, the public address system was brought into action, with every Manava residing in Madhavpur having an option to send their messages and queries via wrist-phone to the address room.

The address was a clearly worded instruction for the migration, and how it was to be completed in a single day, before much bigger tectonic disturbances could sweep Madhavpur. Elected council from each block were texting their queries, which in turn were being answered by Shyam.

'To make an endeavour successful, it is not about how firm your leap of faith is, rather how firm your faith in your leap is…' was Shyam's closing sentence of the address.

The next morning (as it had for aeons) began with splendid sun rising across the eastern horizon of Madhavpur. The first and the most glistening sunrays of the day gleamed on the foot of Mount Meru. With which the upper part of the chrome-plated arch also sparkled in brilliant golden hues.

Each house was cleaned by their occupants and things inside each building placed in order, just in case, if they would ever return to their homeland.

Everybody was dressed in his or her best, to make it look like a happy farewell saga. This way they also got to carry their best and precious clothing along, apart from whatever little essential they carried in a bag on their back.

Radhika excused herself and rushed towards the mobile command centre just below the arc, leaving Vallabha behind with Raghav.

'What are your plans, once we reach Prithvi?' Vallabha asked Raghav.

'To hold that someone special's hand and enjoy the new landscapes,' he said with a poker face.

She smiled and held his hand, reciprocating the same feeling. They looked each other into eyes until a loud voice over public address system started blaring through the cool morning air of Madhavpur. It was an announcement for the row formation according to serial numbers already allocated.

Thousands of people at a time could comfortably pass beneath the arch. A total of about 101 Brahmportation batches were to be run. The generators still had fuel to power around 140 batches.

'Look! My batch number is in among the first few, I don't want to leave without you,' Radhika said to Krishna.

'Women and elderly people are always evacuated first. I need to handle the whole exercise. Don't worry I will join you as soon as the whole exercise ends.'

While her big, bright and starry eyes were fixed upon his, Krishna ordered her, 'Now go and join the formation.'

As soon as the first batch of Brahmportation completed, Krishna and Mohan breathed a sigh of relief. People had to step in quick and each successive batch was to be executed at a fairly fast pace. As time on 1408 was still many times faster (in spite of the slow phase of Omechta), the Manava population on Prithvi had to be filled in fast. The lower the number on Prithvi, the more vulnerable they will be.

Within a matter of an hour, all but one batch of the Manavas were Brahmported. The place where they were to land could be seen on the big screen in the command centre. It was a lush green tract of land, on some big island surrounded by tropical lake on all sides. A spiral cloud like formation could be seen over the island. It was the gateway to the realm (in between Bhoomi and Prithvi) and was shimmering with various colours like an eye of a peacock feather. The gateway was connecting the Bhoomi with Prithvi through the Omechta realms in-between.

Even though the whole operation took just an hour, still on screen, hours of the day could be seen passing on Prithvi.

Radhika was clearly spending time looking toward the spiral cloud formation. Her eyes were glistening with an eager expression of waiting.

As soon as the last batch stepped within a few metres of

the arch, the ground shook vehemently. It was another quake. Everybody stopped and stood, with Krishna holding his breath and hoping that the quake wouldn't harm the structure.

The quake subsided soon. The arch and the command centre were intact, but one of the two generators collapsed. Noticing that, Krishna screamed 'Don't stop, move.'

The last of the batch moved and with clockwork-like precision got Brahmported to Prithvi. But then the indicative lights on the arch started flickering in colours never seen before on that structure.

'We are losing power. The other generator is also yielding,' shouted Mohan. Everybody except Mohan, Krishna, and the Empowered Council was now on Prithvi.

Meanwhile, the spiral cloud, the Prithvi side of gateway to the realm started shrinking.

'Uncle, take everybody including Mohan and just jump across the arch,' Krishna ordered.

Mohan protested and said, 'Krishna you leave along with everyone, I will shut down the module and will join you all.'

'No, the final phase of Kakudmi module needs sophisticated manoeuvring; I will have to handle that. You have to leave now,' Krishna persisted.

Shyam held Mohan by his wrist and said, 'No more discussions. Heed to what he is saying, son.'

Shyam was right; with each passing second the arch was struggling in want of power. There wasn't enough fuel left to waste, and there was no workforce left to work on repair of the systems.

Krishna handed over a pen like device to Mohan and said, 'This contains every useful data, to start everything from scratch if the need be.'

They then passed through the arch and were now visible on the screen by the side of command centre. Krishna quickly booted the final phase of the programme; he couldn't have left the systems open. That would have interfered with the Omechta realm.

The final phase was now up but only a minute or so worth of fuel was left. After the final press of the button to shut all the modules, Krishna slowly walked towards the arch. Meanwhile, he connected his Mani-Bandh to the command centre's terminal. He could see on it, Radhika and everybody else waiting on the other side.

As he reached the arch, he patiently stood there in front of it. His sight was alternating between the lights atop the arch and visuals of Radhika on his Mani-Bandh. He could have moved and gone through the arch, but he did not. Eventually, the indicative lights atop the arch stopped glowing. The arch de-energized and the generators came to a screeching halt.

Krishna then seeing the Brahmportation arch powering down, sighed and walked back to the command centre. He then watched the last few glimpses of Prithvi. He could see Radhika standing there beneath the spiral-cloud formation. Then the last auxiliary power to the command centre too went out.

He then turned his wrist and checked his Mani-Bandh; the visuals (of Radhika waiting on Prithvi) held for a second or two and then flickered away. They were now gone from there too. Those were probably the last visuals of his beloved that he was to ever see.

He was now speechless, motionless, and emotionless.

The spiral cloud on Prithvi, meanwhile, shrunk further.

As Radhika's eyes moved from the glowing spiral cloud to Mohan in utter disbelief, she began to lose consciousness and fumbled, when Mohan and Shriram caught her in time.

The gateway to the realm was now closed.

Glossary

1. Manavas – A highly evolved and immortal successor of the Modern Man. They have evolved to the point where they do not easily give in to primordial emotions like anger, rage, and jealousy.
2. Bhoomi – The planets where Manavas reside. It was earlier called Earth during the reign of Manava's predecessors.
3. Jambhu-Dweep – A relatively small sea-locked continent on Bhoomi. Almost all of the Manavas on Jambhu-Dweep live in and around Madhavpur.
4. Madhavpur – The only known inhabitable city on Jambhu-Dweep. On its Western borders is the Sumeru Hill range, comprising many hill peaks like Govardhan, Meru, etc.
5. Purva-Dweep – Another small sea-locked continent on Bhoomi. Almost all of the Manavas on Purva-Dweep live in and around Ayudhpur.
6. Ayudhpur – The only known inhabitable city on Purva-Dweep. It is situated fairly close to the sea separating the two continents.
7. Kali-Yuga – The era of the Modern Man's (Manava's predecessor) reign. It ended around the year AD 2050 and the world then entered a transition phase, during which a change of Yuga followed.
8. Swarnim-Yuga – The Golden era of the reign of Manavas. This Yuga still continues and was established after a brief transition

period around the later part of the twenty-first century.

9. Bhoomidium – A special compound developed by Krishna to transform the Modern Man into Manava. The first iteration Bhoomidium-1007 was slightly radioactive and decayed with time. It was improved upon by forming Bhoomidium-1008, which was more stable under all conditions. It keeps the Manavas healthy and prevents them from ageing. Also gives them their superior brain and minds.

10. Xididium – A preservative, like food additives, developed in the twenty-first century by a for-profit company. It was meant to keep farm produce fresh but ended damaging soil microbiome. This poisoned the food meant for the Modern Man and caused an outbreak of massive diseases.

11. Epi-Cortex – This is the part of the brain, which is placed atop the cerebral cortex. This part of brain is unique to the Manavas and was not present in the Modern Man. This gives the Manavas the extra wisdom and control over emotions that the Modern Man never had.

12. Cortical Development or CD – The Epi-Cortex in every Manava differs in terms of development. The thicker and more functional the Epi-Cortex, the more wise the person. The Cortical Development or CD is measured on the following scales:

    a) CD1++: Highest level of intelligence, currently possessed only by one person in the whole stock of the Manavas. Apart from exceptionally high intelligence and wisdom, their memory spans not only across wake-time incidences but also across what they see in dreams during sleep-time. They also tend to be well-connected with Nature and their own higher consciousness.

    b) CD2++: Forty per cent of the Manavas are currently

CD2++. They have immense brain and mind power and can choose to deploy their capabilities to vocation of their choosing.

c) CD3++: Almost 60 per cent of Manava population is CD3++. Although fairing the lowest on CD scale, they still are immensely wiser then the erstwhile Man.

d) The CD3++ can move up to CD2++ with planned administration of Bhoomidium. It is a tiresome and painful process and offers very few real life benefits, if any. If a person chooses to bump himself up to CD2++, then City Council can reassign him more work (often time arduous). These additional responsibilities can hamper work-life balance for the newly up-bumped Manava. So, the procedure does not find many takers.

e) Meanwhile, any deficiency of Bhoomidium can lead to lowering of a Manava's CD category. Dehydration being the primary source of the deficiency, as water is primary source of Bhoomidium.

13. Yocto-Particles – A special microscopic particle developed in Krishna's Lab—Café Evolution. The particle measures as small as 10^{-24} part of a metre. The particles are then used to make Yocto-Suits and other fabrics with almost magic-like properties.

14. Yocto-Suits – A special suit made out of Yocto-Particles. These suits are often merged with the daily wear robes, and are usually kept hidden until put into work. The Yocto-particles of the suit hide in the voids between the fabrics of the suit, when not in function. When called to function they move out of the fabric voids and join with each other, forming the suit. The suits can provide many functions such as—thermo insulation for

harsh climate, invisibility for stealth operations and can even be sometime modified to form signal receiver. The access to the suit was mostly restricted to Krishna and Mohan. And they used it for research purposes.

15. MagVahn – The magnetically levitated (train-like) public transport, crisscrossing the city of Madhavpur. MagVahn was the only allowed form of transportation in Madhavpur. The Manavas in general were discouraged from having any private mean of transport. So, they either used MagVahn to get around or walked. It was designed with the sole purpose of being environment-friendly. When the MagVahn crosses the section just beneath the Sumeru Hill range on the western front of the city, it is a beautiful scene to behold.

16. Omechta – Up until AD 2050, the Modern Man knew only about four dimensions—three of space and one of time. But Krishna then stumbled upon work of some of his coworkers (from his NYCAR days), which hinted toward a fifth dimension. Krishna, in his leisure time in Madhavpur, developed that theory further and finally discovered Omechta—the fifth dimension. This hidden dimension used to separate one universe from another. For example, if space coordinates remain constant and time alone changes, a person moves in time (past, present or future) while being at the same place.

If time remains constant and space coordinate changes, a person in the same moment gets transported to a different location.

And if both change, the person will move to a new location in new time.

Now, if Omechta coordinates change, a person can be in the same time and place but get Brahmported to a new universe. Changing Omechta is a very tough manoeuvre and can only be accomplished by a big computer or a Manava with CD1++ intelligence.

17. Omechta Realm – The inter-universe space, through which a person (or object) being Brahmported has to travel. Any person (or object) if stuck in such realm will get suspended in stagnant space and time. His life shall come to pause, with exception of mind and that too in exceptional cases only.

18. Brahmportation – A complex manoeuvre through which Omechta coordinates are changed to teleport an object or person to a different universe of choice.

19. Samganak – A supercomputer built by Krishna for his Café Evolution. The Samganak was funded and approved by the City Council. The system is way superior to any super-computing facility that the Modern Man ever had.

20. Paramganak – A supercomputer, only slightly less powerful then Samganak, built by Vasudevan for his personal ambitions. It was neither funded nor approved by the Council.

21. De-Acceleration Chamber – State-of-the-art facility in Krishna's Café Evolution lab, where he studied and searched new planets for life. Such set-ups in the lab used to fasten the pace of a Manava mind (by altering his brainwave frequency a million to billion times) to let it better understand other worlds with different pace of time.

22. Wrist-Phone – A hand-worn sophisticated device issued to every Manava in Madhavpur. It could be used for communication purposes, entertainment purposes, and as a personal assistant. It is also referred to as the wrist-watch or wrist-device. An exception being, one issued to Krishna. It was customized for him to assist him in his lab work and is called the Mani-Bandh. Although it looked quite similar to other wrist-phone(s), it excelled in its functionalities and capabilities.